PRAISE FOR DENNIS GREEN'S
THE TRAVELER CHRONICLES

PRISONER

"*Prisoner* packs one helluva punch... time and time again! - Rachel Aukes, Amazon bestselling author of *100 Days in Deadland*.

"A gripping dimension-hopping mystery that absolutely refuses to be put down." - Adam Whitlatch, author of *The Weller* and *War of the Worlds: Goliath*.

"Green takes a mystery, colors it with an urban fantasy ambiance, teases it with sci-fi, and adds a spritz of romance for a perfectly styled read." - A.R. Miller, author of *Disenchanted*.

"*Prisoner* picks up where *Traveler* left off as Green takes you for a roller coaster ride of action, science fiction, and good ol' fashion detective work, and then slaps you in the face with an ending that you never see coming. This is a must read for sci fi fans!" - Michael Koogler, author of *Antivirus* and *Convergence*.

"Fast paced, intelligent, and wildly entertaining, Prisoner grabs your attention from page one and doesn't let up until the very end. A thoroughly satisfying sequel to Traveler, Dennis Green expands on an already infinite universe to give us new characters, numerous worlds in need of saving, and the kind of relationship problems that only exist when multiverses collide. Trav Becker's world has just got a whole lot bigger and a whole lot more complicated, and I for one couldn't have enjoyed it more."
-Jed Quinn, author of *Orchard* and *Kingmaker*.

TRAVELER

"A complex thriller that will literally keep you on the edge of your feet. I honestly could not step away from this book until the very end! 5 Stars!" - *Terry's Book Addiction.*

"I can't wait to read the next one! - *Book Lover's Life.*

"What if Law & Order, Harry Dresden and Sliders had a baby? A fantastic page burner!" - David Adam Suski, author of *The Wired Man.*

"...intriguing, roller-coaster ride of a thriller that was action packed and engaging throughout." - *Avid Book Collector.*

"The traveling between parallel universes is neatly explained and the plot draws you in. Mystery lovers and science fiction fans should get a kick out of the novel. Traveler gets a solid thumbs up." - *Second Run Reviews.*

"...a fun novel that fans of either sci-fi or crime fiction can see themselves shifting into." - *Iowa City Press-Citizen.*

"Dennis Green has written a very entertaining book in "Traveler," one that appeals beyond the science fiction genre where it started." - *Cedar Rapids Gazette.*

"Phillip Marlowe meets Philip K Dick in an intriguing mystery that crosses shifting planes of reality." - Denny Lynch, ICON.

"Plenty of thrills await readers as they journey with the traveler." -Rob Cline, author of *Murder by the Slice.*

"Traveler succeeds with surprises at every turn."
    -Lennox Randon, author of *Friends Dogs Bullets Lovers.*

PRISONER

Dennis W. Green

ISBN: 978-0-9977452-1-4
LOCN: 2015910230

Editing by Elizabeth Humphrey
www.bookwormediting.com Littleton, Colorado USA

Cover art and design by Drew Morton
www.drewmadestuff.com Iowa City, Iowa USA

HAPPY HOUR
PUBLISHING

www.happyhourpublishing.com

To Lennox Randon, the most inspiring man I know.

And always to Debbie, whose beauty, wit, and intelligence live in every female character I write.

1

*T*HEY'RE COMING."

BRIGHT, arterial blood spurted from the shoulder of the man standing at my door. It contrasted with a darker stain that soaked his abdomen. The arm that wasn't gushing blood was wrapped around the stomach wound, trying to hold his guts in.

He swayed a couple of times and crumpled to the ground.

I managed to catch him before he hit, lowering him to the floor as gently as I could. I cradled his head as his mouth worked, but all that came out was a rusty wheeze.

"Don't try to talk," I said. "I'll get help."

He focused on me with some difficulty, reaching for the collar of my shirt with a bloody hand. He pulled me close to his face.

"They're *coming*," he whispered again.

And died.

I gently laid his head back and placed the hand that had grabbed my shirt on his chest. I laid two fingers on his neck to verify there was no pulse, but I knew there was no life remaining in his blank, staring eyes.

I rocked back on my haunches and regarded the dead man on my living room floor.

I knew him. His name was Trav Becker. Thirty-two, eleven year veteran of our town's police department, last four of those a detective. Single, but with a girlfriend totally out of his league. He was thinking of asking her to tie the knot.

I knew he'd broken his elbow jumping off a play set at his eighth birthday party.

I knew that he was still coming to terms with the death of his dad, even though it had been more than two years.

And that he was now strictly a beer drinker because of some very unpleasant memories involving vodka.

I knew a lot more about him than that.

In fact, I knew everything about him.

Because Trav Becker is also my name.

And this was not the first time I had found myself staring at my own dead body. In fact, it wasn't even the first time in this room.

It is not something you get used to.

Strange as it may seem, as I regarded the corpse with my face on my (our?) living room floor, I wasn't wondering how he had gotten here, or even why he was wounded. I was thinking, *Thank God, Mary just missed him.*

The day had begun quite normally–actually, better than normal. As my mind swam slowly up from the grey depths of a restful sleep, I had become aware of a bare leg lying across mine. And I soon realized what had woken me up was a slight muscle cramp in my left arm, due to the fact that it was wrapped around the owner of the leg. Her cheek lay on my shoulder, her breath making a tiny, cool breeze across my bare chest.

I ignored the ache in my arm for a few minutes, breathing in the scent of Mary's hair and enjoying the feel of her soft, warm body wrapped around mine.

She'd shown up at my place about ten-thirty the previous night. I was watching an old *Stargate* episode on Netflix, dozing a little, when her keys rattled in the lock. I hopped up, and met her at the door.

She dropped her purse and violin case on the floor, spying the lemon drop martini I held.

2

"God, I love you. Gimme."

I handed her the glass and she took a slightly-more-than-ladylike sip, eyes rolling back in her head as she moaned with delight.

"Ooh, I needed that. C'mere, you."

She slipped her free hand around and hooked the back of my neck, pulling my face to hers. Mary put everything into her kisses, and a hot thrill coursed through my body.

We unclenched just long enough to move to the couch. Mary plopped down and kicked her pumps off with a grateful sigh. She shrugged out of her jacket, revealing a white camisole underneath. Reclaiming her drink, she swung her bare feet into my lap. I grabbed the nearest one and began to firmly massage her instep and footpad. She sighed appreciatively.

"Remind me again why I haven't married you?" she murmured, eyes closed.

"You haven't asked me yet."

She cracked one eye open. "Don't tempt me. I just might."

I changed feet, and this time her throaty moan was downright sexual. I was not so much of a gentleman to resist sliding my gaze along her bare legs, still tanned from the summer, to where they disappeared into her short pencil skirt, now hiked up far enough to reveal several inches of equally-tanned thigh. It seemed a fair recompense for the outstanding foot massage.

Mary had long, wavy brown hair. Eyebrows that might be just a trifle thicker than current fashion topped her otherwise-fine features. Even dog-tired after a six-hour rehearsal, she was movie-star pretty. At least, to me.

"Long night?" I asked.

"You don't know the half of it," she sighed. "Putting the orchestra and opera together for *Carmen* looks good on paper, but is turning out to be a cluster.

3

"Theoretically, the orchestra is just supposed to be the pit band, but Rodney is having to work more and more with the stage director, and Phillip thinks they're talking behind his back."

Our town was blessed with both a symphony orchestra and an opera company that were far better than you would expect from a mid-sized Midwest college town. A few years ago, the two had begun collaborating on a couple of productions a year. The two maestros, Rodney and Phillip, always made nice for the cameras, but in private, hated each other's guts.

"Sounds like fun."

"Yeah, and add to that the personnel manager asking me every five minutes how I think the vote on next year's contract is going to go. I am about ready to have a certified, complete snit worthy of my lofty position as concertmaster and head diva."

"In that crowd, no one would even notice."

"Hmm. In my next life, no musicians." She straightened up and, like a cat sneaking into your lap, maneuvered her upper body so that she was snuggled into the crook of my arm. She turned her face up for a kiss, and I obliged.

"Anything new at work?" she asked.

I shook my head.

"Shit. Those poor girls." She watched me for a minute, knowing me well enough to see the frustration behind my neutral expression, but also seeing I was not ready to talk about it. It had taken a long time for her to learn to suppress her natural inclination to try to draw me out, but she knew I didn't like to talk about some things until I had fully processed them myself, and she respected that.

She squeezed my knee with her free hand, and looked at the TV.

"*Stargate?* Which one?"

"Third season."

"Are you close to the one where O'Neill and Teal'c get into the time loop?"

I thought for a minute. "That's the next season, I think."

"Too bad. I like that one."

"Me, too."

Well, it *had* been one of my favorites. The last time I had watched, a couple of the scenes had struck a little close to home.

"You really into it?" she asked.

"Not really."

"Good." She raised herself a little and put her lips next to my ear, one of my top five erogenous zones. "Because as soon as I finish this excellent martini, I am going to take you into that bedroom and take out my frustrations by doing things with you that would make your mama forbid you from ever seeing me again."

In times of fatigue and tipsiness, the four years Mary Logan had spent at a conservatory in Texas started to come through in her voice, which of course, did exactly zero to diminish its sexiness.

"I don't know," I said doubtfully, "Mom's pretty liberal."

"We'll see," she whispered.

She stuck her tongue out at me. As long as it was out, she decided to use it to trace the outline of my outer ear.

Which caused *me* to growl in a way that was downright sexual.

She smiled and snuggled against my chest again.

Five minutes later, she was sound asleep.

I watched the show for a little while longer, finally gathering her up in my arms and carrying her into the bedroom. She mumbled something about needing to brush her teeth as I eased her out of her clothes, but tumbled into bed with an appreciative sigh when I held the covers open for her.

It didn't seem like she had moved at all during the next eight hours, other than to seek out my side of the bed and wrap herself around me.

I was not complaining.

But the ache in my arm wasn't going away, and as much I enjoyed just lying here, I was going to have to move soon. I was just getting ready to gently roll her over when I heard her whisper.

"You put me to bed."

"Uh huh."

"And you didn't even take advantage of me."

"You don't know that."

"Oh, I'd know, believe me. But you forgot something."

"What?"

"My pajamas."

She stretched, which had the side benefit of allowing me to flex my arm enough to get the blood flowing without having to remove it from her smooth back. Her pretty mouth stretched into a wide yawn as she wriggled even closer to me.

I realized that one of the things that had made my slow journey to wakefulness such a pleasure had been the pressure of her small but firm breasts pressed into me.

Which had the side benefit of causing the blood to flow to *other* areas of my body.

"What makes you think I forgot?" I murmured.

"Mmmm. Looks like you forgot *your* pajamas, too." Her hand snaked across my body and her fingernails danced across the rapidly-growing erection in my boxer briefs.

"When do you have to be at work?"

"Swim lesson this morning."

"Oh, too bad," she said with a frown. She squeezed me, causing me to groan, and not with pain. "I hate to see this go to waste."

"Oh, it's not going to waste," I growled, rolling over and reaching for her.

She was expecting this move, and quicker than she should have been able to do, unwrapped herself from me and rolled out of bed.

"*You* have to meet your boss. And *I* can't show up at work wearing yesterday's clothes. I'll just jump in the shower."

She padded toward the bathroom, turned and looked at me over one bare shoulder.

"You're not going to make me shower alone, are you?"

Shower sex doesn't last long, but boy, is it intense. I was still tingling forty-five minutes later, as Mary and I sat across from each other at my small kitchen table, sipping coffee and trading sections of the paper. The fruity scent of Mary's shower gel filled the air. And it was probably just as well I was headed to a chlorine bath, as the flowery scent that now emanated from my skin probably would have gotten me some ribbing at the station house.

As we sat in companionable silence it occurred to me, not for the first time, that I wanted this domestic scene on a daily basis. And despite Mary's jest from the night before, it was up to me to make the next move. It had been sitting at the top of my to-do list for some time, but I just hadn't been able to pull the trigger.

Mary rose and stretched. She wasn't wearing yesterday's clothes after all, having located a track suit she kept at my house for workouts and lounging.

I rose as well, grabbing our breakfast plates and tossing them into the sink. When I turned around, she was right behind me, and glided into my arms.

"Seems to me you've already had your water workout," she giggled.

7

"Yeah. I'm probably ruined for the day."

I walked her out into the living room. "Dress rehearsal tonight, right?"

She nodded. "It'll be another long one. Could be late."

"Text me when you're done and I'll come over."

"You just want to put me to bed naked again."

"Darn right."

She gave me one more coffee-flavored kiss and spun out the door.

I had shut it behind her and turned around just in time for a blood-soaked Trav Becker to collapse into my arms.

I went into the kitchen and got some paper towels to blot up the blood a little. Fortunately, my place has hard wood floors. Bloodstains on the carpet would have been really tough to explain. I tidied up the area where he'd been standing when I had entered the room. He couldn't have been there more than a minute or two when I had wandered in, or there would have been even more blood to contend with.

I took the dirty paper towels into the kitchen and threw them away, knowing I was just postponing the inevitable. I went back into the living room and stood over the body, getting the distinct feeling of déjà vu.

Of course, *déjà vu* is the *feeling* you've done something or been somewhere before. Which this technically was not, as I had been in this *exact* situation before.

The last time was with my friend Sam, a particle physicist who had just gotten done explaining that he had pulled me in from a parallel universe to help him stop a killer. One who had done in the Trav lying in almost this exact spot.

Yeah, that's right. Parallel universes. Sam called them streams, and the fact that he had produced an exact replica of myself, only not breathing quite so much, combined with a lot of other crazy crap that had been happening to me, lent more than a little credence to his story.

And if you're confused hearing about it, imagine what it was like to live it.

That had been almost a year ago. Fortunately, I'd made it out of the adventure without joining what ended up being a rather long line of deceased Trav Beckers.

My life since had been normal to the point of boring, or at least as normal as a cop's existence could be. And I liked it that way.

But it looked like my boring and happy life was going to get weird again.

I bent to examine Dead Trav. Normally, I would have put on a pair of rubber gloves, but since any DNA I would leave on the body would be the same as the victim's, I didn't see the need to bother.

The first thing I noticed were his clothes. The last Dead Trav I had examined was dressed identically to me, right down to the socks. This guy... well, his socks were the only part of his clothing that looked familiar.

Instead of the jeans I normally favored, he wore a pair of black cargo pants that had a vaguely military look to them. His t-shirt was black as well. Over it was a dark, gray cotton shirt, long-sleeved, and unbuttoned. It too had kind of a BDU-ey look to it. On his head perched a baseball cap, also black, with of all things, a Star Trek logo on it.

That sent me searching for clothing tags, but all of them had been cut off, except for the t-shirt, which was the tagless kind.

There was an empty holster strapped to a gun belt that wrapped around his hips. The holster looked like it would fit the Glock that was my service weapon.

His pockets were empty, except for a keychain. The key on it was familiar. It was to my car, a Mustang of recent vintage, with remote lock key fob.

No wallet, either. There are two things no American male is ever without. His wallet and his cellphone.

And he had neither. That was weird.

A glint of silver at his wrist caught my eye. I pulled up his shirt sleeve and saw something extremely curious.

It was a silver bracelet. Thick, almost more of a wrist cuff, about three-quarters of an inch in diameter and not quite half an inch thick. It was smooth and featureless. It was like a fitness band from the future. No watch face, inscription, or anything to identify its purpose. I don't go in for jewelry. My own watch was a cheap sport thing.

Which caused me to look at said watch. *Crap*. I was out of time. A more thorough examination was going to have to wait. In the meantime, though, what the hell was I going to do with the body?

Fortunately, my previous experience with Dead Travs provided an answer.

I got my arms under his armpits and dragged him over to my living room's only closet. I balanced him on one hip, in an odd parody of the cross-chest carry lifeguards used, while I worked the door open with my free hand.

Once that was accomplished, I propped him up in a semi-sitting position on top of some boxes of out-of-season clothes. I pulled the cap's brim down to hide his staring eyes. On impulse, I slid the bracelet off his wrist before shutting the closet door.

I pulled my smartphone, a fairly recent surrender to modern technology, out of my pocket and poked at it for a few seconds, then grabbed my gym bag and car keys.

I didn't want to be late for swimming lessons.

Fifteen minutes later, a hot mix of humidity and chlorine filled my nose as I entered the natatorium at the university that also calls our town home. I had a towel thrown over one shoulder, and carried a water bottle and a pair of short bladed fins. A pair of goggles flapped against my thigh, held in place by the strap stuffed up one leg of my suit.

Two octogenarians water-walked in the near lane. At the opposite end of the pool, a college student in a lifeguard suit was in the water giving lessons to two young children.

A lap swimmer occupied the center lane. He barely disturbed the surface of the water as he sliced through it, his stroke relaxed, but Phelps-like in efficiency.

I set my gear down at the end of his lane and slid into the water. He pulled up just as I finished applying anti-fog solution (spit) to my goggles.

He pushed his own goggles up onto his forehead and we regarded each other.

"Morning."

"Hey, Leon."

"You ready?"

I nodded.

"500 easy free to warm up."

I nodded again and settled my goggles into place. He took off. I waited a couple of seconds, then followed.

I tried to keep the vision of Leon's smooth, controlled stroke in my head as I made my own way down the pool. But in contrast to Leon's smooth glide, I was sure I looked more like a dinghy propelled by a box fan with part of the blade missing.

Captain Leon Martin is my boss in the PD, which should explain why an appointment with him, even though not technically work-related, was important enough to keep that I would leave behind a corpse in my apartment.

A few months previously, I had raced in my first triathlon. I'm a pretty steady runner, and had invested in a decent bike. But I hadn't spent nearly enough time working on the swim portion. I had survived it, thanks largely to a wetsuit giving me some extra buoyancy, but I had swallowed about half the lake in the process.

After that, I'd asked Leon to help me with my stroke. He was a nationally-ranked Masters swimmer, with a couple of state records in the 50+ age group.

However, I failed to realize what I was getting into. Leon interpreted "give me some tips" as "make Trav a real swimmer."

So, for the last month, I'd been meeting him before work three times a week at the pool. He was as calm and patient a coach as he was a boss, but had made it clear that he'd only help me if I took it seriously. If I hadn't shown up for our workout, he'd wonder why.

Which was why Dead Trav had to go into the closet until I had time to deal with him.

So, I tried to forget about the body in my apartment as Leon put me through a series of stroke drills designed to improve my efficiency and feel for the water. This was followed by some 100-yard repeats, each one getting a little faster than the last. Leon swam with me in addition to coaching. Somehow, he managed to finish each repeat with plenty of time to watch me and prepare the next set.

On anyone else, it would have looked like showing off.

By the end, I was breathing just as hard as if I had been running wind sprints. The funny thing about swimming is that because you don't sweat, sometimes you fail to realize how hard you're working until you find yourself panting so much your throat hurts.

Leon nodded at me approvingly. If he was amused by my wheezing, he hid it well.

"That last set looked good. You're holding your streamline pretty well. Remember to fully extend your arms, even when when you're increasing turnover. Stay long in the water. Imagine you're reaching for something on a high shelf, and get some torque by driving from your hips."

I shook my head ruefully. "God, so much to remember."

"It's simple really. There are only three rules in swimming."

I'd heard this before. "I know. Technique, technique, and technique."

"And they told me you couldn't be taught."

He clapped me on the shoulder and heaved himself easily out of the pool. I shook my head, hoping that I was as limber when I got to be his age, and followed.

In the locker room, we talked baseball while showering and getting dressed. As we finished up, however, Leon quit keeping up his end of the conversation, responding to my comments with increasingly vague grunts. I knew why.

"Task force this morning?"

He nodded, lips compressed into a tight line. "Feebs are bringing in a new profiler."

"Lovely."

He raised his eyebrows and gave a "What can you do?" sigh as he slung his gym bag over one shoulder. I followed him out into a clear, early fall day.

"You know, Leon, we can skip for a few days if you want. Even weeks. You don't really have time for this right now."

"Are you kidding?" he replied. "This is the only place I don't have the Feds or the news media, or both, following me around. It's the highlight of my day. No, you're going to have to find a better excuse than a double kidnapping and interagency task force if you're going to wimp out on me."

"You see right through me."

"Besides," he continued, "they've asked me to add some manpower to the task force. You and Adam are up."

"Now what have I done to you to deserve that?"

Leon chuckled, but then his expression turned serious. "Sorry, Trav. This is a real tar baby. Everyone who touches it gets sticky and dirty. The press is making me out to be ineffective at best. The governor has gotten involved. I would like nothing better than to dump it into the Feds' laps and go home. But there is still a chance those little girls are alive, and I would offer donuts and coffee to the Devil himself if I thought it would help. Nobody kidnaps kids in our town."

There was steel in his eyes and, not for the first time, I could see why he had closed nearly all of his cases when he had my job.

"I need you, Trav."

"You've got me. You know that."

He nodded. By now we were at our cars.

"See you at the ranch," Leon said, opening his door.

I nodded and did the same.

Leon Martin was not much for speeches. It was a measure of just how much the Patel-Day case had gotten under his skin that he had just given, what was for him, major oratory.

As I drove to work, I mused that if the media had heard what he had just said to me, Leon might be having a better time of it. He barely tolerated the press, only giving statements when he absolutely had to, and taking as few questions as he could get away with. He did his best to keep all his emotions out of it, which unfortunately made him seem cold and distant on the air. Online forums had started calling him a variety of unflattering nicknames.

I generally shared his opinion of the FBI guys who'd been assigned to the case, but they at least did a better job of letting the media believe they were part of the team. Leon could not care less about his PR image, but this was the kind of case that could be a career-killer.

Leon just wanted to find the little girls. If bringing Adam and me in could help, I was on board.

14

2

I DROVE THROUGH a McDonalds, wolfing down an Egg McMuffin as I left my car in a small gravel lot beside the station. It was home to an odd assortment of vehicles, including two wrecked black and whites, a half-dozen impounds, our personal vehicles, and four dark sedans. I would describe them as nondescript, except they pretty much screamed "Fed." Or maybe *Men in Black*.

Heading into the building, I swiped my key card on the panel next to the entry door. It opened onto a narrow staircase. The landing at the top of the stairs opened into the squad.

It was a big, open room in need of a coat of paint. Beat-up desks, most of them pushed together in facing pairs, crowded the floor space, leaving only the narrowest of paths in between. The air smelled of burnt coffee, making me grateful for the Mickey Dee's in my free hand. Not exactly Jamaican Blue Mountain, but better than the tar I drank most mornings.

Most of the desks were empty and missing their chairs, which had been pushed up toward the center of the room, where a large conference table sat. You could get a dozen people around the table, but there were easily twice that in the room. Some had been able to get chairs around the table, others had pushed desk chairs into whatever gaps were available. A few more people perched on desks and, in one case, a low filing cabinet.

Five FBI agents stood ramrod-straight at the far end of the room from me.

I'll say this for the Feebs, at least they didn't try to grab the chairs near the donuts.

Leon hadn't been joking about that. He knew sugar and fat were as important to meetings as markers and a whiteboard.

One of the Feds actually held a cup of coffee, the first time I had witnessed an FBI agent consume food. I had begun to wonder if the FBI treated a cop shop like humans in Fairy Land: eat or drink nothing lest you be trapped there for eternity.

In front of the white board stood a woman. She was trim, a few years younger than Leon, so mid-forties, and African-American. She wore the standard fem-Fed uniform of dark suit, skirt and low heels. Straight hair, shoulder-length, framed a face that was probably expressive in her off-hours, but gave nothing away in this environment.

Leon perched on the corner of a desk to her right.

"I think everyone's here," he said.

She nodded, and looked us over, her gaze sharp, her mouth a tight, narrow line.

"Special Agent Kelly will be conducting the briefing this morning," Leon continued.

"Thank you, Captain," Kelly said with a small nod. "Thank you all for coming. We have some new faces with us today, both from the Bureau and the Department, so with apologies to those of you for whom this will be a repetition, I will start pretty much from the beginning. There have been some inaccurate and speculative reports in the media, so don't be surprised if you hear some things that are different from what you think you know about the case."

She flicked her fingers up the screen of a black tablet she held in one hand.

"Fifteen days ago, Sophie Patel, age twelve, was babysitting her neighbor, Ella Day, age eight, while Ella's mom was at work. This was a common arrangement between the families when Ms. Day had to work during the day on a weekend.

"At one thirty-eight p.m. Sophie sent a text to Ms. Day saying she and Ella were going to bike to the playground, about twelve blocks away.

"Ms. Day arrived home a little after four. Finding the house empty, she texted Sophie that the girls should start home. After a half hour, she grew concerned. She went to the Patel's house next door. The Patels had not seen their daughter, and a phone call to Sophie's cell went to voicemail.

"Ms. Day and Mr. Patel drove to the park. Ms. Patel stayed behind in case the girls showed up. The girls were not in the park. The parents retraced the girls' assumed route, but could find no sign of them.

"They contacted local law enforcement, who issued an Amber Alert. Captain Martin dispatched two black and whites, one to the Patel residence, the other to begin canvassing the neighborhood.

"More officers were added to the search throughout the night. The decision was made to treat the case as a potential kidnapping, and the Bureau was called in. A neighbor two blocks over, a Mr..."

Another flick on the tablet.

"...Taggert, was mowing his lawn and reported seeing two girls on bikes ride past his house at about two p.m. Sophie's cell phone was found about three blocks from that location, near a residence at 2891 31ˢᵗ Street. The cellphone..."

She held up the device, encased in an evidence bag.

"...was still powered on. No damage, other than some scratches. No prints other than Sophie's. Several texts and voicemails received but not viewed. No outgoing traffic other than the text to Ella's mother prior to their departure.

"To date, we have received seventy-five calls to the tip line, but none have been helpful. We've talked to every person along that route who was home at the time. No one saw anything suspicious. No strange vans, no unfamiliar people."

"All of that you know," Kelly finished. Her eyes swept the room, ending with the knot of Feebs next to her. "I have asked the Bureau's field office for some extra assistance and I'm pleased to report they have sent us a senior profiler to lend a hand. This is Special Agent Matthew Ward."

She indicated the Fed who was holding the coffee cup. He tilted it in our direction with a nod.

"Special Agent Ward is new to our field office. We hope a set of fresh eyes might shake something loose. He will be working with a subgroup Captain Martin has assigned. While this case is still a high priority, as we all know, the chances of finding victims alive decreases exponentially with each passing day. Both our agencies also have other work. The subgroup will focus on this case only, with the ability to request other personnel and resources as needed. All tips and leads will go to them. Captain Martin will continue to be our chief liaison to the media."

I heard a soft snort behind me, followed by a sneeze.

Except it wasn't actually a sneeze. In the soft exhale, I could hear the word *bullshit.*

I turned around and saw the raised eyebrows of my partner, Adam Yount. He was leaned back in his desk chair at my ten o'clock.

"Shut up, you asshole," I whispered back. "You don't know they're cutting us loose."

He rolled his eyes. "Right."

"Something you gentlemen want to share with the rest of the class?"

I hastily turned back. Kelly was fixing me with an icy stare.

Trying to keep from looking like a kid caught passing notes, I shook my head.

"No, ma'am. Sorry."

Her eyes shifted to Adam. "Are you suffering from allergies, Detective?"

Now it was Adam's turn to try and keep a straight face.

He cleared his throat.

"Not that I know of, ma'am."

"Maybe you should have your throat looked at."

She continued to stare at us for a beat longer, then turned toward Leon, who was also trying to look impassive.

"Special Agent Ward will team with two officers Captain Martin has selected."

She scratched at the tablet some more.

"Detectives Becker and Yount." She looked up, eyes scanning the room.

Adam and I raised our hands.

She nodded, the look in her eyes saying she thought Leon could have made a better choice. "Of course. Well, if you gentlemen aren't too busy, perhaps you can join us in the captain's office to discuss the next phase of the investigation?"

We nodded.

"All right, then. Thank you to those who gave up office and desk space for our staff. We'll try to clean up and be out of your way before lunch. Thanks for your cooperation and hospitality. Remember, this is just another phase of the investigation, no one is quitting. Full resources are still being expended to bring those girls back to their families safely. We'll all stay in close touch. Anything else?"

There wasn't. People stood up, chairs scraped on the tile floor.

"You know how you can tell when a Feeb is lying?" Adam asked softly, as we pushed our own chairs back to our desks. Leon was huddled with Kelly, Ward, and the rest of the FBI folk. It would obviously be a few minutes before we were needed.

19

"Don't," I warned, glancing over at the brass.

"Her lips are moving."

"Christ, Adam. What is wrong with you? She already demonstrated she has super hearing. You trying to make this even worse?"

"How much worse can it get? She pretty much just told us we're on our own."

"She gave us this Ward guy."

"Yeah, a profiler who is 'new to the field office.'" He snorted, making air quotes. "What do you bet he's fresh out of the Academy, and the reason we're getting him is because no one with actual mojo wants any part of this mess."

"You don't know that."

"Sure, I don't. And Leon is going to be the media liaison because he is so skilled with the press."

There wasn't much I could say to that. I shook my head, thinking how my partner had changed in the last year.

Adam was a couple inches taller than my five-ten. He'd been skinny, almost gangly when we'd first met, but had been putting in some pretty serious time in the weight room. He'd filled out quite a bit. He was still slim, but was now all muscle. He wore his wavy, blond hair longer than most cops, but it suited him. His lean, gristly physique and sleepy blue eyes gave him kind of a surfer-dude look.

When he had first been assigned to me as a detective trainee, I felt like I had been given a Labrador puppy, all curiosity and energy, tripping over paws he hadn't grown into yet. Adam had been wounded in the line of duty last year, and it had changed him.

Like I said, he'd started hitting the gym after his shoulder wound had healed, and as his body had gotten harder, so had his attitude. He didn't suffer fools gladly, and bristled at anything he thought stood in the way of doing his job.

A year ago, I would have had to force an opinion out of him. These days, I worried that shooting off his mouth at the wrong time would hurt his career. Bureaucracies only reward the right kind of truth telling. I had learned that the hard way, and had been trying to keep Adam from repeating the mistakes I'd made.

"Look at the bright side," I said. "We're on this full time, don't have to work it in between other cases. And who knows, maybe Ward will be all right."

"Don't hold your breath."

"Trav, Adam." Leon called us from where he stood with the Feds. "My office."

We stood up. Kelly and Ward split off from the other agents, and the five of us headed into Leon's office.

It was a tight squeeze. Leon's office was maybe the size of two office cubicles. There were two guest chairs in front of his desk, but no room to bring in any more. We knew better than to offer the chair to Agent Kelly. So instead, we pushed them back toward the wall. I put my foot up on one, and rested my arms on my knees. Adam learned against a filing cabinet that filled one corner of the room. The Feds stood between us.

Agent Kelly looked us up and down.

"Captain Martin tells me you are two of his best." She put just the right amount of doubt into her tone.

"You might have gotten off on the wrong foot with them, Ms. Kelly," Leon said. "But I wouldn't have recommended Detectives Becker and Yount if they weren't two of my most focused, serious investigators…"

Leon might have continued singing our praises, but he was interrupted when my pocket broke into song.

Specifically, the Eighties chestnut *Don't Forget Me (When I'm Gone)*, by that legendary Canadian supergroup, Glass Tiger.

I dug into my jeans pocket with difficulty, finally prying the phone out, desperately trying to silence the notification tone, but the song went on and on as I fumbled with it, getting to the seven-word contribution to the production by that other Canadian superstar, Brian Adams, before I was able to get it shut off.

I think I mentioned my smart phone was a fairly recent upgrade to my personal tech. Sam had procured it for me and helped me set it up. But he had buried some bug in it that, without warning, caused the ring and notification tones to change from the defaults to a random selection of some of the absolute worst songs from the 1980s, my pick for the decade when popular music reached its lowest point.

I refused to give Sam the satisfaction of knowing he'd got me with a good one, and had been trying to fix it myself. I actually thought I had gotten it licked, but obviously not.

"Problems, Detective?" Kelly inquired sweetly. Adam had one hand over his mouth, desperately trying not to burst out laughing. There was no smile on Leon's face. He just shook his head. Ward looked from his superior to mine, but obviously decided the wisest course was to stay out of it and kept his mouth shut.

"Just a task reminder, sir. Ma'am. Sorry."

"Must be pretty important, to have such a...distinct ringtone."

"Just a friend's idea of a joke, ma'am. I..."

My attempt to slough off my *faux pas* died in my throat. My poking at the phone had finally resulted in the display revealing the reminder I had put in before leaving my apartment.

The text said *Remember to clean out your closet.*

3

OKAY. QUICK PRIMER on pan-dimensional cosmology:

It turns out that we don't move through time, from birth to death, in a straight line. We're more like twigs being carried along a stream. When we make a decision, or a major event happens, the stream forks. Sometimes the twig that is you goes into one stream, sometimes another. But both streams continue to exist.

And so do you. A version in each of the streams. Your consciousness rides one or the other, but both "yous" continue to exist as well.

I'm sure you've read the books or seen the endless movies and TV shows that tell parallel reality stories. None of them have ever gotten it right. Which is funny, because each and every one of us have experienced the shift to a parallel universe.

Here's the proof: Have you ever been looking for something–your car keys or maybe a book? You look everywhere, and can't find it. Then all of a sudden, there it is. In a place you could have sworn you already searched. Or even more unnerving, maybe you were staring right at it, but for some reason, didn't see it.

Congratulations. You just experienced a shift from one parallel reality to another.

It happens to all of us. Dozens, even hundreds of times a day. But the reason we don't know it is that our minds smooth over these incongruities to keep us sane.

When the book you were looking for shows up in the pile where it was not, you shrug, hope you're not suffering from early onset

Alzheimer's, and move on. And this can happen no matter how big, or glaring, the aberration.

Yes, even one as big as a dead version of yourself you had to leave in the closet.

I had suspected I could not trust my brain to keep the dead body in my closet front and center. Which was why I had entered a reminder in my phone before I left Dead Trav. Every couple hours, it was to chirp so I didn't get busy with my regular life and forget the trouble lurking just outside the realm of my perception. Of course, I hadn't counted on Sam resurrecting the MTV era for anyone within earshot.

"Trav? Is something wrong?" Leon's words were solicitous, but his tone was hard.

"Sorry," I said, pocketing the phone. "Should have put that on vibrate."

"Sure it can wait?" Kelly asked. "If you need to get your oil changed, or pick up milk, we don't mind putting the case on hold."

I shook my head. She gave me the kind of look you give the cat when it coughs up a hairball in the middle of your living room, before finally looking down at her tablet.

"Anyway, Special Agent Matthew Ward. Detectives Becker and Yount."

We shook hands all around.

"I won't kid you guys," Kelly continued when we had finished. "This is one of the most frustrating kidnappings I've ever worked. As you know, despite what you see on the morning news shows, off-the-street kidnappings by strangers are rare. Nine times out of ten it's a non-custodial parent or boyfriend covering up some atrocious act. Less often, a neighbor or friend of the family."

"We've cleared the family. And the neighbors," Adam said.

"Exactly. Two weeks and we have exactly nothing to show for an investigation that has involved two municipalities, state DCI, and the Bureau."

"So, the three of us are supposed to succeed where fifty investigators failed?" Adam made no attempt to hide his sarcasm.

"I know how this looks, Detective," Kelly replied. "I can only reiterate what I said out there. We are not giving up."

"Tell that to the Patels and the Days."

"Adam," Leon said. My partner wisely clammed up.

"We will all stay professional here," Leon continued. "Bottom line is, Kelly is right. We can't throw unlimited resources at one case forever. But you three are on this full time. Start at the beginning. Read Ward in. Maybe a set of fresh eyes will jar something loose. We've moved all the case files to Interview Two. Work out of there. Anything else you can think of right now?"

We shook our heads.

"Get to it."

We filed out, waited for Ward to collect his laptop case from the conference room, and led him to the room Leon had set aside for us.

Our station had four interview rooms. They look exactly like you've seen on TV. Square box with a beat-up table and a few chairs. The only thing missing in Interview Two was the huge one-way mirror you always see the other cops watching interrogations through. Instead there was a small video camera which sat in a bracket in a corner of the ceiling. It was linked to a monitor in the adjoining room. Because it didn't have the two-way glass, it served more as a multi-purpose room, only used for interviewing witnesses or suspects when no place else was available.

The whiteboard from the conference area had been moved into the space, and there were a couple of binders on the table, along with a laptop.

"Home, sweet home," Adam said as we arranged ourselves around the desk.

"You guys have Kelly all wrong," Ward said. He had fairly recent Middle Eastern ancestry. Olive complexion, short, dark hair, slight and about my height.

"Yeah?"

"Yeah. The regional office wanted the Bureau out of this completely. Kelly went to the wall to keep us in. She's serious. We come up with something concrete, I can have a full contingent back here in an hour."

"Then the thing to do is find something," I said. "And do it soon. Kelly was also right that every day that passes makes it less likely we find the girls alive."

"All right," Adam said. "I'll leave it alone. Let's get to it."

For the next hour and a half, we went back through every note, photograph, interview, tip, and theory about the case. The table quickly became covered with papers we unclipped from the binders and re-arranged. The whiteboard was filled with enough notes, circles and arrows to teach organic chemistry.

As the ancient HVAC system labored unsuccessfully to keep the room from getting moist and stuffy, Ward–proving he was in fact, human–tossed his coat in the corner and loosened his tie. We switched out empty coffee cups for water bottles, or in Adam's case, Mountain Dew.

The FBI agent proved to be a quick study, and while he didn't talk about himself, it was obvious he was not some accounting major recruited into the Bureau to fill out the diversity goals. In fact, I noticed that he kept rubbing the back of his neck and cheeks. The room wasn't that warm.

"You just come out from undercover?"

His eyes narrowed. "What makes you say that?"

"You rub your neck and face like there used to be a lot more hair there."

"Can't talk about it," he replied, giving me a long look. "You did some undercover work yourself last year, didn't you?"

I frowned. Why would an FBI profiler know anything about my activities from a year ago?

"Yeah," I said after a pause. "Didn't last that long."

"But it did result in us taking down one of the biggest organized crime rings in the Midwest," Adam put in.

"We had a CI inside," I said. "It was mostly about keeping him alive. He did all the heavy lifting."

Ward nodded.

I wanted to get off this topic, so I asked, "You're a profiler. Can you work up anything that might help us?"

"There's not a lot to work with yet," he replied. "Anything I would say now would be pretty general."

"Anything might help," Adam said.

Ward thought a minute. "On average, we're looking for a white male, thirties or forties. Trouble in a relationship, or a history of troubled relationships. Other than that, as we discussed, kidnappings like these are rarely executed by strangers. Particularly in broad daylight in a quiet neighborhood."

"That points to a family member or friend," I said.

"Who, as you say, you've cleared. Although we should go back and look again."

"You don't think we know how to do our jobs?" Adam asked.

"I know how to do *my* job," Ward replied calmly. "And that means looking at everything myself."

Adam started to object some more, but I quieted him with a raised hand.

"Assuming family comes up dry, what then?"

"We widen the net. Chances are it's someone the girls knew. But it might be an acquaintance we aren't aware of. Someone they might trust who wouldn't be obvious to us. The guy who volunteers as a crossing guard after school. Or someone who would present themselves as a trusted figure, even if they were not well known to the girls."

Adam and I exchanged a confused look. "You lost me," I said. "A trusted figure who is not well known by them?"

"Someone who would be trusted as a result of their job or position," he explained. "Someone from school or church. A teacher or guidance counselor. Or some other authority figure in the community. Anyone like that turn up in your investigation?"

I shook my head. "No one comes to mind that we haven't already mentioned."

Ward tapped a paper he had picked up out of the interview pile.

"This guy. Uhh... Alan Taggert."

"The guy who saw the girls bike past his house," I said.

"Either of you guys do the interview?"

I took the paper and glanced at the initials at the bottom of the report. "No, it was Stevens."

"Should we try him again?"

"All he said was he saw two girls bike past his house," Adam said doubtfully.

"He's the only person who saw them," Ward pointed out. "If nothing else, it's the one location we know for sure the girls were at, at least briefly. I'd like to get a look at it. Then maybe we can talk to the parents."

"Okay," I replied. "You want to go now?"

Ward looked at his phone. "Sure, but let's drive separately. I'll probably leave right from there to check in to my hotel."

"Sounds good. Adam, you want to drive or want me to?"

"Uh, actually, I was going to meet Kim over lunch. We have to look at flowers. Or maybe it's flowers on the invitation. I'm starting to lose track."

"Doesn't sound like something you need the best man for."

"God, no."

"Congratulations," Ward said. He shrugged back into his suit coat.

"Thanks... I think." Adam shook his head. "It's a wonder any groom ever goes through with a wedding. It's like the entire process is designed to make the man run as far away as he can."

"That's what engagements are for," I said lightly. "If you can stay with her while she's a bride, you can make it through anything."

"The only thing keeping me going is the anticipation of watching you go through the same thing," Adam said, chucking me on the shoulder.

I didn't reply.

Ward broke the sudden silence. "I'll, uh... meet you at Mr. Taggert's residence at one-thirty?"

We nodded and went our separate way–Adam and me to the staff lot, Ward to wherever he had parked his Feebmobile.

"Did I say something wrong?" Adam asked as we descended the stairs.

"Just leave it alone," I said.

"Something I should know about you two?"

"I said, leave it alone."

"Okay! Okay." He held his hands up in surrender. "I'll see you over there."

I fished in my pocket for my car keys as we split, hitting the unlock button.

My pocket vibrated as I opened the door.

Two hours since my last reminder about the body in the closet. Not that I needed one right now.

Because curled in the cramped back seat of the Mustang lay a bleeding Trav Becker.

4

O*H, CRAP.*

I looked around. Fortunately, Adam and Ward had both moved out of sight. There was no one else around, but I had to be careful. There was a camera on this lot.

I opened the back door and leaned in, careful not to put any weight on him. I checked his pulse. Nothing.

Great. Another dead body on my hands.

I just stood there for a while, staring into his lifeless eyes. He was dressed exactly like the first one, all in black. He also wore a gun belt, but in addition to a holstered gun on one hip, there was a long, narrow leather sheath hanging from the opposite side.

It was a scabbard and sword. What the hell was he doing with a sword? I'd never held one of the things in my life, despite *The Princess Bride* being one of my favorite movies. I was certain if I ever picked one up, I'd be lucky if I didn't cut my own thumb off.

Well, I couldn't think about it right now. I had to get moving. But what was I going to do with my rapidly-cooling friend? I didn't dare leave him in the back seat. If Adam or Ward happened to look inside, it would all be over.

I got into the car, and pulled around to a small alley that exited the parking lot. It was narrow, and quite close to the building, so it was rarely used. It was also out of range of the security camera that watched the rest of the parking lot.

I squeezed out of the car and, doing my best to keep his blood from getting on my clothes, managed to maneuver Dead Trav Number Two out of the car and into the trunk.

I got back into the car and took a deep breath. I had to go. Adam and Ward would be waiting at the witness's residence. But I had one more thing to do before I could join them.

I pulled out my phone, and poked the picture of a smallish, red-haired man with a half-day's growth of beard that had taken him two weeks to achieve.

"Hey," Sam Markus said.

"Good morning. Just calling to tell you good luck, Mr. Consultant. Got everything you need for your first day on the job?"

"I'm a knowledge worker," my best friend replied loftily. "I carry all the tools I need in my head."

"Are you going to be ready for D-Day?"

"I better be. I told them when they hired me I would have their site up, legal, and uncrackable on the first day of online gaming."

Sam had spent pretty much his entire career in academia. He'd been doing research in particle physics for nearly a decade. Recently, his work had veered off into a new direction, as some of the work he had done had applications in a branch of mathematics related to something called quantum computing.

Meanwhile, after years of lobbying by the casino industry, the state legislature had passed a law making online gaming legal.

While a big business, online gambling had historically been pretty shady. Anything based in the U.S. had to technically be "for entertainment only," although many sites had ways to get players to cough up money in order to unlock certain benefits or access to better games. There were a few true online gaming sites, but they were generally run offshore by countries who could ignore threats from American law enforcement. As such, you could almost guarantee they were crooked. You had to be really dumb, or really addicted to gambling, to go anywhere near them.

A few states, beginning with the gambling capitals of Nevada and New Jersey, had taken some tentative steps to offer the gambling industry a way for online casinos to go legit, offering clean games in the same way real-world casinos did, inspected and regulated by the state. Smelling tax revenue, our state–which in recent years had gradually let more and more communities build casinos–decided to join the parade.

But in a world where stories about a company's credit card database getting hacked was a daily occurrence, convincing people the games were honest was the one thing standing between a gaming site and big, big money.

It turned out that Sam's work had an application for online casinos. Using this quantum computing, he could write gambling algorithms that in theory made the games truly random and honest, not to mention totally uncrackable.

With the growing Hispanic market in mind, a local group was developing an online casino they called *El Juego Grande*, The Big Game. The group had approached Sam to lead a small team to write secure gaming algorithms for them. They had also thrown a huge donation at the university, making his department head only too happy to loan him out.

But there was pressure to produce that he had never experienced before. Four or five other casino operators were working on their own online sites. Conventional wisdom said if you weren't there on opening day, you could lose out.

The new law took effect in just two weeks, and one member of Sam's team had been very distracted.

"Have you talked to Sanjana?" I asked.

"Yesterday. She said she was coming in. I told her it wasn't necessary, but she said it beat staying home staring at the phone."

Sanjana Patel was another mathematician Sam had recruited to help him with *the El Juego Grande* project.

She was also the mother of Sophie, the elder of the missing girls.

"I guess I can understand that. Anything to take your mind off it for even a little while. I'm doing everything I can."

"I know you are. Anything I can do?"

"Well, now that you ask, there is something going on I could use your advice on."

"About the case?"

"Not exactly. Look, I know you are balls to the wall, but I have something I need you to look at."

"What kind of something?"

"Something related to our fun last year."

"Oh, shit."

"Yeah."

"Can you tell me anymore?"

"Not over the phone."

"Right," he said. "Umm… well, I was planning to work through lunch, but I could probably sneak away."

"Adam and I are headed out to re-interview a witness. How about I text you when we're done?"

"Sounds like a plan."

No sooner had I hung up than my phone started playing the opening piano riff to Springsteen's "Thunder Road."

"Hey," I said.

"Wow. I guess the magic really is gone," Mary teased.

I must have sounded more worn out than I realized.

"Sorry," I said. "Been a long day."

"It's not even half over."

"I know. It's been… some morning."

"Buy me lunch and tell me about it?"

"Sorry, meeting Adam in a few minutes. Leon is keeping us on the missing girls."

"That's good, right? Weren't you two worried they were going to close the investigation?"

"Yeah. But instead Leon put Adam and me with an FBI guy to go through everything again, hoping to find something we all missed. We're going to start over with some of the witnesses."

"Leon is smart. He knows you won't give up. Tell me that you will get some lunch, though."

"Of course."

"Because breakfast after swimming was the drive-through, right?"

"Uh…"

"Trav. You can't save the world if you're not going to take care of yourself. Don't make me call your mother."

"Fine, fine. No need for the nuclear option. I'll stop for something on the way back."

"Promise?"

"Yeah."

"All right then. Will I see you tonight?"

"I hope so. Maybe after your rehearsal?"

"It might be late."

"That's not a problem. Text me when you're done."

"Okay. Love you."

"Love you, too."

Wishing I was headed to a lunch date with my girlfriend instead of to a witness interview that was probably a dead end, I tossed the phone onto the passenger seat and flicked on the radio.

Unfortunately, instead of the particular brand of album rock I tune in for, I was treated to talk.

Crap. Just when this day couldn't get any worse.

When I was a teenager, my dad had turned me on to his favorite music, marginal and obscure album rock bands of the Seventies and Eighties. I'd inherited his extensive album and CD collection when he'd died a couple of years ago, but honestly didn't pull them out all that much because our town had an increasingly rare media jewel.

A great radio station.

Axe 106.9 had managed to avoid the homogenization of music radio that has happened over the last fifteen years or so, playing a unique blend of classic and modern rock, blues and jazz that had become the soundtrack to my life through high school, college and into adulthood.

When the longtime owner had decided to retire, he did something unexpected. Rather than cashing out and selling to a giant media company, he had done some sort of deal where the station was transferred to a non-profit board and became part of the public radio system.

Which also eliminated commercials, in favor of corporate underwriting announcements ("Support for this program comes from World of Wheels, the Tri State's local bicycle shop and organic deli…"), and the occasional pledge drive.

I considered it a fair trade-off, and was happy to send them a few bucks a month.

But apparently, I was one of the few who did. Because more and more news and talk programs started showing up on the air.

Blame Pandora. Blame the iPhone. Blame Google. But I guess that even in the non-commercial world, you have to worry about ratings. And with people turning to the internet for music, broadcast radio turned more and more to talk and news shows.

First it was the Wing and a Prayer Morning Battalion, a truly great morning music show, replaced by NPR's Morning Edition.

Now, apparently, the midday DJ had been replaced by some talk program.

I was just about to switch the radio off, when I realized I recognized the voice of the host. I turned the radio back up.

"Leah, I definitely sense a male energy surrounding you. When you asked me that question, it was like your words were actually a color. And can you guess what that color was?"

"No, Morgan."

"The color was blue. I think you're having a boy."

"A boy!" Even through the speakers, you could hear that the caller was near tears. "That's wonderful. Thank you!"

"You're welcome," the host replied warmly. She smoothly shifted into announcer mode. "You're listening to *Second Sight* on KAXE. I'm Morgan Foster. What does *your* future hold? More of your calls after the news."

Now I did switch the radio off. I wasn't sure which bothered me more. That my favorite radio station had put a talk show featuring a psychic on the air...

Or that the psychic was someone I knew.

I might have been even more offended if I hadn't known Morgan Foster was the real deal. She actually did have a gift that allowed her to see beyond the physical world most of us see.

Like Sam, she had played an important role in my adventures last year.

When I had realized I was bouncing from stream to stream, it had been Morgan who had given a name to what was happening to me, and helped me understand it. She even had a name for people like me. Travelers.

(Yeah, I know… Trav is a Traveler. That weirds me out to this day.)

Morgan had advanced a theory that seers, prophets, and mystics throughout history did not foretell the future so much as they perceived events in another parallel reality, one where time was flowing at a slightly faster rate. And many of the unexplainable occurrences and mysteries which most of us dismissed as urban legends could in fact be explained by the notion that people sometimes physically moved between streams.

Then, after shifting streams myself, I had met *that* reality's version of Morgan, who had helped me even more. Without her help, I probably would have just kept drifting, or sometimes getting pushed from stream to stream. Morgan had helped me figure out a way to direct my Traveling to the stream of my desire.

I had also met a third Morgan Foster. And in some ways that had been the strangest experience of all.

Anyway, with a lot of help from Morgan (each version) and Sam, the bad guys got what they deserved, and the hero got the girl. Everyone (well, almost everyone) lived.

But I had learned a valuable lesson about meddling with events in the Multiverse. In each reality I spent time in, any move I–or another version of Trav–made to save a life, or avert some form of disaster, caused unforeseen ripples down the line.

In one reality, my partner Adam had died in a shootout. In another, I'd managed to save him, only for him later to be involved in a car accident where a little girl died.

After the dust settled, Sam and I agreed to do nothing further to disturb the natural progression of events.

I had kept that promise. But turning away from everything associated with Traveling had also meant not talking to Morgan Foster.

In fact, I had never even told her thank you. She had asked me to tell her how everything had turned out. But I had felt the wiser course would be to stay away from her.

So now I was feeling pissed that another of my favorite music shows was gone and, at the same time, feeling guilty about showing up in Morgan's life, blowing her mind about how the universe worked, and then never speaking to her again.

I sighed. Just another item to add to the list. Right after figuring out why dead versions of myself kept appearing.

And, finding those missing girls.

Alan Taggert lived in a nondescript but well-kept, single-story ranch with attached two-car garage. The house was that light green which was all the rage for about eighteen months in the early Sixties, preserved forever by those owners who had made the unfortunate choice of permanent siding.

But the yard was immaculate. The grass was the kind of lush, blue-green that only comes from daily watering and exacting amounts of carefully-applied fertilizer. It looked softer than my living room carpet. A colorful flowerbed lay along the house's front.

A hedge you could have used as a drafting table ran along one side of the yard and disappeared behind the house.

Adam's SUV and Ward's Feebmobile were already parked in front of me. I got out at the same time as Adam and Ward. We made our way up the sidewalk, the grass along its edges razor-straight.

"Mr. Taggert?" I said to the man who answered the door. He looked to be in his early seventies, paunchy, with silver hair and little glasses. He wore a white, short-sleeved shirt, tucked in, belly hanging over a pair of black pants that had seen better days. His waist had long since ceased to be effective in holding up said trousers, so he'd resorted to suspenders.

"Yes?" he said, a little uncertainly, looking from one to the other of us.

"I'm Detective Becker, this is Detective Yount and Special Agent Ward from the FBI. I'm sorry to bother you, but we'd like to ask you a few questions."

"This is about the girls?" His voice was low and gargly, like there was a perpetual frog in his throat.

"Yes." I answered what I knew would be his next question before he could ask it. "I know you've already given a statement…"

"Three times."

"Right. But, we've been asked to kind of go back to the beginning and go over everything again. I hope you don't mind."

"Of course not. I want you to find them as much as anyone." He opened the door fully. "Do you want to come in?"

"Actually," Ward said, "Could you come outside and show us exactly where you saw the girls?"

"All right."

We moved aside as he stepped onto the porch and shuffled across it, stepping down into the front yard.

"Can you tell me where you were when you saw the girls?" Ward asked.

Taggert nodded, and led us toward the right side of the house, which was opposite the garage. He stopped at the corner. There was about ten feet of side yard, ending at the hedge, which seemed to extend all the way to the other end of his property.

"I was right about here, watering the mums." He waved a hand toward the flowers along the front of the house. "Two little girls rode past on bikes."

He turned back toward us.

"And that's it."

"What time was this?" Ward asked.

"Two or two-thirty."

"How do you know it was the missing girls you saw?" Ward asked.

"When they ran the pictures on the news, I recognized them."

The FBI agent turned to Adam and me. "How far away are we from the Patel residence?"

"A half mile," Adam supplied.

Ward nodded. "Fits the time line. What else?"

"That's it," said Taggert.

"Do you remember seeing any unfamiliar vehicles in the neighborhood?"

"No," Taggert replied.

"People you didn't recognize?"

Taggert sighed. "No. I keep telling you people. I just saw two little girls. I would like to be able to help more, but there just isn't anything else."

"But the woman with the kids in the inflatable pool—" Ward consulted his tablet, "—Mrs. Rodriguez, did not see them. And she was only two blocks over."

"That's what I understand," said Taggert.

It was obvious that, while Mr. Taggert wanted to help, he was tired of telling the same story over and over again.

Ward thanked Taggert, and we made our way back to our vehicles.

"What next?" asked Adam.

Ward consulted his tablet again, paging through the notes he had made back at the station.

"Families, I think." He glanced in the direction of the house, making sure Taggert was back inside before he continued. "They'll be frustrated that we keep asking the same questions, too, but maybe we'll shake something loose."

"That'd be nice," Adam said. "Trav, you ready?"

"Trav?"

But I wasn't listening. I was watching a multitude of Trav Beckers lining the sidewalk ahead of me.

5

MY HEART SANK as I watched more than a dozen ghostly figures move around in a seemingly random fashion.

If I looked closer, however, there was some rhyme and reason to their motion. Some seemed to be in conversation with an unseen second person. Another was going through the motions of unlocking a car. Still another was focused intently on the ground.

The figures had varying degrees of solidity. Some were wraithlike, others looked nearly normal.

The one thing each figure had in common was a glowing outline, like someone had traced around them with a fluorescent piece of chalk. The outlines were all blue.

Except one.

I knew two things.

One, I was the only one who could see this little Trav-mob. I knew that Adam and Ward were staring at me, wondering what I was looking at, but I couldn't reply, not yet, because…

There.

The second thing I knew was that there would be one figure outlined not in blue, but in red. And that was important.

"Trav?"

I didn't answer right away, just stared at the milling figures, in particular the red one that was crouched down, looking under one of the hedge plants that lined the sidewalk.

I had hoped never to see this sight again.

I'd been getting along just fine without the hocus-pocus for the last year. And damned if I was going to start depending on it now. Who knew what can of worms it might open? Better to work this case the old-fashioned way.

I closed my eyes, took a couple of deep breaths.

No, thank you.

I opened them again. The knot of scurrying bodies was gone.

"Trav. Are you okay?"

"Yeah. Sorry. Just... uh, trying to visualize the route they might have taken that would have missed Rodriguez."

I mentally went back over the conversation I had missed. "Yeah, families. That's probably our next step."

We got back into our vehicles and drove to the Patel place.

The Patel home was on a cul de sac, same street as Taggert's, but in a newer section. Their house was bigger, with a three-stall garage. The yard was well-kept, but not to the same degree as Taggert's.

Mr. Patel answered the door. I watched his eyes light up. But they quickly dimmed, his shoulders slumping as he realized we were not bringing any good news. He invited us in, managing a gracious, if hollow, smile.

I introduced him to Ward, then asked, "Mrs. Patel isn't home?"

He shook his head. "She decided to go in to work. I am working from home today. You know, just in case there was some news."

Riswan Patel was around forty, with just a touch of gray at the temples framing his wide-set face. His Indian heritage was clear, but he spoke with no accent. He wore suit pants and a white dress shirt, sleeves rolled to just below his elbows.

Ward was a little smarter this time, emphasizing that we would probably be going over familiar ground, and apologizing in advance for asking questions he had answered dozens of times previously.

"Please, come in and sit," Patel said.

He motioned us to the living room, where we arranged ourselves–Ward and I claiming a soft, overstuffed couch, Adam in a wingback chair. We declined the usual offer of something to drink. Patel sat in a love seat opposite the couch.

Ward walked the man through the day of the girls' disappearance.

No, he had not seen any strange vehicles or people in the neighborhood.

No, Sophie had not been acting oddly.

No, it wasn't strange to allow Sophie to bike by herself to the pool.

"We've always believed parents live too much in fear, never letting children be unsupervised," Patel said. "Some families don't even let their children walk three blocks to school. We were proud of Sophie's independence. We never dreamed that here, in this neighborhood, those paranoid fantasies were the truth..."

His voice trailed off. He squeezed his eyes shut. It took some time to get himself back together.

"I'm sorry," he finally said, voice hoarse from holding back tears, "what else can I tell you?"

Ward shook his head. "I don't think I have any more questions right now. Can we see Sophie's room?"

Patel nodded. "It's upstairs."

He led us to the second floor and into a room just to the right of the stairs. It was painted robin's-egg blue, with the standard collection of posters of cats and boy bands on the wall. A neat desk sat near the window, with a MacBook at its center.

"Computer Forensics has been through it completely," Adam said. "No strange email or chats. All her Facebook friends check out, real people. They even traced the IP addresses of every computer that visited her profile for the last six months. Nothing."

Ward nodded. He made a show of poking around a little bit, but didn't find anything.

We trooped downstairs and stood by the door.

"Are you going to see Michelle now?" Patel asked.

"Yes," Ward replied. "Then we will want to talk to your wife. Can we visit her at work?"

Patel nodded. "I'll call and tell her to expect you."

"Anything we should know before we talk to Ms. Day?" Ward asked. "Tell me a little about the relationship between Sophie and Ella."

Patel didn't answer right away. When he did, his voice was tight once again. "Sophie doted on Ella. From the time she and Michelle moved into the neighborhood, Sophie was always looking out for her. And Ella idolized Sophie. When Michelle asked Sophie to watch Ella this summer while she was working, both girls were thrilled."

"Twelve is a little young to be a full-time sitter, isn't it?" Ward asked.

"Our daughter is very mature for her age, Mr. Ward," Patel said. "All you had to do was watch the two together to see how good Sophie was with Ella. But the truth is, while Michelle was paying Sophie for her time, it was understood that my wife would be keeping an eye on the girls as well."

"But your wife wasn't here the day the girls disappeared."

Patel shook his head. "No. Sanjana worked from home much of the time, but on this particular day, she needed to go into the office."

"I see," Ward said.

Patel leaned forward in his chair. "Gentlemen, please. If I can ask just one thing of you. When you talk to my wife, try not to bring up this topic. It has been tearing her apart that she wasn't here."

"We don't know that it would have made any difference. The girls would still have biked to the pool," I said.

46

"Even so. You will have an easier time interviewing her if you don't upset her any further."

Ward nodded. "We'll do our best."

He looked at his device again, flipping his finger upward to page through his notes. "Now, what about Mr. Dawson? Ms. Day's boyfriend?"

"We don't know Joshua well," Patel said. "But he and Michelle had been seeing each other for some months. She has not had very good luck in men. Please don't misunderstand me. It's not like there was a parade of men coming and going from her house. There have been a handful of boyfriends since we have known her. Joshua seemed, well, a cut above the sort of man she had previously been seeing. He has a good job, doesn't spend a lot of time in bars. He has always seemed trustworthy. We were happy for Michelle."

"He didn't seem unusually interested in Ella?" Ward asked.

Patel's lips wrinkled in distaste. "We watch television, Special Agent. We know it is almost always the father or the boyfriend who is found to be guilty in cases like these. I have had to answer questions—" He closed his eyes and pinched the bridge of his nose. "—that no father, no *man* should have to think about, let alone hear. I have given your investigators complete access to our house, my computer here at home, and also at my office. My understanding is Joshua has done the same."

Ward glanced at Adam and me. We nodded.

"You understand I have to ask?" Ward said gently.

Patel nodded. "It is worth noting that Joshua has stood by Michelle through this entire crisis. Even though, as I said, his entire life history and actions have been scrutinized by the police and the media."

Ward nodded. "Well, sounds like Ms. Day could use someone like that. And it sounds like you have been good friends to her as well." He pulled a business card out of his breast pocket.

"I know that you have answered these questions again and again, and I am sorry that the investigation hasn't borne much fruit. But, we are doing everything we can. If you can think of anything, *anything* that might help us, please call me. This is my cell number. You can call it anytime of the day or night."

Patel nodded. "Thank you."

"We'll stay in touch."

On the street, Ward turned to us.

"Do you agree with his take on Dawson?"

Adam and I exchanged glances. We both shrugged.

"Patel was right, it *is* often the boyfriend," I said. "He's been under a microscope since the first day. But no one has found anything the least bit dirty about him."

Ward ran a hand through his hair. "The more you dig into this, the fewer clues you have."

"That's why they pay us the big bucks," Adam said. "So, the Day place?"

Ward nodded. "How far?"

"Just down the block. We can walk."

We started down the sidewalk. A flash of movement caught my eye, and I turned back towards our cars, to see a faint, red-tinged image of myself getting in the Mustang.

Dammit.

NO.

I turned my back on Red Trav and followed Ward and Adam along the sidewalk.

The neighborhood had obviously been developed in stages. Taggert's place was late Fifties or early Sixties. The Patel's was only maybe ten years old.

Michelle Day's was somewhere in between. It was a single-story ranch, with a two-car garage. It had redwood siding that was a little faded. The grass was long, but not unkempt.

An older Nissan SUV was parked in the garage, and a little Subaru sedan was in the driveway behind it.

Ward raised his hand to ring the doorbell. But before he even touched it, the door swung open.

"Finally!" exclaimed the woman who opened the door.

Like the Patels, Michelle Day was around forty. Average height, with light brown hair cut in a short bob. She wore faded jeans and a Packers sweatshirt, and greeted us with an exasperated sigh.

"It's about time. We've been waiting for you!"

"Excuse me?" Ward began. "I'm not..."

Ms. Day cut him off. "Please. We know why you're here. And we're anxious to get started."

"Started?"

She waved a hand. "You'll understand. Please, come in."

Ward narrowed his eyes and glanced back at us. He raised an eyebrow.

Adam and I both shrugged.

We all trooped into the house, taking a left into the living room.

"Here they are, just like you said," Ms. Day said proudly.

Ward and Adam looked confused. Fortunately, I was still behind them, or they might have seen *my* jaw drop. I wasn't confused at all, just stunned.

On the couch, sipping from a bottle of water, and looking at us with interest, sat Morgan Foster.

6

WARD STUDIED THE two women.

"And you are...?" he said to Morgan.

"Morgan Foster," she replied. She rose and put out her hand.

Ward automatically took it. "Special Agent Matthew Ward. These are Detectives Young and Becker."

Morgan Foster hadn't changed much in the last year. She was petite, with a mass of curly, blonde hair that encircled her head like a cloud. She wore a close-fitting, leotard-like top with a scoop-neck collar, a long cardigan sweater, and black leggings that ended in a pair of Chuck Taylors in sparkly silver.

Morgan inclined her head to Adam, then at me.

"Detectives."

She held my gaze for a beat longer than necessary, and turned back to Ward, who you could tell was trying to figure out why she was here.

"Are you Ms. Day's attorney?" he tried.

I opened my mouth to explain, but Michelle Day beat me to it.

"Morgan is a psychic!" she exclaimed. "She can help us find my daughter!"

To his credit, Ward took this news without missing a beat.

"I see," he said slowly. "And... Ms. Foster, is it?"

Morgan nodded.

"How long have you known Ms. Day?"

"We just met."

50

"Has Ms. Day… er, retained your services?"

"We haven't gotten that far."

"We were just going to go up to Ella's room," interrupted Michelle. "Morgan is going to try and pick up some vibes from touching Ella's things."

"Actually, Ms. Day, we would prefer to ask you some questions."

"I have answered your questions every day for weeks," she retorted, "and you're no closer to finding my daughter. Isn't this what you people do sometimes when you've reached a dead end? Bring in a psychic?"

"Just on television, Ms. Day," Ward replied patiently. "To the best of my knowledge, the Bureau has never involved psychics in any investigations."

"Well, maybe it's time you started."

"Be that as it may, we would like to talk with you for a few minutes, and it's probably best if we do so privately."

"Nonsense," Michelle replied. "Anything you can say to me you can say in front of Morgan."

"No, it's fine," Morgan interrupted. "I'll go."

She stood up, and turned to Michelle Day. "You have my number. Why don't you call me later and we can pick up where we left off? I tend to work better when there aren't a bunch of people around, anyway."

Michelle moved to escort her from the room, but Morgan held up a hand.

"No, you should get started. I can let myself out." She crossed to Michelle and took her hand in both of hers.

"I have a good feeling, Michelle," Morgan looked earnestly at the other woman. "Stay strong."

"Thank you," Michelle whispered.

"Special Agent, Detectives." Morgan nodded to each of us in turn.

I was closest to the entryway, and stepped aside to let her pass. She paused for a moment, raising both eyebrows, and stared deeply into my eyes. It was just for a few seconds, but I have a girlfriend, not to mention a mother. I knew what that look meant.

We need to talk.

Great.

Just great.

I looked up from Morgan's gaze to meet the eyes of Agent Ward, who was watching the petite psychic thoughtfully. He looked at me and I could see the beginning of a question in his eyes. But he just turned and started questioning Michelle Day.

Which was just as fruitful as the previous interviews, with an extra dose of belligerence, as Michelle was still a little sore from what she saw as our brusque treatment of Morgan.

Finally, just to try and get some cooperation out of her, Ward promised to float the idea of consulting the psychic to our bosses. That seemed to mollify her, but after the same round of questions and looking over Ella's room, we left with little to show for the day.

We were at the front door when a beautiful car pulled up and parked in front of the garage.

It was a classic. A Plymouth Road Runner, powder blue, 1969 or 1970, so cherry it looked like it had just been driven off the showroom floor.

I'm a Ford man myself, but this car was enough to make me think about going Chrysler.

A man got out and walked toward us.

"Josh!" Michelle called. She pushed past us and stepped off the porch, running to him and throwing her arms around his neck.

Joshua Dawson returned the embrace.

"Is there some news?" He looked from Michelle to the three of us, frowning, trying to assess whether we were bringing good or bad tidings. Unlike the car, he was a nondescript fellow. Average height, kind of pale. Dark hair peeked out from under a brown cap.

"No, nothing new," said Michelle, "but Special Agent Ward here is going to talk to his boss about letting Morgan help with the investigation!"

"Is that so?" Dawson looked surprised. "Is that normal procedure?"

"They're making an exception!" she gushed.

"Er, we'll have to see," Ward said. "Mr. Dawson, can we ask you a few questions?"

"Why?" Michelle asked. "Josh wasn't even in town that day!"

"Just procedure, Ms. Day."

Her expression darkened. For a moment it looked like she was going to go off again, but Dawson put a hand on her arm.

"No, it's fine, hon. You go inside. I'm sure this won't take long."

She looked doubtful, but finally shrugged and bid us goodbye.

Dawson leaned against the white railing that encircled the small porch and looked at us.

"Okay. I'm all yours."

"When was the last time you saw Ella?" Ward asked.

"Day before they disappeared. I took her and her mom out for supper."

"Where did you go?"

"Applebee's."

"You don't remember any strangers or strange vehicles in the neighborhood?"

Dawson shook his head.

"How would you characterize your relationship with Ella?"

Dawson's eyes went flat.

"Cordial." His voice was carefully neutral.

"What do you mean by that?"

"Just what I said. Cordial. You don't know what it means, look it up in the dictionary."

"Mr. Dawson, I'm just asking you to describe your relationship with the girl."

"No, I know exactly what you're doing," Dawson snapped. "Look. Ella was... *is* the daughter of my girlfriend. That's it. The three of us went out for ice cream a couple of times, but both Michelle and I knew better than to push it. You ever dated a woman with a child, Agent Ward? You don't do it exactly right and she either resents you for trying to replace her dad or gets too attached too fast. If you break up, she gets hurt all over again."

He stopped, took off his hat and ran a hand through his hair.

"Look. I know I'm a suspect. The boyfriend always is. But you can ask anyone. I've never laid a hand on Ella. Never been alone with her. I know you guys are just doing your job, but you're barking up the wrong tree. I've let the police search my house, my computer, my car. What else can I do?"

"It's nothing personal, Mr. Dawson," Ward said. "We're asking every..."

"It's not personal to *you*," Dawson exploded. "It sure as hell is to us! It is to *her.*"

He pointed toward the house. "That woman is desperate. Desperate enough to consult a psychic. I know how she comes off, but she is *scared to death* that the next knock on the door, the next phone call, is the one that ends everything for her.

"*Please.*" His voice turned pleading. "Find her."

"We're doing everything we can, sir," Ward said.

"Nice car," I said to change of subject.

"Thanks," Dawson replied, relaxing a little.

"Restore it yourself?"

He gave a modest shrug. "It was in good shape when I got it. There were some rips in the upholstery, which I fixed. Someone had put an after-market stereo in. Took me awhile, but I finally found a factory unit on eBay."

"Nice."

This exchange defused the atmosphere enough to cool things off to the point where we could do the "if there is anything else you can think of, please don't hesitate to contact us" dance.

We piled into our cars, agreeing to meet back at the station. We would head over to see Sanjana Patel after Ward got back from checking in to his hotel and Adam got done with his flower mission. I had hoped to be able to sneak away and meet Sam, but there wasn't going to be enough time. I would have to connect with him later.

Upon my arrival, I found a plastic sack sitting on my desk. I hung my jacket across the back of my chair and opened it. I pulled out a bottle of water, along with a sub sandwich. Turkey on wheat, spinach, onions, olives, all the peppers, and spicy mustard. My standing Subway order. A Post-It note was stuck to the wrapper.

I knew you were lying about getting lunch.

I smiled. Mary knew me too well. I zipped off a thank-you text.

You're welcome. Still on for tonight?

Wouldn't miss it.

I then tried a new trick, at least for me. I sent her an emoji, one of those happy face things.

She responded with a pair kissing lips.

I kept up this exchange while wolfing the sandwich down, discovering in the process Mary had included a small bag of Cheetos, my favorite guilty pleasure.

An angel. The woman was an angel.

Bolstered by the food and the prospect of some romance after Mary's rehearsal was over, I dove back into the case. I quickly typed up my notes from the interviews, such as they were. Ward was back by this time. I sent Adam a text, asking for his ETA.

Might be awhile. Flower crisis.

"Adam got hung up," I said to Ward. "Why don't we head over to *El Juego* and he can catch up later?"

"Sounds good. You want to drive, or do you want me to?"

At that moment, my phone buzzed with the arrival of a message. I thought it was Adam, acknowledging what I had just told Ward, but it was a reminder. Fortunately, I had silenced the phone, or we would have been treated to more Glass Tiger.

Don't forget to clean out your closet. And the trunk.

"Uh, let's take your car."

"What do you know about this place?" Ward asked, after I had given him directions.

"It's a startup. Only been around a few months."

"That's weird. In most of the states that have legalized online gaming, it's the big gaming companies that have gotten there first."

"That's what I understand. But the CEO is hooked into the venture capital crowd, and they bought into his vision that a lean, limber company could get there first with a superior project when the new law took effect. He hasn't had any trouble finding investors."

"Who's the CEO?"

"His name is Christopher Clark. He made a boatload of money with his first company, which was designing hospital websites or something. Sold it just about the time they started talking about legalizing online gaming. Decided to get into the game, so to speak."

"Funny. And the office is here?"

We had arrived in The District, which we locals called an area of town that formerly had housed decaying warehouses. Gradually, developers had been reclaiming more and more buildings, until the area now housed a pretty lively mix of unique restaurants, urban lofts, and night clubs. Just a year ago, there had been places in this neighborhood it was unwise to go after dark. Now there were people on the streets until all hours.

"Yeah. It's an up and coming neighborhood. A lot of businesses and people are moving down here."

"Probably a lot easier now that Anton Kaaro doesn't own most of it."

"Ah. You've heard of Kaaro."

"Oh, yeah. He was a thorn in our side, too, until you put him away. Nice work."

"Thanks."

"How long were you undercover with him?" he asked.

"A few months."

"That had to be a tough gig. From what I've heard, Kaaro is a sharp cookie. You'd have to be a pretty good actor to fool him."

I had to tread carefully here. It was true Trav Becker had been undercover for several months, pretending to be a crooked cop in the crime lord's employ. But it hadn't been me. It had been the Trav Becker who had originated on this stream, killed by a version of Sam Markus, who had come to believe Traveling was dangerous and had taken it upon himself to eliminate that danger—one Trav at a time.

I had never fully understood the relationship between that Trav (Trav One in our naming scheme) and Kaaro.

"Things did get pretty hairy at a couple of points," I said simply.

Time to change the subject. "Ironically, the building Clark's company is in is the very one we took Kaaro down in."

"Really."

"Yeah, it went cheap, needless to say. Clark put a ton of cash into re-habbing it. His company is on two of the floors, and he also hosts a new business incubator in some unoccupied space."

"Did you spend a lot of time there? You seem to know a lot about it."

I should. I had blown it up on another stream. Clark had been lucky there was something here to remodel at all.

But I just shrugged and said, "Some. But Clark is one of those guys whose every move is covered by the business reporters. Plus, he hired a friend of mine to help him design the computer algorithms that will underpin the site."

"That's an interesting coincidence."

"Well, it's a small town."

"Your friend must be pretty smart," Ward observed. "Making the math honest is the one thing keeping online gaming from going mainstream."

"That's what Clark says will be the difference between El Juego and the other online casinos."

"Isn't Sanjana Patel in the math end of this, too?"

"Yeah. In fact, my friend, his name is Sam Markus, is the one who brought her into the company."

Ward grunted. I got the feeling he was about to say something else, but we had arrived.

"It's right up here," I said. Ward swung into a parking spot.

I hadn't been in the building since the remodel, but I noticed immediately upon entering that Clark had kept the building's signature feature.

Before Clark (or Kaaro) got hold of it, the building had been the warehouse for Sieman's Department Store, one of those pre-mall downtown department stores that had a little of everything, from furniture to lingerie. Back in the day, the store had also featured a unique cash-handling system.

There were no cash registers anywhere in the store. A customer's money or check was put into a latched metal container, about the size of a soup can. The container was clipped to a fast moving belt, which was surrounded by a narrow wire enclosure, not much wider around than the container itself. The store's ceiling was covered with a complex spider web of the tracks, like a tiny monorail system, which zipped the little box to the cashier's office, where the purchase was recorded and change made, before being sent back.

The cash railway was eventually moved to the warehouse, and Clark had kept it. In fact, he had kept it operational. The first thing you heard when you walked in was the low hum of the belts moving within a spider web of the wire enclosures all along the ceiling.

One ran down a wall just inside and along the right side. It terminated just behind the control desk, where a young woman smiled at us.

"Sanjana Patel, please," I said. "She should be expecting us."

She pointed to a clipboard in front of her. "Certainly. Can you sign in?"

After we had done so, she wrote our names on a notecard, folded it, and put it in one of the cash railway cars. She flipped a couple of switches and affixed the car to the belt. After a moment, it engaged and zipped up the wall, along the ceiling, and careened through a couple of junctions before it went out of sight.

A couple of minutes later, Sanjana Patel, accompanied by Christopher Clark himself, came down a set of stairs in the center of the first floor.

Sanjana Patel was a few years younger than her husband. She wore jeans, a royal-blue top, and a pair of flat sandals—gold, with glittery bangles. Her black hair was pulled back away from her face, which was drawn and tight.

Christopher Clark looked every inch the dot com millionaire. He was around forty, slightly pudgy, with brown hair and beard. His red flannel shirt was open over a vintage Pac-Man t-shirt.

"Christopher Clark," he said to Ward, stretching out a hand. Proving that even if you're a jeans-wearing CEO, you still turn to the guy wearing the suit first.

"Special Agent Ward," Ward said. "This is Detective Becker."

"Do you have any news?" Sanjana asked.

I shook my head. The tiny spark of hope that lit her eyes as she approached us went out. But she managed a gracious, if hollow, smile.

"What can I do to help?"

"Special Agent Ward is new on the case," I explained. "We're going back over everything."

She nodded.

"Please come upstairs," Clark said. "You can use my office."

"You don't have to do that, Chris," Sanjana said. "We can use one of the conference rooms."

"Nonsense," he replied with a sniff. "My office is much more comfortable. Besides, I spend too much time in there anyway. Do me good to get out and wander around."

We headed toward the stairs. A chill ran down my back as I realized I was walking over the exact spot where I had watched Anton Kaaro use a young officer named Amy Harper as a human shield, taking four bullets meant for him.

Granted, Amy had, in the words of Obi-wan, gone over to the Dark Side. In both this and the other stream, she had been in Kaaro's employ. But she had deserved better, and I was grateful that on this stream, she was still breathing, even if she was in prison.

"Interesting intercom system you have," Ward said to Clark.

The other man smiled. "Pretty retro, isn't it? When I bought the building, the architect told me I was crazy to keep it, but the idea of our high-tech workflow juxtaposed with something so quaint appealed to me. Plus, it's an object lesson. Disruption is the rule in technology. I'm sure the guys who invented this thing told themselves again and again that cash registers would never catch on. It's good for us to keep that in mind. Just because you're on top today doesn't mean you won't be pushed aside by The Next Big Thing. Plus, it's way more fun than sending email."

As we neared the top of the stairs, he turned to me. "You're Sam's friend, right?"

I nodded.

"He's a good man. There's no way we'd be ready for launch day without him. The algorithms he's written? I graduated from MIT, and I can barely understand them. It's like they're from some other universe."

"What?" I said sharply.

"Uh, the math is... well, way complicated." His voice trailed off as he gave me a perplexed look.

"Sorry," I said. "I thought you said something else."

He nodded. "Turn left here."

The second floor was divided into two halves, which from this angle looked pretty much alike. Rows of tables, each with multiple computers on top. There were white boards in front of almost every table. The high-tech look of the place was slightly ruined by the index cards and Post-It notes that festooned the whiteboards and about every square inch of wall space. Not to mention the wires and pulleys of several cash railway stations, some of which dropped down from the ceiling to a desk right in the middle of the room.

"This is our main work area," Clark explained, as he ushered us into the left-side space. "The other side is a co-working space that we rent out to start-ups and individuals looking to work in an environment more professional than a coffee shop."

About half the workstations were occupied. Most of the workers were young, although there was one guy busily typing away who looked about fifty. It appeared to be an even split between male and female. A few of them were standing, and I realized the tables were adjustable and could become standing desks. Most wore headphones and did not look up from their screens as we passed.

Except Sam, who I saw sitting at one of the work stations. He jumped up as we approached. I introduced him to Ward.

Sam Markus was three or four inches shorter than me, and may have just barely tipped the scales at one hundred-forty pounds. He looked up at us through the forest of spiky red hair that sprang out from his head in uneven clumps.

He wore the standard geek uniform: jeans, gray hoodie and a t-shirt with a science joke. Today's read *I am uncertain about quantum mechanics.*

"Don't let me hold you up," Sam said, after pleasantries had been exchanged. Sanjana nodded, and the three of them kept moving.

"I thought you were going to call me," he said softly.

"Didn't have time," I replied. "I will as soon as I can."

"Okay."

I caught up to Clark, Sanjana, and Ward.

"Everything all right?" Ward asked.

I nodded.

Clark held open the door to his office and ushered us in. "Take as long as you need," he said. "Please let me know if there's anything I can do."

We thanked him, and he withdrew.

The office was not large by CEO standards, but also not quite as stark as the workstations outside. His desk was of the same design as those outside. It was just a tabletop, also adjustable to work standing up, I assumed. I found myself wondering, as I often do when I see work areas like this, where people kept all the stuff I kept in my desk drawers. Even in the computer age, you need to keep pens, a stapler, and occasionally a fifth of something where coworkers or visitors won't happen onto it.

Sanjana and I sat down in two comfortable chairs surrounding a low table. Ward leaned against a foosball table that took up one corner of the room.

"Special Agent Ward has just been assigned to the case," I began.

She nodded. "That's what my husband said."

I apologized for what seemed like the hundredth time about going over the same territory again.

"When was the last time you talked to Sophie?" Ward asked.

"It was shortly before one o'clock, on the day when..." she stopped, holding a hand up.

"Mrs. Patel..." Ward began.

"No," she said a catch in her throat, "it's all right. Just give me a minute."

She collected herself, and began again. "It was just before one. Sophie called me, said she had finished lunch, and had been helping Ella practice her reading. They wanted to bike to the pool. She was trying so hard to be grown up. I had been working from home a lot this summer, to not leave the girls alone all the time."

She smiled tearily. "But Sophie begged me to let them stay alone, and I finally said yes..." She coughed and squeezed her eyes shut, trying to stay composed, but her face screwed up in a grimace, and though she tried to keep her breathing under control, tight sobs burst out.

There was a box of tissues on Clark's desk. I offered one to her. She nodded her thanks and pressed it to her eyes.

"I'm sorry," she finally said.

"It's all right, Mrs. Patel," Ward said. "I know this is hard for you. And there was nothing unusual in the days prior to the disappearance?"

The door opened. "Everything okay? Sanjana, are you all right?"

Christopher Clark's bearded face peered around the doorframe.

Sanjana's eyes darted toward him, then back to Ward.

"I'm fine, Chris. No, Mr. Ward. There's nothing else." She stood up.

"Thank you, Mrs. Patel. We'll stay in touch," Ward said.

"Let me show you the co-working space on the way out," Clark said.

He led us to the door that opened into the other side of the space, but stopped with his hand on the knob. "When I bring tours through here, I tell them to keep their phones in their pockets. There are some startups using this space and they can get a little nervous if they think people are taking pictures or recording. I just mention it so you don't take it personally if monitors get shut off and you get stared at."

"We don't have to go through there," I said.

He shrugged. "No, I like guests to see the whole operation. You never know where the next good idea is coming from. The more people who know about our space, the better."

He conducted us through the opposite side of the office. The area looked similar to the Juego side, except there were fewer Post-It notes.

The space was more crowded, too. Nearly all of the workstations were occupied. Most of the occupants were my age or younger, except for one grizzled old-timer in his forties, who looked up from his monitor and watched us suspiciously as we crossed the room.

"I...I better go see if Sam needs me," Sanjana said. She turned quickly and went back the way we came.

Clark escorted us to the door.

"Sanjana is just a contractor, but that doesn't mean she isn't important to the team, and to me," he said. "If there is anything I can do, *anything*, please call me."

My phone vibrated. Ward's pocket chimed at the same moment.

"My contact information," Clark said. "I was serious. Call me anytime."

We thanked him, and signed out.

"How did he push his contact information to our phones?" Ward asked.

"I was going to ask you."

"Pretty neat trick. So, what's next?"

"No idea."

Back at the station, we joined Adam in Interview Two.

"You guys weren't kidding when you said the investigation hit a wall," Ward said, leaning back in his chair. He threaded his fingers together behind his head. "Any ideas on where to go next?"

"We didn't really go over the girls' computers," I said.

"Go over computers? Who are you, and what did you do with Trav Becker?" Adam asked suspiciously.

"I didn't say I knew *how*, just that it needed to be done."

"Do you have their computers?" Ward asked.

"No. Our computer forensics guy cloned their hard drives," Adam said. He reached for a laptop that was hooked into the department's network. "Which one do you want to see first?"

Ward and I looked at each other. We both shrugged.

"Sophie's, I guess." I finally said.

Adam poked at the keyboard for a while. After a moment, he grunted with satisfaction, and swiveled the computer so the three of us could see it.

The desktop background was a riot of color, to the point that it was hard to pick out the shortcuts and apps. Eventually, I realized it was a CD cover, featuring the current boy band flavor-of-the-month. I couldn't remember their name, but recognized the dimply faces peering out from behind rainbows and flowers. It was kind of Magical Mystery Tour-esque. At least they'd swiped from quality.

Music started to play, which was not a surprise, but as the tune unwound, and I looked again at the faces on the computer, I frowned.

"That's weird."

"What's weird?" Ward asked.

"The music."

"What about it?"

I pointed at the laptop screen. "She's got a boy band on her desktop background. Why is her computer playing Billy Joel?"

"Billy Joel? Are you sure?"

Adam snorted. "You're new around here, so we'll forgive you, but never question Trav on old music. He's an expert on anything more than forty years old."

"You're just jealous of my vinyl collection," I responded. "Turn it up."

He did, punching a key on the computer that made a little burping sound as the volume increased.

"Yeah," I said after listening a little more. "It's early, pre-'Piano Man'."

"Never heard of it," Ward said.

"Trav's specialty," Adam put in.

I flipped him off absently, searching my memory for the identity of the tune.

"You're sure you know it?" Ward asked.

"Yeah. It has kind of a funny title, not really a part of the lyrics," I mused.

What was it?

Adam pulled out his phone. "I have that app that IDs songs."

But before he had the chance to load it, I snapped my fingers. "Miami 2017."

Adam shook his head. "See? With Trav Becker, who needs the Internet? He's like Wikipedia."

"Asshole," I growled.

"You're right," Ward said. "It is a funny title. Weird that you know it."

He was right. It was weird. Not that I knew the song–Adam was right. Old rock was my passion. But very weird that it was on this girl's computer. Could her dad have turned her on to it, as mine had me? I made a mental note to ask Patel the next time I saw him.

"But I doubt liking old rock and roll is what got her kidnapped," Ward said. "Anything else?"

Adam shrugged.

"Lots of innocuous Facebook chats. No other messaging program. Her phone wasn't backed up to her laptop, so nothing there."

"In other words, a dead end, like everything else?"

"Pretty much."

"I've never seen a case with fewer clues," Ward said. "It's like..."

"Like what?" I asked.

He shook his head. "Nothing."

For a few minutes, there was silence. The only motion in the room was Ward rocking back on his chair, flipping his finger up and down on his tablet.

"The psychic," he mused. "Morgan Foster."

"What about her?" I asked.

"Maybe she should be interviewed."

"Why?" Adam asked. "Do you believe in that mumbo jumbo?"

"Psychic powers may be mumbo jumbo," he replied, "but psychics themselves tend to be extremely observant and good judges of people. It's how many of them stay in business. They make their predictions based on physical and emotional cues they read from their clients. Who knows what she may have picked up from hanging out with Michelle Day?"

"The press will have a field day if they find out we're bringing in a psychic," I pointed out.

"Yeah. We don't need that. We should interview her off-site. Becker, you know her, right?"

Wow. Someone else was pretty observant, too. Of course, many of the things he had just said about psychics also applied to profilers, so I shouldn't have been surprised he'd picked up an emotional subtext between Morgan and me.

I nodded, trying to keep my tone off-hand. "I interviewed her last year, as a witness to an altercation at a bar. Next block over from El Juego Grande in The District, as a matter of fact."

"Will you call her?"

"I can do that."

"Today or tonight, if you can do it."

I didn't need Ward telling me time was of the essence, but I let it go.

"I'll call her."

Ward packed his laptop up and put his suit jacket back on.

We had already exchanged cell numbers, in the event that something popped up after-hours. Ward bid us good night. Adam and I walked out to our desks.

I pulled open a drawer and pulled out a business card. It was deep blue, white letters against a field of stars, with Morgan's name, phone number and website. She'd given it to me when we had met last year, and even though I had never called her, I had kept the card. I dialed her number.

"Hello?"

"Hello," I said, very aware of Adam's presence. "This is Detective Trav Becker."

"Why, Detective," she chirped. "What a surprise to hear from you."

Her tone indicated she was not surprised at all.

"Uh... yes," I said. "I was, um, wondering, if I could..."

"Geez Trav, what are you doing, asking her for a date?" Adam said.

I glared at him. "I—we—have a few questions. I was wondering if you had some time this evening."

"I would be happy to answer your questions. Do you want me to come to the station?"

"No, that's not necessary. I can meet you wherever you like."

"How about the Kremlin? That seems appropriate."

"Uh...yeah. That will be fine. Seven?"

"It's a date."

The room suddenly felt very warm. "I'll, uh... see you then."

Adam looked at me curiously as I hung up. "How well do you know her?"

"Not well. Why?"

"Sounded to me like she was expecting you to call. You only met her that once, like you said?"

"That's what I said, wasn't it?"

He looked at me thoughtfully. "Well, maybe she actually is psychic."

"We don't believe in psychics, remember?"

"Right. Well, I hope she's observant like Ward says. We need a break. You ready to head out?"

I nodded.

A friend is someone who will help you move. A good friend is someone who will help you move a body.

Fortunately, I had just such a friend.

As I walked to my car, I sent a text to Sam, and he said he would meet me at my place. I got home a few minutes ahead of him and waited in the car, searching the radio dial in vain for some good music to listen to.

I kept meaning to figure out how to hook my phone up and play my own music, but I hadn't gotten around to it, although this new talk format on The Axe might mean I would need to.

I took a short mental break from the two mysteries I was working on, and instead spent a few pleasant minutes anticipating seeing Mary that evening.

We'd been talking about moving in together. But we hadn't done anything about it, which was fortunate, considering what had happened today.

I didn't like keeping secrets from Mary, but I had never come up with a way to tell her about the existence of the different reality streams. Explaining two extra Travs would have been really hard.

I hoped I could resolve whatever was going on without involving her.

Sam pulled up in his Prius. I popped open the trunk, and we looked at its grisly contents.

Sam gave a low whistle. "Shit. That is something you don't get used to seeing."

"That's what I thought when the other one showed up."

Sam's jaw dropped. "The other one? There's another one?"

"Yeah. We'll take a look at him in a minute. I want to search this one first. I didn't have time earlier."

I handed the bloody towel I had covered the body with to Sam, who took it somewhat gingerly.

This Trav was dressed like the first, all in black, quasi-military style, except he had no ball cap. Or a bracelet.

"This is like some weird reboot of *Weekend at Bernie's,*" Sam muttered. "What's with the sword?"

"No idea."

I drew out the blade. I don't know a hell of a lot about swords, but it reminded me of the kind I had seen cavalry officers carry in the movies. The blade slightly curved, with a simple hand guard. But it was not just for decoration. The edge was firm and sharp.

"What are we going to do with him?" Sam asked.

"I don't know. But I do know I want the other one out of my closet. Come on."

I shut the trunk and Sam followed me inside. I swung open the closet door.

Sam took a step back as Dead Trav One came into view. "Yuck. Talk about *déjà vu.*"

"I know. Grab his feet." I got under DT1's shoulders and we lugged him outside. I had purposely parked the Mustang as far from any streetlights as I could, and was trusting to both the quiet street and twilight to cover our suspicious activity.

"You don't have much time before they start to smell," Sam pointed out, huffing a little under the load. "You're going to have to do something a little more permanent."

"If I can't think of anything else, maybe I'll just firebomb the car."

"You have very strange problems, my friend."

I balanced DT1's shoulders across a knee propped up on the bumper while I got the trunk open, and we rolled the body into the trunk.

It was a tight fit. We soon understood why the Mustang was not the vehicle of choice for contract killers. The car bounced up and down on its struts as we pushed and shoved.

"Okay, now this one's leg is hanging out."

"I know, I know. Here, I think I can push his arms into the back corner."

"Careful! You don't want to get blood all over you."

I wedged DT2 as far forward as I could, holding him in place with one hand while I swung DT1's thigh into the trunk with the other.

"Got it," I said with a satisfied grunt.

"Not quite."

Sam pointed to DT1's head and right shoulder. They now hung over the left tail light.

"God, it's like trying to put toothpaste back into the tube."

"Car trouble?"

A young man holding a pizza box looked at us curiously.

Sam and I snapped around, nearly bumping heads. I tried to put one foot up on the bumper, failed, making it on the second try. Sam quickly stepped in front of DT1's hanging limb.

The kid was in his early twenties, on the thin side, with wavy brown hair that was pushed into place rather than styled. He wore jeans and an unbuttoned denim shirt over a Superman t-shirt. A black Ford with flashers blinking was parked a couple car lengths behind us.

"No," I stuttered, "I mean yeah, uh…"

"Flat tire," Sam offered.

"Right," I agreed. "I hate those doughnuts, don't you?"

He frowned at us behind a pair of gold wire-rimmed glasses. "Doughnuts?" he repeated.

"Temporary spare," I offered. "Instead of a full-sized tire."

"Oh. Do you need some help? I know a guy who's pretty good with cars."

"No!" Sam and I said in unison. I gave him a sour look before turning back to the pizza guy.

"I mean, we're fine. We got it."

"Okay," he replied doubtfully. He looked at the ticket on his pizza, then at the building we were parked in front of. Behind his thick glasses, his eyes suddenly widened.

"Oh no! This is West Jefferson, isn't it?"

I nodded.

"I'm supposed to be on *East* Jefferson."

"Ouch," Sam said. "I hope you don't have a thirty-minute guarantee."

"No, just a boss who thinks delivery drivers don't have to obey the laws of physics."

He sprinted back the way he had come. "Good luck with the tire," he called.

"You, too."

He hopped back into his car. We shielded his view of my trunk until he had pulled away, tires squealing.

"Whew. That was close," Sam said.

I shook my head. "We make *Weekend at Bernie's* look like geniuses. Flat tire."

"You didn't come up with anything better," Sam replied.

"Come on. Let's figure this out before someone else shows up to help."

Finally, we managed to get both bodies wedged in. Sam stood back while I managed to hold all eight limbs in place and slammed the trunk lid shut. I used my phone as a flashlight, making sure no articles of clothing, or God forbid, fingers were showing.

"Trav..." Sam said.

"I know," I sighed, not turning around "This is just temporary. Tomorrow I'll figure out a more permanent solution."

"No," he continued, "That's not what I meant. Uh..."

"What's the matter?" I turned around to discover Sam's face had gone even paler than when he had been arranging corpses.

Almost as pale as that of the bleeding Trav Becker who collapsed into his arms.

7

"TRAV!" SAM YELPED.

I leapt to assist him.

"Let's get him inside," I said, now extra grateful Pizza Guy had departed.

We each got under one of the wounded man's arms, and slowly walked him along the sidewalk and into my building. Once in my apartment, we carefully lowered him to the floor.

In pretty much the same exact spot I had placed Dead Trav One, come to think of it.

And at first I thought I had a third corpse on my hands, but when I checked his pulse it was weak, but steady.

Like the other two, he was dressed all in black, right down to the black ball cap. Although this one featured a different movie logo, Indiana Jones. I opened his vest. Blood flowed from a nasty gash that looked like it went deep into his abdomen. There was a corresponding tear, only larger, in the material of the vest.

"Pretty bad abdominal wound," I said. "Go in the bathroom and get me a towel."

He returned with one of my bath towels. I folded it and pressed it to Hurt Trav's stomach.

"Aaggh," he groaned, eyelids fluttering open.

"Easy," I said, pressing the towel into place. "I'm going to zip your vest over this. Think you can add some pressure?"

His eyes darted from side to side in panic and confusion. He squinted, trying to focus on my face.

"O'Connor?" he asked.

"Look, take it easy. We can figure everything out later. First thing is to keep you from bleeding out."

I zipped the vest back up, and crossed his wrists over it.

"Try to hold that in place."

His eyes were closed again, and I wasn't sure if he understood. I put my hands over his, and applied gentle pressure.

"What now?" Sam asked.

"Well, I can hardly show up at the hospital with my identical twin."

"We can't leave him on the floor."

"Especially right there. It's a bad luck spot. All right, let's get him up and into bed. Get his other side."

Sam moved into position.

"Time to get up, pal," I said.

Sam put a hand under his neck. I worked an arm underneath his upper back. We both put our arms under his knees.

"On three," I said. "One, two, *three*."

Sam and I stood, as gently as we could. Which did not keep Hurt Trav's eyes from bulging open. His body tensed in pain.

"Oh, Goddd..." he moaned.

"I know. Can't have you bleeding all over the floor, though. It's only a few steps. You can do it."

He gritted his teeth and nodded.

Sam and I carefully negotiated my narrow hallway, only causing a few agonized moans from our patient.

I steered us to the spare bedroom. It was mostly set up as an office, but there was a bed for guests. I got him laid down, then sent Sam back out to the car. The department issued a first-aid kit to all officers who used their own vehicles on the job. It was a lot more comprehensive than what was in my medicine cabinet.

Sam came back in and handed me the medical kit. I unzipped the vest again, tossing the towel aside, and cut away his shirt. Sam was ready with gauze, and he put pressure on the wound. The trip to the bedroom appeared to have exhausted whatever reserves Hurt Trav had left, and he was unresponsive. I checked his pulse again. Rapid and weak.

I leaned down, giving the vest a close examination, along with some sniffs. When I sat back up, Sam was looking at me curiously.

"What?" he asked.

"The tear in his vest doesn't conform to a bullet hole. I can't smell any powder residue. If I came on him in the street, I'd say it was a knife wound. But after seeing Dead Trav Two..."

Sam's eyes got wide. "You think he got that from a *sword?*"

"I wouldn't have until today."

I had Sam gently pull the gauze away from the wound. It was ugly. A jagged tear over three inches long. He was very lucky he hadn't bled out. I wet some gauze with disinfectant, and cleaned it up the best I could. Mercifully, he didn't regain consciousness while I worked.

After cleaning him up, I packed the wound with more gauze, and attached a dressing. I went to my medicine cabinet and grabbed a bottle of ibuprofen. Again, not great, but all I had. I shook him awake.

"Take these."

I helped him lift his head just far enough to get the pills and some water in him.

He needed antibiotics. And a couple of units of blood. Even if there was no slug inside him, the wound was certain to get septic.

"What now?" Sam asked.

"Let him rest. That's about all we can do."

He nodded, and we went out into my small living room. Sam sat down on the recliner, I took the couch.

"What the hell is going on?" he asked.

"I wish I knew."

I started at the beginning and told Sam what little I knew. I didn't hold anything back. Sam was the only person I could turn to for help. He also had some experience with parallel dimensions.

In fact, it was a version of Sam who had discovered the existence of the streams, and the multiple versions of himself and his friends who populated them.

Unfortunately, that knowledge had also caused him to become mentally unhinged.

This Sam and I had managed to defeat his extra-dimensional analogue, who we had dubbed Sam Zero, in honor of the fact that the entire mess had originated in that Sam's corner of the Multiverse.

Sam and I had started off in a branch we called Stream Four. But the events of the past year had ended up with *this* stream being short one Trav Becker and Sam Markus, requiring us to take up permanent residence here, rather than return to where we had come from.

I wasn't complaining. On Stream Four, I was a drunk, about to be fired, and damn close to suicidal. Here I'd been promoted, I still had Mary, and I was totally off vodka. No mystery as to why, given the chance, I had moved in to this time stream.

Sam had made the adjustment just fine, too. But he had sworn off research into the streams, frightened that it would drive him mad, too.

I was very nervous about dragging him into this, but there was no one else to turn to.

"*'They're coming,'*" Sam mused. "*Who's* coming? More Travs?"

"I hope not. I'm running out of places to keep them."

"No shit." Sam chuckled, but then got serious. "So, what now?"

I glanced at my wall clock, an LP of Dave Brubeck's *Take Five* with a clock mechanism in the center.

"I'm supposed to meet Morgan Foster at seven."

"Morgan? Why?"

I explained.

"You need to go then," he said when I had finished.

I turned my head in the direction of the bedroom. "I don't feel like I should leave."

He waved a hand. "Don't worry about it. There's nothing you can do here. I'm happy to stay here with him if you think talking to Morgan might help Sanjana's daughter. And while you're gone, I can wake up my software and see if there is anything that looks strange."

"You don't have to do that."

"It's okay, bro. Just looking at some data won't make me go all Dr. Evil. I promise." He lifted an eyebrow. "What about you? Any, uh... hocus-pocus?" He waggled the fingers of one hand.

I shook my head. "The only other Travs I'm seeing right now are the ones we've been lugging around all night."

"Do you think it might help if you... you know, opened up to it?"

"No," I said, my lips tightening into a thin line. "We're not getting into that again. We just barely survived last time. No more."

Sam jerked his head toward the bedroom. "That's obviously not what *he's* doing. Not to mention the other ones."

"Yeah, and look where it got them. I'm serious, Sam. We figure out just what we need to know to get this to stop. We're out."

He sighed. "I know that's the smart move. But don't you want to know what the hell is going on?"

"Not enough to get involved." I looked at my watch. "I gotta go."

"Let me go out and get my laptop."

While Sam was gone, I looked in on Hurt Trav again. He was pale, barely breathing. Hell, on the whole, the Dead Travs looked better.

"You're sure you don't mind me leaving?" I asked when Sam returned.

"Scat." He made a shooing motion. He plopped down on the couch and stared intently at his laptop.

Hoping the next time I came home it would not be to find a third Trav corpse, I grabbed my car keys.

So, for the second time that day, I found myself headed toward The District.

Once again I marveled at the transformation of the area. A year ago, the gentrification had only just begun to take place, affecting maybe a half dozen buildings. Go left instead of right coming out of the funky, vintage clothing boutique and you could find yourself in front of a bombed-out structure full of homeless squatters.

A case in point was the club where I was headed. The Kremlin had long served as Anton Kaaro's headquarters, and it sat squarely on the Mason-Dixon line between the old and the new. The dichotomy meant it had been a trouble spot, as the nouveau cool and Kaaro's goombahs had never mixed well.

All that had changed, though. More commercial development had improved the buildings abutting the club. The new owner seemed to be squeaky clean, and the Soviet theme was now just for ironic hipsters, not refugees looking for a taste of home.

Morgan stood near a small knot of people gathered under the building's only outside feature, a scarlet square of red neon (Red Square, get it?). She waved as I drove slowly past.

I found a parking spot and walked back toward the bar. She met me halfway.

"Good evening, Detective," she said. "What a pleasant surprise to get your call."

"Please, it's Trav. And why do I get the feeling you aren't surprised at all?"

"Why Trav, that sounds like you believe I'm a real psychic. Unlike your friend."

"Not my friend, just a colleague. And one whose world doesn't include psychics."

"Or Travelers?"

"Definitely not. And neither does mine. At least, not anymore."

"Hmm. Then why did you call me?"

I stopped walking and turned to face her. "Since you know Michelle Day, you know we're pretty much at a dead end. And time is running out. I... we thought if there was a chance you might have observed something or picked anything up in your interactions with the Day family, it was worth looking in to."

She nodded and cocked her head toward the bar. "Buy a girl a drink?"

I couldn't help but chuckle. "Sure. It'll be nice to go into the Kremlin without a gun in my back."

We were both silent during the short walk. I held the door for her and entered the Kremlin for the first time in a year.

It had changed a lot.

Not in the decor. The red neon theme from the sign outside was repeated throughout the club. Dozens of long tubes of light, all red, provided the majority of the illumination, punctuated by pinpricks of white from small lamps at tables and booths.

Under the Kaaro administration, the Kremlin had been home to a lot of Eastern European ex-pats, most of whom were either Kaaro's gunsels or their hooker girlfriends. So I was expecting an empty, sad assembly of tired barflies. But the only thing this Kremlin shared with that one was the lighting scheme.

The place was packed.

Each table was full. Several with couples hunched toward the center, in intimate conversation. Other tables had been pushed together to accommodate larger, more raucous groups.

The pulsing beat of bass and spinning lights leaked out from the dance floor, which was to our left. It was enclosed by glass walls, with bar stools around the outside, which meant the music could be deafening inside and you could still hold a conversation away from the music.

Whatever the new owner was doing, it was working.

There were a few empty seats at the bar, and we claimed two of them. There was a huge mirror behind it, which took up most of the entire rear wall of the room. Dozens of bottles of liquor lined three shelves under the mirror. I knew that the owner's office was on the other side of that mirror, which was two-way, and that the occupant of that office had a clear view of most of the room. But as long as it wasn't Anton Kaaro watching me, I didn't care.

I ordered a beer and a white wine for Morgan.

She stared at our reflections in the mirror, not speaking until our drinks arrived. She clinked her glass against my bottle and looked away.

The silence went on for what felt like a very long time.

"It is you, right?" she finally asked, looking at my reflection, not at me. "The Trav I met last year?"

I nodded.

"I wondered. The day after we talked, Mr. Kaaro and his gang all get arrested. You testified at the trial, so I assumed that was what you were working on."

"More or less."

"But then I never saw you again." She tried to keep her tone light. "I started to wonder if I had imagined the whole thing. Or…"

"Or what?"

"Or that the Trav who ended up on this plane of reality hadn't ever met me."

"It wasn't that. It's just..." My voice trailed off. She raised an eyebrow, not speaking but not letting me off the hook, either.

"Well, like you saw, the next couple days were pretty busy. And after that..."

I paused again.

"After that?" she finally prompted.

I picked at the label on my beer bottle. "What happened to me last year was really, *really* strange. I got through it, but a lot of it was just dumb luck. When it was over, I just wanted to forget about the hocus-pocus and go back to living a normal life."

"I was pretty worried after you left me that night," she said. "It would have been nice to know you were okay without looking for your name among the casualties in the paper."

"I know. That wasn't fair. But as more time passed, it got harder and harder to pick up the phone. And it got kind of foggy for me, too. There are some days *I* wonder if I imagined the whole thing."

She nodded. "*That* I get."

"I'm sorry," I said. "We should have had this conversation months ago, and it's my fault."

"Well, like you said, you did have a few things going on."

She narrowed her eyes and made a show of analyzing me. It was cute as hell.

"Okay," she pronounced. "You're forgiven."

My apology was sincere, but I wasn't telling her anything close to the real truth. The fact was, even though the universe kept conspiring to make me forget the dead bodies in my closet, I remembered every moment of my stream-jumping adventures from the previous year. Actually, due to some really weird multiverse hoodoo, I had some parallel sets of different recollections for the same set of circumstances. So in a way, I had *extra* memories, not fewer.

But the reason I hadn't called her last year, and the reason I wasn't telling her the full story now was because I couldn't figure out how to explain to someone I barely knew that on another stream of reality, we were a couple.

The Morgan of Stream Zero had shown up like the cavalry just when things were dire and saved her Trav and me. It was soon obvious they were much more than friends.

People always wonder about the road not taken, how their lives might have been different if they ended up with another person. I *knew,* and to say it made me uncomfortable around this woman was a vast understatement. She freaked the hell out of me.

But if Morgan sensed my discomfort, she gave no sign.

She took a sip of her wine. "Tell me what happened that didn't make the papers."

I shrugged. "There wasn't a lot. I kind of had a practice run the night before."

"You what?"

"It's a long story, but suffice it to say, I was in that same warehouse on another stream, and all hell broke loose. The building blew up. Kaaro and his gang didn't make it out. I learned from the experience. Nobody died the second time. I called it a win."

"Wow." She slumped back in her seat. "You think you can handle the weirdness, but hearing it like that, it's still mind-blowing."

I changed the subject. "So, how did you get hooked up with Michelle Day?"

Now it was her turn to shrug.

"She called the radio station. Not during my show, thank God. I don't know what I would have done if I had to talk to her live on the air."

"Congrats on that, by the way."

She gave me a wan smile. "I'm sure you think a radio psychic is a pretty silly thing. And to be honest, most of the time I'm just confirming for people something they really know. They just don't want to admit it to themselves."

"Like the sex of their unborn baby?"

"You heard that, huh? Actually, that was totally real. As soon as I heard that woman's voice, I knew what she was going to ask, and what the answer was."

"Does that happen a lot?"

"Not as much as you'd think. Or as much as I'd like. Trav, I have a gift, I really do. I know it, and I think you know it, too."

"I'm not arguing with you, just asking."

She fiddled with the stem of her wineglass, coming dangerously close to sloshing its contents onto the bar. "But it's not something you can count on. Sometimes, no matter how much I meditate and mentally prepare for a reading, I sit down with the person, take their hand, listen to their questions, and..."

"And?"

"And nothing. My mind is a blank. Or worse, I've got the latest Katy Perry song stuck in there."

"That *is* bad. What happens then?"

"Then I ask more questions, study the person's face and body language. Like I said, people often come to me not because they really need help choosing the right path. Deep down, they probably know what the correct choice is, but for whatever reason, they're not admitting it to themselves."

"What do you mean?"

"Well, a woman comes in and wants to know if her husband is cheating on her. Obviously, there is already something going on that is making her think that."

"His behavior has changed. Doesn't want to talk about where he's been, secretive about his phone or credit card bill."

Morgan nodded. "Or sometimes it's the woman herself, projecting her own dissatisfaction with the marriage onto him. Either way, there's something that's not right. Even if I can't see into her mind, I can try to help her understand that."

"But the bottom line is, you're helping her. What's the problem?"

"I just feel like I'm a fraud sometimes."

"You're not a fraud."

"That's nice of you to say."

"In fact, that's why Ward suggested we talk to you. He wanted to get your read on the case not because he thinks you have psychic powers, but because he figures you're observant and a good judge of people."

"That's nice... I guess. So I am a fraud. Just a smart one."

"Don't be so hard on yourself. But I need to ask. Do you know anything, *anything* that might help with the case?"

She shook her head. "No. What about you?"

"Nada. It's like those little girls just disappeared into thin air."

"No, I don't mean the investigation. I mean what is your gift telling you?"

"Nothing," I said, lips tightening across my jaw.

"Oh, come on Trav, this is me, remember? I'm not going to go tell the FBI or anything. What are you seeing? I mean, you know, *seeing*?"

"I told you. Nothing beyond what anyone else does. Whatever I used to have, I don't have it anymore."

Her eyes narrowed. "Last year, you were slipping between planes of reality. You fought a gun battle in a building that was on fire, then crossed over and did the same thing all over again here. And you're telling me it just stopped?"

I nodded.

"Those kind of gifts don't just go away, Trav. Tell me, what is really going on?"

I sighed. "Last year, everything worked out. Just about everybody survived. I promised myself when it was all over that I was done. And I am."

She looked skeptical. "And you can turn it off, just like that?"

"Well, I did."

"And no visions, no glimpses, or whatever it was you saw that showed you other streams?"

"At first, some. But if you ignore them they go away."

I didn't mention the glimpse I had gotten of Red Trav earlier in the day.

"You just walked away."

"I've *seen* what screwing around with parallel realities gets you," I said fiercely. "Crazy. Or dead. I lucked out last year. A lot of other people weren't so lucky. And I was very nearly one of them. Trying to play God doesn't end well. You fix one thing, something unravels somewhere else."

"But you said what you learned on that other stream last year, in the warehouse, helped you here. No one died."

"And I also said it was luck. What I really learned was *quit while you're ahead.*"

I tipped the beer bottle to my lips, glad for the chance to look away from her.

She didn't say anything for a moment. But then she whispered, *"But what if you could help those girls?"*

I closed my eyes, trying to pretend I hadn't heard, wishing she would let it go, but knowing that wasn't going to happen.

"Trav," she persisted. "There is more to it, isn't there?"

I didn't say anything.

She leaned toward me, putting a hand on my arm. "I don't know you all that well, but I can't imagine you wouldn't use every possible tool at your disposal to solve this. You have a gift, something that could help, and you're not using it. Why?"

"Look," I tried to keep my voice steady. "Anything I do will create ripples that I can't control. I may be able to improve one outcome, but it could screw something else up beyond all recognition. Better to just work the problem the old-fashioned way. We're good at what we do. We can solve this without any hocus-pocus."

She looked uncertain. "I can understand that. But nothing else is working, right?"

I shook my head.

"Then don't you owe it to yourself, and those girls, to bring out the big guns?"

"I guess a girl who owns a Desert Eagle knows a thing or two about big guns."

"How did you know...? Oh." Her eyes narrowed as this sank in. "What were you and I into on that other plane that included me needing my gun?"

Before I could answer, I felt a vibration in my pocket, followed by a loud *squelch*. The educated listener would recognize it as the sound made by the giant foot which signals the sudden end of the *Monty Python* theme. In this situation, however, it signified a text from Sam. I held up a finger and pulled my phone out of my pocket. Two words glowed against the phone's wallpaper.

He's awake.

8

"I HAVE TO go," I said, still staring at the screen.

"Does it have to do with the case?" she asked quickly.

"No. But it's something I have to take care of. I'm sorry."

She nodded, and bit her lip with a look of indecision darkening her elfin features.

"What?" I asked.

She shook her head. "I'm sure it's nothing."

"Doesn't look like it's nothing."

"Well," she sighed, "when you called, and we were thinking of a place to meet?"

I nodded.

"I thought of this place."

"So?"

She gave a little *humph* of impatience. "I mean I *thought* of this place. The same way I *thought* of that baby's gender."

I knew better than to dismiss her concern. I didn't know if Morgan was an actual psychic, but she was tuned in to the same kind of wavelengths I was, albeit on a slightly less bumping-into-other-versions-of-yourself scale. Which meant when she had a feeling, you were wise to pay attention.

I looked around the room now, more carefully than I had when we walked in.

"Any idea why?" I asked.

She shook her head. "No, and it could just as easily be that I associated this place with you because it was where we first met. But you said if I could think of anything, I should tell you."

"I appreciate it. I don't know what it means, but..."

I scanned the room a third time, and this time, it did seem like there was something niggling at the back of my mind. I swept my gaze back and forth across the room, trying to nail it down. But whatever it was, I couldn't get it to track.

"Well, it might mean something, it might not. But I'll have to think about it later. I'm sorry to have to leave so abruptly." I waved a hand, trying to attract the attention of the bartender.

"Oh, don't worry about it, it's on me," Morgan said. "This is the most entertaining time I've had in weeks."

She hopped off the bar stool and stood very close to me.

"But I'm giving you a warning," she continued, poking me in the chest with a manicured finger. "The two times I've talked to you, you've totally blown my mind, then you've split without another word. The next time I see you, I'm not letting you go until I get the whole story. Or else..."

"Or else what?" It was impossible not to smile.

"Or else I might have to introduce you to my gun on *this* plane."

"I'll be careful," I replied. I paused, looking at her.

"What?" she asked.

I had been waiting for her to answer me by saying *You'll be dead!* But the Morgan of this stream had never seen *Star Wars*.

"Nothing."

I turned to go.

"Trav." She put her hand on my arm again. I swung around to face her, inclining my head.

"Think about what I said? About using *every* tool at your disposal."

I pressed my lips together, but nodded. "I will. You can get home okay?"

"Oh, please," she snorted. "I used to come here when it was a front for the Russian mob. I don't think I'm in much danger from a bar full of hipsters."

Still holding my arm, she drew me toward her and put her lips near my ear.

"But next time," she whispered, "the whole story. I mean it."

"Fair enough."

I left her there, chatting amiably with the bartender.

My phone chirped again as I walked down the street to my car.

Just about done here.. finally. My place?

Mary.

I had forgotten all about our date after her rehearsal. Was it just this morning I had woken up next to her? It seemed like a week ago.

A pang of guilt soured the beer in my stomach.

Something's come up on the case, I thumbed. *Heading into work. Sorry.*

It's okay. Hope it leads to something.

Lunch tomorrow?

It's a date. Pick you up at the station?

Yeah. Love you.

Love you, too.

Trying to convince myself that I hadn't blown her off, just postponed, I headed for home as quickly as traffic would allow. I pushed the guilt at not being honest with Mary, or Morgan for that matter, out of my mind.

I rushed into my building, and unlocked the door to my apartment.

Sam sat stiffly on my couch. He looked up at me as I entered, but didn't speak.

"So, what's going on?" I asked. "Has he said anything?"

"Not yet," said a voice behind me.

I felt the barrel of a handgun against the back of my neck.

"Hands," the voice continued.

I raised both arms above my head. A hand snaked into my jacket and eased my own weapon from my shoulder rig.

"Turn around. Slowly."

As I did so, I was only mildly surprised to find myself staring into my own face.

Well, almost. This Trav sported a good-sized scar that went from his right eyebrow up and under his ball cap, which displayed the *Jurassic Park* logo.

The scar brought a jolt of recognition. I had seen the wound when it was fresh. I knew this Trav. He had appeared to help Trav Zero and me at Kaaro's warehouse, but disappeared right after the action.

"Have we met before?" I asked.

"More or less," he grunted. He waved with the gun, motioning me to sit next to Sam.

"Sorry, man," Sam said softly as I sat. "They showed up right after I texted you."

"They?"

"Oh yeah."

"It's getting kind of crowded out here," Jurassic Trav called. "Is he mobile?"

"Mobile enough," rasped a third voice.

Another Trav, this one sporting a *Matrix* cap, appeared in the doorway, supporting *Indiana Jones* Trav. Indiana had fresh dressings applied to his stomach wound, and one of my shirts was draped loosely over his shoulders.

"Come on," Jurassic said impatiently, "we've already been here too long."

The other two crossed the room, moving slowly, because it was clear Indiana really shouldn't be up and about.

"You coming?" Jurassic said.

"What?"

"Are. You. Coming," he repeated, emphasizing each word as if he were speaking to a child.

"You're kidding, right?"

He didn't reply, just raised an eyebrow.

"Let me get this straight. You want me to go voluntarily where that happens?"

I gestured at the wounded Travs.

"I didn't say it was easy work," he responded. "But I remember you're pretty good in a fight. We can use you."

"I'm retired."

"Aren't you just a little curious about what the hell is going on?"

"Nope."

That made him chuckle. "Yeah, we all start out that way. But when you get motivated, give me a call." He flicked his wrist and something silvery arced up and toward me. Without thinking, I raised a hand and snatched it out of the air.

It was one of the silver bracelets like I had taken off of Dead Trav One.

"And what am I supposed to do with this?" I asked.

"You'll figure it out."

"We gotta go," Matrix Trav said, glancing at Indiana. The wounded man's complexion was turning gray.

"All right. You guys ready?"

Matrix and Indiana nodded. All three men closed their eyes. A second later, they winked out of existence.

I felt a slight breeze as air rushed in to fill the vacuum left by their disappearance, but other than that, it was as if they had never been there.

Even though he had seen Traveler magic before, Sam stared at the space where the three Travs had been, mouth hanging open, for what seemed like a long time. He blinked a couple of times, shaking his head.

"Did he actually quote Han Solo at you?"

"That's what you got out of all this? *Han Solo?*"

"'You're pretty good in a fight. We could use you,'" he quoted, sounding neither like me nor Harrison Ford.

"Hey, it's your fault," I pointed out. "You're the one who turned me on to all this nerdy stuff. I'm sure that's the case in every stream."

"You acted like you knew one of them. The one with the Jurassic Park hat."

"I think so. He was on Stream Zero. He wouldn't talk about how he got hurt or where he was from. But he lent us a hand, then disappeared before we had a chance to ask him any questions."

"So, whatever it is he was involved in that got him injured is still going on. And is pretty hard on Travs," Sam observed.

He paused, frowning. "Remember when we joked about some pan-dimensional strike team that went around fixing whatever was wrong on the streams. Is it possible one not only exists, but it's made up entirely of *you?*"

"We don't know that," I said.

Sam made a clucking sound through his teeth. "Well, whatever it is, it doesn't seem to be going too well for the home team. What did he give you?"

I opened my palm and handed him the bracelet. It was exactly the same as the one Dead Trav One had worn.

He examined it for a minute. Suddenly, his face opened in a huge smile.

"Ah-HA!" he crowed. "I understand it all now! It's so simple."

"What?"

"No idea," Sam replied, tossing the bracelet back to me. "I'm just messing with you. I got nothing."

"Ah, Christ," I groaned.

"Did you really think I could solve the whole mystery that easily? You obviously have a lot of respect for my deductive ability."

"Jackass."

Sam raised his hands in surrender. "Hey, just trying to lighten the mood. Seriously, what now?"

"Now? I go back to work. This has been a distraction I don't need. I can get back to focusing on the kidnapping."

"What about your trunk?"

In the excitement, I had forgotten that Jurassic had actually removed only thirty-three and one third percent of the extra Travs on this stream.

"Ah, crap," I muttered

"What are you going to do about them?"

"I don't know. But I am wiped out. The whole mess can wait until morning."

Sam was looking at the bracelet, which I absently twirled on one finger.

"What are you going to do with that?" Sam pointed at it. I shrugged.

"Mind if I take a look?"

I shrugged again and handed it to him. "But be careful. We have no idea what it's supposed to do."

He nodded.

"Promise," I insisted, holding his gaze. I didn't totally trust Sam's ability to keep his curiosity in check.

"Of course," he replied. "Trav, you don't need to worry about me. Honest." He yawned. "I don't know about you, but I think I have had enough excitement for one day. Unless you need me for something else?"

I shook my head.

We bid each other goodnight, and I locked the deadbolt behind him. Not that a locked door would do much good if the Ghosts Of Travs Past showed up again, but it still felt satisfying to hear the solid *thunk* of the lock sliding home.

I puttered around, tidying up until I couldn't put off going into the spare bedroom any longer.

There were bloody towels and gauze everywhere. It looked like a MASH unit. And the bed looked like someone had performed major surgery on its surface. I wadded everything up and stuffed the whole mess into a garbage bag. I would sneak it into the building's dumpster later.

By now, I was yawning myself, and dragged myself into my bedroom, shedding clothes as I did. I tumbled into bed.

And lay there, completely unable to fall asleep.

This is not a problem I usually have. I've done shift work most of my life, and can usually grab sleep whenever the opportunity presents itself. But no amount of rolling over or jamming my fists into the pillow to fluff it into a more comfortable shape helped.

I lay on my back, the ghostly images your eyes create in a dark room swirling above me.

I knew I had made the right decision in not going with the other Travs. Most of my contact with other versions of myself had gone just about the same way today's had. I got treated like a kid you had to keep shushing in church. But when the shit hit the fan and *they* needed *me*? They were only too happy to pull me in.

Not anymore. Their war was not my problem. Sophie and Ella were.

And just like that, the eddies my optic nerve projected into the darkness of my room seemed to coalesce into the fine features of Morgan Foster. And my ears now entered the game. The hiss of air entering through the furnace vent became her soft voice.

But what if you could help those girls?

It had been months since I had seen a manifestation of the red-outlined Trav that had guided me in the past.

Until today.

I pushed myself out of bed and started pulling my clothes back on. I had sworn to never meddle in parallel realities again, but I had been kidding myself.

Morgan was right. If I did not use every tool at my disposal to find Sophie and Ella, I was just as guilty as their kidnapper. And if diving back into the weird sea of changing causality made me uncomfortable, it was a small price to pay.

I shrugged into my jacket and grabbed my car keys.

Time to see just what Red Trav had found so interesting in Alan Taggert's neighborhood.

9

IT WAS A clear, cool night. In fact, the weather called for unseasonably cold temps for September, maybe even an early freeze. This was good news for me, as it meant the macabre load in my trunk would keep longer. This would not be a good time for an Indian summer heat wave.

I parked a couple houses down from Taggert's place, grabbed the big flashlight I kept in the car and slowly made my way up the sidewalk, waiting for the cloud of hazy Travs to appear. I had no way of calling them up or directing them. In the past, they had just shown up, a tangled ball of blue outlines, except for the one in red.

Sam had once theorized that the way my mind visualized my desired stream or outcome outlined in red meant that somehow I was connected mentally to the thousands of Travs taking all possible actions in a given situation, and somehow my mind sorted through these thousands of connections, aided by all the others, in a kind of unconscious gestalt that showed me the correct path.

Which, I thought with a mental chuckle, would be a great name for a band.

But apparently, Unconscious Gestalt had a gig someplace else this evening, because the night remained dark and quiet, with no glowing Travs to light my path.

We were going to have to do this the old-fashioned way after all.

I headed over to the approximate spot where I had been standing when I had seen Red Trav. As I recalled, all the other Travs had been upright, walking or standing. But this one had been on all fours, examining something on or near the sidewalk.

At the time, I had been focusing more on making the vision go away, but I hoped I could reconstruct the scene.

I peered along the sidewalk I had just come down, trying to place where Red Trav had appeared along the sculpted hedgerow. Had he been just north or south of that sidewalk crack?

North. I picked my way back along the walk to the spot that looked right. I glanced up at Taggert's house before I switched on the flashlight. There was no reason for me to hide my presence, but no sense in causing a commotion if I didn't have to. The house was dark, so unless Taggert was in the habit of wandering around the house with no lights on, I could assume he was asleep, or not home.

I got down on my hands and knees, moved the bottom of the hedge out of my way, and shone the flashlight along the ground. Part of me felt this was a huge waste of time. We had gone over every inch of this area with the proverbial fine-toothed comb. Multiple times. But that's police work. Sometimes you just keep going over the evidence time and again, hoping to find what the last guy missed, or even to jar something loose in your mind.

In my more cynical moments, I was reminded of Einstein's comment about how the definition of insanity was doing the same thing over and over again and expecting a different result. But right now I was feeling insane enough just showing up out here to retrace the path of my extra-dimensional double.

I shone the light and felt along the edge of the sidewalk, back and forth in the same ten feet several times, with nothing to show for it but dirt up my sleeves and a solid ache in my lower back. I was just about to expand the search area when my hand rubbed against something that was neither sidewalk nor soil.

The dirt underneath this particular part of the sidewalk had washed out somewhat, probably from incessant watering by Mr. Taggert. The area right under the cement had eroded away, creating a small, hollow pocket underneath. It was not much of a surprise that other searchers had overlooked it.

I couldn't shine the flashlight down there, so I had to search by feel. I was certain I had brushed up against something, but when I stuck my hand back down, there was nothing. I leaned over, trying to stretch my wrist out at an angle that was definitely unnatural, while I felt around the entire cavity.

My fingers were starting to cramp when I grabbed something that wasn't a rock or part of the sidewalk. I pulled it out, taking some skin off in the process.

It was a key ring.

I directed the beam of the flashlight to it and gave it a good look. I could immediately tell I hadn't unearthed something old. The key was shiny and the leather flap attached to the ring was supple, not dark and dried out.

I stood up and turned my find over in my hand, shining the light on it from every angle. Belatedly, I realized I should have put on gloves, standard procedure in any kind of search. But I hadn't really believed I would actually find anything useful.

Of course, there was no proof this had anything to do with Patel-Day. It could have been stuck down there for weeks prior to the kidnapping, or dropped just yesterday.

But as I stared at the Road Runner logo embossed on the leather fob, I couldn't help but wonder if this key fit Josh Dawson's muscle car.

I stuck the keychain in a Ziploc bag I kept in my jacket pocket for just this purpose. Not exactly proper chain of evidence, but my theory was pretty tenuous at this point anyway.

I got back in the car and, before I could talk myself out of it, headed toward Michelle Day's house.

Red Trav seemed to have deserted me, but the fates hadn't. Dawson's immaculate car was parked in front of the house. Like Taggert's, it was dark and looked empty.

I parked across the street, shut my engine off, and tried to decide if this was a good idea. If the key in my pocket did fit the Road Runner, it did not necessarily implicate Josh Dawson. And I would have a devil of a time explaining what had led me to finding the key where I did.

However, I was here, and was hardly going to drive away now without checking. Part of me hoped the key didn't turn the lock. All I would be out was some sleep, and no one the wiser.

I slipped out of the car and crossed the street, sliding the key ring out of its bag. I looked at it for a second, marveling at how tiny it was compared to today's monster keys with their gigantic, plastic, theft-deterring heads. My first try at putting it in the keyhole was wrong, of course. It also dated from the time before keys could be inserted with either side up. I turned it over, and tried again.

This time, the key slid in like it was greased. When I turned it, I was rewarded with a soft *pop* as the silver post inside the car popped up.

I was just about to re-lock the door and head back to my car to plan my next move when I was shoved from behind.

"What the hell are you doing?"

I stumbled as I tried to keep my balance and turn at the same time to look at my assailant.

Josh Dawson glared at me.

"I asked what the hell are you... Oh, shit. It's *you*."

The anger fled his eyes, replaced by surprise and fear. He saw the key still in the lock, and grabbed for it.

"Don't touch that, sir."

"Or what?" he replied belligerently. He pulled the key all the way out. I took a step toward him, but he slashed his arm across the air between us, brandishing the key like a weapon.

I put up my hands. I wasn't too afraid of his key sword, but the man was definitely agitated, and I needed to calm him down.

"Please don't make this harder, Mr. Dawson. I just have some questions to ask you."

"Questions? That's what you have? *Questions?*" He lunged for me, and before I could block his hands, he snatched the front of my shirt, pulling me close to his face. He was a little taller than me, so I got a much closer look at his nostrils than I ever could have wanted.

"Questions?" he repeated, voice dropping to a whispered growl. "*Questions?* After what you took from us? How dare you show up here!"

The grip he had on my shirt prevented me from easily getting to the gun in my shoulder rig, so I tried to keep him talking.

"Took from you? I don't know what you mean."

He pulled me closer. "You said you were going to help us. Is that what you told the others?"

He smelled of sweat and garlic.

"Others?"

"Everyone who believed you, you bastard."

Now he was shouting. "*Just tell me!* What were you going to do with them?"

"Mr. Dawson, please calm down. If you think you have a problem with me, why don't we call my captain? He'd be happy to listen to you."

"Don't give me your shit!" he hissed.

And with strength I wouldn't have imagined in a slim guy, he pushed me away with such force I tumbled ass over teakettle.

As I smashed into the ground, I was able to tuck my head and roll enough for my shoulder to take most of the impact, rather than my head or neck. But it cost me time. By the time I was able to sit back up and draw my weapon, Dawson had already wrenched open the door and hurled himself inside.

The legendary 440 that powered the Superbird roared to life, and the brake lights lit as I scrambled to my feet.

By the time I stood, he was pulling away. I ran for my car, jumped in, started it, and whirled the wheel in the fastest three-point turn I could manage.

My Mustang is not new, but it wasn't a classic like Dawson's Road Runner. And even though I had a V-8 engine of my own, it was no match for the big block wedge with a six-barrel carburetor, manufactured in the years when speed limits were high and gas was cheap.

But we also weren't on the Salt Flats. I might be able to catch up on these winding, narrow streets.

I could just see his tail lights in the distance, and as I floored it myself, I flipped the switch on my portable light, which rested on the center of the dash. It was small but powerful, and cast scarlet shadows in the car as it revolved.

I was driving fast enough that I needed to keep both hands on the wheel, but took the time to snake my right hand under the dash. I had a police radio under there. I hoped it still worked. As an investigator, my job didn't usually entail responding to squeals. I used my cell phone much more than the police band, but this was a matter for dispatch, and the fastest way to get them was the radio.

In fact, it had been long enough since I had used the radio that it took me a minute to remember my call sign. Finally it came to me.

"Three-Bravo-Tango-Four, Dispatch."

"Dispatch. Three-Bravo-Tango-Four," came the response.

"In pursuit. Suspect assaulted me, then took off. He's driving a 1970 Plymouth Road Runner, blue. Don't have the tag. Eastbound on Brooklyn Avenue. Just passed... uh... Seventeenth."

"Roger." There was silence for a few moments before the radio clattered to life again with the all-call.

"All units. Three-Bravo-Tango-Four is in pursuit of a 1970 Plymouth Road Runner. Eastbound on Brooklyn, approaching Fifteenth. Officer's vehicle is a 2010 red Mustang, license Yankee-Romeo-Oscar-Eight-Zero-Eight."

"Four-King-Lincoln-Six, Dispatch. I'm just two blocks away."

In our department's nomenclature, the middle letters of the radio call sign were the officer's initials, last name first. After a moment, I was able to put a face to the initials. He was a capable guy, about Adam's age, named Larry Kudej. Pronounced, believe it or not, *KOO-jee*. A guaranteed stumble by any new co-worker. Sometimes he bought coffee as a prize for someone who came up with a particularly creative pronunciation.

"Kooj, it's Trav."

I used the radio rarely enough, I figured I should introduce myself. "I just passed Fourteenth. He's about two blocks ahead of me."

"Roger that. I'll come up Tenth and cut him off."

"Roger." I kept hold of the mic but added three fingers from that hand to the wheel. It had been a long time since I had been involved in a chase. It was all I could do to hold the radio and keep the car pointed the right way, while avoiding parked cars that choked each side of the narrow street.

I had managed to close the distance between us to a little over a block. I lost sight of Dawson as he swung around a blind corner, but had started to breathe easier, knowing Kudej was just on the other side.

But I still took the corner at speed, the Mustang's wheels squealing in protest. As soon as I cleared the turn, I could see Kudej's whirling red, white, and blue lights up ahead, blocking the next intersection.

Dawson had certainly been agitated, crazed even. But I didn't think he would slam head-on into a parked patrol car. We had him boxed in. I slowed down as I got closer, but...

Kudej's black-and-white was the only vehicle in sight.

I wrenched my head right and left, looking for Dawson's car.

The street was empty.

I pulled up to the patrol car. Its door opened and Kudej climbed out. He was tall, with coal-black hair.

"Where is he?" Kudej asked.

I shook my head. "I saw him take the corner, Kooj. He isn't here?"

Kudej raised an eyebrow. "Does it look like it?"

He spread his hands to encompass the empty street.

I turned around, peering back the way I had come. There had to be an alley, even a dark driveway...

"You sure you didn't see anything?"

"Nothing to see," he replied. He looked at me without expression. "What were you chasing again?"

"Blue Road Runner. A real classic."

"Hmm."

"He must have turned into an alley, or driveway or something. Can we look?"

He shrugged and got back into his car.

We drove down the deserted street, me in the lead. Kudej had a spotlight mounted by his driver's side mirror, and shone it along the left side of the street. I peered into the gloom on the right, but it was not so dark that I couldn't see that there was no space big enough to hide even a small car, let alone one the size of a Seventies coupe. But the uniformed officer gamely followed me all the way down the street and around the corner. We stopped about where I had seen the Road Runner's taillights make the turn.

We got out of our cars. Kudej leaned against his fender, looking up and down the street. I did, too, hope fading that we had missed something simple and obvious.

"You're sure he didn't turn off on one of the other side streets?"

I shook my head. "I saw him make this turn. I was only a block or so behind him."

"Well, I don't know what to tell you. The first car I saw make that turn was yours." He was actually doing a pretty good job of hiding his skepticism.

"I don't know, either."

"What were you chasing him for again?"

"Well, you know I'm on the Patel-Day case?"

He nodded.

"He's Michele Day's boyfriend. I... I was poking around near her house when he showed up and got aggressive with me."

"Did you badge him? Maybe he thought you were a prowler."

"No, he recognized me."

"Why'd he take off?"

"That's what I was hoping to ask him."

I thumped my hand against the Mustang's fender in frustration. "Well, he's gone now. Sorry to waste your time."

Kudej shrugged. "All pays the same. I'll keep an eye out for your car. Who knows? Maybe he'll come out from his hiding place and decide to go get breakfast."

I thanked him with a chuckle I didn't really feel. Kudej was being nice, but I had no doubt the story of the detective chasing a car no one else could see would soon make the rounds.

We both got back into our cars. Kooj resumed his patrol, and I headed to the station. I didn't think Dawson or his car were going to turn up, but I filed a BOLO, a *Be On The Look Out*, anyway.

Despite a promising beginning, the only thing my work tonight was producing was paperwork.

I was yawning as I finished and headed home, turning up the radio to keep myself awake. Mercifully, The Axe had not cancelled my other favorite show, a late-night retrospective that avoided an artist's hits, focusing on lesser-known chestnuts.

Coincidentally, tonight's feature was on Billy Joel. I warbled along with "Travelin' Prayer," one of my absolute favorites. As I did, the puzzle of the Billy Joel song on Sophie's computer niggled at the back of my mind.

The other thought that wouldn't let go, of course, was Josh Dawson. Not just his disappearance, but the cryptic outburst that ended with him attacking me.

He had acted like he knew me. Knew me much better than the short interview we had shared that afternoon. And he was pissed.

At me.

I was no stranger to situations where people started spouting what seemed like nonsense. But where most cops experienced this while arresting druggies riding high on meth or PCP, for me it was from jumping between different streams of reality.

Was that possible? Had I interacted with a Josh Dawson from another stream? Had he jumped streams?

Had I?

The Patel-Day case was enough of a bitch without tossing parallel realities into the mix. But as much as I didn't want to admit it to myself, it was starting to look like my mundane, if potentially tragic, case had a supernatural aspect.

Shit.

Was this what Jurassic Trav had been referring to when he had hinted that I would join Team Trav when I got "motivated"?

With this cheerful thought in mind, I tumbled into bed. And despite my frustrating and confusing night, this time I dozed off almost immediately.

I dreamed of Billy Joel.

10

I WAS PERCHED on a barstool in the Kremlin, but instead of the bar, I was leaning against a grand piano. I could see my reflection in its shiny, ebony top.

Billy Joel sat at the piano. It was the Seventies Billy, all skinny tie and gigantic helmet of black hair. He sang about seeing the lights go down on Broadway.

"This is one of my favorite songs," Morgan Foster said.

She took a drag from her cigarette, and blew smoke into my face. It did not sting my eyes.

"Mine, too," I responded.

"What kinda car you got?" she continued, loudly smacking a mouthful of gum. The cigarette, fortunately, had disappeared.

I didn't want to answer. My Mustang had a pitifully small engine. It was embarrassing.

"Wanna ride?"

A leather key chain with a Road Runner logo suddenly dangled between us. We looked up into the face of Trav Becker. The Road Runner also adorned his black ball cap.

"Cool!" Morgan exclaimed. She hopped off her stool, smoothed her poodle skirt, and took Trav's arm. I watched them go.

At a table by the door, Sam sat beside a Dead Trav. He had tied a string to the corpse's wrist and used it to make the limp hand wave bye-bye.

"Man, what are you doing here?" Billy asked. He looked at me, then to his left. I followed his gaze.

Mary sat at the other end of the piano, head bowed. She looked up, tears creating little half-moons of mascara under her eyes.

I tried to speak, but again no words would come out. My own throat started to tighten and now my eyes did burn.

Coming awake was like swimming up through a lake of Jell-O.

It was one of those dreams that, even though the events didn't really make a lot of sense, the emotional impact was very real. I lay there, convinced that I had disappointed anyone who had ever cared about me.

The dream, and the depression it brought with it, refused to fade. I pushed the picture of Mary's tear-filled face out of my mind and thought about the rest of the scene.

It was no surprise the Piano Man had played a supporting role. The Billy Joel retrospective had been just about the last input my brain had ingested prior to falling asleep. But something was bothering me about it.

It was the song he'd been playing as I'd sat near the piano. The tune had not been a part of the retrospective I'd been listening to the night before. But I knew it immediately, having heard it just that afternoon.

"Miami 2017 (I've Seen the Lights Go Down On Broadway)."

As I had told Adam and Ward, "Miami 2017" was early stuff, released during the rather long hiatus that began after *Piano Man* and ended when *The Stranger* started Joel on the road to rock legend.

The song had been inspired by a financial meltdown New York City had experienced in the Seventies. Joel said it was written from the point of view of a retired New Yorker in the twenty-first century telling his grandchildren about the late, great Big Apple. And since most New

Yorkers retire to Florida, he titled it Miami 2017, and referred to it from then on as his science fiction song.

And it had no business on the computer of a twelve-year-old girl.

By itself, this meant nothing, but when you put it together with my strange encounter with Josh Dawson last night, an encounter that seemed to indicate the man had come from another stream, the whole thing had a different light.

A Seventies album cut on a little girl's computer would mean nothing to anyone, even a highly trained investigator.

Unless that investigator had a thing for old, obscure rock music.

Was it possible that song was a clue meant for me?

I hopped out of bed and showered quickly. I wanted to go over Sophie's hard drive again before Ward or Adam got in.

Grabbing an energy bar in lieu of stopping to make breakfast, I locked up and headed toward the car.

The station was quiet, and I anticipated at least an hour of uninterrupted work on the computer, but as I approached the door to Interview Two, I spied the dark head of Larry Kudej across the way. He saw me at the same moment, and gestured for me to come over.

Kooj was seated at one of the desks used by uniforms who didn't have their own workstations. The man he was interviewing had his back to me.

As he heard me approach, the man turned in his chair.

It was Josh Dawson.

"Detective Becker, right?" Dawson asked.

I nodded.

"Maybe you can tell me what's going on here."

Either Dawson was a marvelous actor, or the Josh who had attacked me last night had, in fact, originated on another stream, because there was no trace of the wild-eyed maniac who had jumped me last night.

"You didn't see Detective Becker last night?" Kudej asked, before I could come up with anything to say.

"Noooo," Dawson said slowly. "I was at work."

"All night, sir?"

Dawson nodded.

"Anyone see you there?"

"Only the entire production line."

"You work third shift?"

"Yeah. At Everlast Packaging."

"And there is someone there who can verify you never left?"

"Yes!" Dawson replied, with growing irritation. "Like I said, my boss and the hundred people I work with."

"You were at work all night? Didn't leave?"

"I told you, no. Look, why the third degree? What's this got to do with my car?"

"Your car?" I blurted.

"Mr. Dawson claims his car was stolen last night," Kudej explained.

"What do you mean, claims?" Dawson continued, now clearly agitated. "It was parked right in front of my girlfriend's house. She called me this morning and asked why I didn't come in to say hi before taking it."

"How'd you get to work if your car was at your girlfriend's?" Kudej asked.

"She dropped me off. Sometimes we grab a late dinner before I have to go in. I can catch a ride to her place in the morning. But today, she called before I left, and I knew the car had been stolen." He looked from Kudej to me. "You didn't answer my question. What's this all about?"

Kudej gave me a puzzled look. When I didn't say anything, he dove in.

"Detective Becker says you assaulted him last night, then took off in your car."

"WHAT?" Dawson whirled around toward me and shot to his feet. "What the hell are you talking about?"

Kudej had also risen. Heads turned throughout the room, eight officers quietly going on alert.

"Please sit down, sir."

"The hell I will," Dawson snarled, "not until I find out what is going on here. I came in to report my car stolen, and you're accusing me of assault!"

"No one's accusing you of anything, Mr. Dawson," I said calmly, hoping my smooth tone would be contagious.

"That's not what it sounds like to me!"

"Is there a problem here?" said a voice behind me.

I turned to see Leon Martin.

Oh, this just gets better and better.

The captain's posture was relaxed, but I knew he was a coiled spring, ready to act if things escalated.

"No, sir," I said.

"The hell there isn't!" Dawson said. "I came in to report a stolen car and this man," he pointed at me, "says I assaulted him!"

Martin raised an eyebrow at me. I thought fast.

"I... was out last night, taking another look at the area near Michelle Day's house. I saw a man near a car I recognized as Mr. Dawson's. As soon as he saw me, he jumped into the car and took off. I gave chase, Officer Kudej responded to my radio call. But we lost him."

"And that's not how you recall it, Mr... Dawson?"

"Hell, no. I was just telling these officers, for the third time, that I was at work all night. I came in to report my car stolen and now I'm starting to think I need a lawyer."

"That won't be necessary, Mr. Dawson," I interrupted. "Honestly, the man I saw last night matched your general description, and he got in the car fast enough it seemed he must have had a key. Now, seeing you here today, I may have jumped the gun in assuming it was you."

This mollified him a little. "Well... I guess it would have been an easy mistake to make."

"Officer Kudej here will finish taking your statement," Martin said. "Trav, gotta minute?"

I followed Martin to his office.

"I had already seen your report," he said without preamble. "Nowhere did you indicate any doubt that it was the owner in the car you were pursuing."

"Leon, I thought it was him. But he says a hundred people saw him at work all night. I must have been wrong."

"It's not like you to jump to conclusions, Trav. What were you doing out there anyway?"

I shrugged. "I couldn't sleep. I drove out there just to soak it in, look for some inspiration, you know?"

He nodded. "Do you think this has anything to do with the case?"

"It's a strange coincidence, I'll grant you that."

That's not the half of it.

"And you're sure it wasn't Dawson in the car? I can assign someone to keep an eye on him."

"No, I don't think that's necessary. I'll call his boss, just to verify his story, but he didn't act like a guy who was hiding something."

Martin looked at me for what seemed like a long time. Leon was no dummy. Between Dawson and me, I was the one acting like he was hiding something.

"Okay. Well, you know where I am if you need me for anything. You're in early, considering you were here pretty late last night."

"I want to go over Sophie's computer again."

At last, I could say something approaching the full truth.

But this caused the captain to raise a sardonic eyebrow. "You, going over the computer?" He pulled his cell phone from his breast pocket. "Should I call my kid and have him come over and help you?"

Leon's son was fourteen.

"Nice," I snorted. "Thanks for your confidence."

"Well, don't let me stand in the way of your computer forensics," he chortled. "Pool workout tomorrow?"

"Fine," I replied. "Like it's not enough torturing me in the office."

He waved me out with a smile. I headed back across the office, noting Kudej must have finished up with Dawson. The interview desk was empty.

If I had ever doubted the Josh Dawson I had met last night was from another stream, this morning had pretty much erased it. And that made it a very special occurrence.

Aside from Sam Zero, who had used a device of his own invention to jump between streams, the only people I had ever witnessed who could shift under their own power were the different versions of me. Was the Dawson I had encountered last night a Traveler? And if so, was the Dawson of this stream aware of his ability?

Questions, all I had was questions. The deeper I got into this case, the more questions I had.

And they just got weirder and weirder.

Maybe I had been too hasty in turning down Leon's offer to have someone watch Dawson. If he was a Traveler, that would be good to know. Although how I would explain to the officer assigned to tail him that the man might have the ability to disappear, I did not know.

Before I dug back into Sophie's computer, I spent a few more minutes on Dawson. No record. Next, because despite what my boss thought about my computer savvy, I turned to Google, a detective's best friend. I had actually cleared a case once because the suspect had posted pictures online that contradicted his stated alibi.

At the top of the search results was a picture of Dawson with the Road Runner, holding a trophy. Waxed and in the sunshine, I wasn't surprised it won awards.

And another article totally unrelated to the car suggested something I hadn't had time to consider the previous night.

I was only a few paragraphs in when the door to Interview Two opened. It was Ward.

"There you are," he said. "Come on. We need to go."

"Go where?"

"Did you connect with that psychic, Morgan Foster?"

I nodded.

"What happened?"

"Nothing. I mean, I talked to her."

"And?"

"And she didn't know much. I was going to fill you and Adam in when you came in."

"Do it now."

"Why?"

"She's gone missing."

"What?" I blurted before I could stop myself.

"Morgan Foster is missing," he repeated. Adam came around the corner at the same time.

"I just heard. I was walking past just as the desk sergeant was telling someone over the phone that it was too early to file a missing persons report. I heard him say her name." He looked at me. "Did you see her last night?"

I nodded.

"What time?"

"We met at seven. Talked for maybe a half hour."

"You left her at the bar?" Ward asked.

"Yes."

"We don't know this has anything to with our case," Adam pointed out.

Ward shrugged. "It may not, but we don't have any other leads to chase down."

"Could she be at a boyfriend's place?" I asked. "She didn't say anything about meeting anyone after I left, but she looked like she intended to stick around awhile."

"The neighbor says no boyfriend."

"That doesn't mean anything" Adam said. "She could have met some guy at a bar."

"Maybe," Ward said. "But she didn't seem that type."

"What type do you think she is?" Adam asked.

"Lesbian."

"*What?*" I blurted.

Ward raised an eyebrow. "That's the profile on women practicing the paranormal."

"You mean every woman who reads books about vampires is gay?" I asked.

"No. I didn't say *interested* in the paranormal. I said *practicing*. Wiccans, psychics, any fringe belief system, tends to have a higher percentage of gays than the rest of the population."

"Wow," I said. "*That's* the kind of research they have you guys doing at Quantico these days?"

"Don't be ridiculous," Ward snapped. "Or do you know something about her sexuality you'd like to share with the class?"

I shook my head. "I just don't like classifying people based on one characteristic."

"I'm a *profiler*. Classifying people is what I do. Now, are we going to stand around debating how politically correct we are, or are we going to check out a lead?"

"What lead?" Adam asked. "All we have is a woman who hasn't gotten home from an evening out."

"Like I said, we don't have anything else to chase down. Or do we?"

Adam and I shook our heads. I still wanted to get a look at Sophie's computer, but this wasn't the time to bring it up.

"I'll drive," Ward said, releasing me once again from the stress of driving my co-workers around with a trunk full of bodies.

I sat up front. Ward had already gotten Morgan's address. Adam and I busied ourselves checking phones as we rode. I was half hoping to hear something from Sam, but no luck.

I tried not to worry about Morgan. She had said she could take care of herself and I believed her. Adam's explanation made the most sense, but the idea that she had left the bar with some random guy bothered me.

Before long, we arrived at Morgan's residence. She lived in an area the locals called Czech Town, in a restored row house originally built for Eastern European immigrants enticed to the New World to work in a long-shuttered packing plant.

A half-dozen or so of the houses had been kept up. They were tiny places, but suitable for a single person who didn't care for apartment living, or maybe a couple with no kids.

Each house was brightly painted and nicely landscaped. Two even had little picket fences.

Morgan's was painted blue, and a gray sign with the words Psychic Readings printed on a background of stars and a crescent moon was stuck into the ground next to the porch stairs.

An older woman, maybe in her mid-seventies, stood on the porch. She wore a hoodie and yoga pants. Her silvery-blonde hair was tied into a loose ponytail.

"Are you the police?" she asked, meeting us halfway up the walk.

"I'm Detective Becker," I said. "This is Detective Yount, and Special Agent Ward."

"The FBI? Oh, of course." She nodded in approval. "You'd be called in the event of a kidnapping."

"Let's not jump to conclusions," Ward said, "Ms...?"

"Cynthia Prevost," she replied. "I'm Morgan's next door neighbor." She pointed to the next row house down, white with brown shutters.

"Ms. Prevost," Adam said. "What makes you think something out of the ordinary has happened? We saw Ms. Foster just yesterday, and she seemed fine."

"Of course," the woman repeated, nodding again. "She was helping you investigate the disappearance of those two little girls."

"That's not exactly the case..." Ward began, but Ms. Prevost wasn't finished.

"No wonder you rushed right out here," she continued as if Ward hadn't even spoken. "You must be as worried as I am."

"Ma'am." It was my turn to try and get us back on course. "Is it unusual that Ms. Foster would be gone overnight?"

"Yes. Oh, I know what you're thinking. Attractive young woman, likes to hang out at that bar..."

"That's the... uh, Kremlin?" Ward had consulted his phone while she spoke. "You mentioned to the desk sergeant that was where she told you she was going last night."

The woman nodded, but then she frowned. "Now do not get it into your heads she went home with someone. Morgan is much choosier than that."

"It sounds like you know her well," I said.

She nodded. "I do. We talk every day."

"*Every* day?"

"Yes." A note of impatience crept into her tone. "That's our arrangement. We're two single women, each living alone. No family near. We check in with each other every day. Usually first thing in the morning, before I go to my water aerobics class and she goes over to her radio station. You know she has her own program, don't you?"

"Yes, we know," I said. "And that's why you called the police? Because she missed her check-in?"

She nodded. "Morgan would never let that go. She knows I would worry. Well, what are we waiting for?"

"Waiting for?"

"Let's go inside."

"Ma'am, I'm not sure that's wise. We will need probable cause to enter Ms. Foster's residence."

"Don't be absurd." She produced a ring of keys from her jacket pocket. "I'm inviting you."

"Ms. Prevost," I said, "even if a crime has occurred, it didn't happen *here*. What reason do we have for going into her home?"

"Well, *I'm* going in. If for no other reason than to feed her cat. You gentlemen can do whatever you like."

She turned and walked purposefully back up onto the porch.

As she unlocked the door, Ward shrugged and followed, Adam and me in his wake.

Prevost had already disappeared into the kitchen by the time we entered Morgan's front room. Ward and Adam followed her. I hung back, sidling over to a small side table next a love seat. Despite being "invited" in, searching the house was out of the question.

But...

I quietly slid open the single drawer in an end table next to Morgan's small couch. If things were consistent from stream to stream, it contained a rather large gun that I knew from experience, the diminutive psychic knew how to use.

I breathed a sigh of relief. Morgan's Desert Eagle took up almost the entire space. In fact, the enormous handgun had to go in the drawer diagonally to fit at all. I chose to believe that since she had left it here, she hadn't been expecting to get into any trouble last night.

I started to close the drawer, but my hand was nudged away by a small black head.

Morgan's cat, which had hopped up onto the love seat, pushed his ears under my hand, angling for a scratch.

I closed the drawer with my other hand and scratched him on the neck. He let me do that for a moment, then walked along the edge of the table so I could stroke along his spine. I did so, concentrating on the spot right where his backbone and tail connected.

"Now, that's odd..." Cynthia Prevost re-entered the room, still trailed by Ward and Adam. "Oh, there you are!"

I started to say something, to give some reason for not having followed the rest of the group, but she wasn't talking to me.

"Noah, didn't you hear the can opener? Detective, you certainly have a way with cats. Usually Noah is standing right by his bowl as soon as he hears a cupboard door open."

"Yeah, Trav," Adam smirked. "Since when did you become the Cat Whisperer?"

I shrugged, giving Noah's back one final rub. Sensing our moment was over, he hopped off the table and trotted into the kitchen.

Ward watched the cat leave with a frown, staring in its direction even after it disappeared into the kitchen. After a moment, he turned to Prevost. "Ma'am, we should go. Nothing seems to have been disturbed."

"But you haven't even searched the place!"

"And we won't. There is no re-"

His phone beeped. He glanced at the incoming text message and frowned.

"We have to go."

"Now?" Prevost asked. "What about Morgan?"

"We will follow up on your tip, I promise. If by some chance Ms. Foster does show up, please let us know."

"Oh, I will."

"Becker, Yount, let's go."

He quickly walked back to his car. We left Cynthia Prevost and the cat behind to lock up.

"What's up?" I asked.

Ward started the car and pulled out. "Ms. Prevost may have been right after all. We sent a man down to that club, the Kremlin, and pulled their security camera footage from last night."

"What did they find?" I asked.

"Didn't say." But he turned his head and gave me a long look. "Just that we needed to see it."

At the station, we were met at the door to Interview Two by one of the FBI agents who'd been a part of yesterday's meeting. He handed Ward a USB stick and left. Ward tossed it to Adam, who inserted it into the laptop.

The machine whirred as it woke up. Adam found the file on the drive, but before he could click on it, Ward turned to me.

"Before we watch this, is there anything you'd like to say?"

"What the hell is that supposed to mean?" Adam said.

I met Ward's gaze. He looked at me expectantly.

"I expect you will see Morgan and me having our conversation. But you knew I talked to her. Why all the mystery?"

"Let's just see what the tape says."

Adam looked at me uncertainly. I shrugged. He launched the video.

As luck would have it, the security camera was located in direct line of sight to where Morgan and I had been sitting the night before. I've seen network newscasts with a sloppier two-shot.

We watched as the text from Sam came in. I got up to leave. Morgan took my arm and a few more moments of intense conversation occurred, before she pulled my head to her. From this angle, it looked like she kissed me on the cheek rather than whispered in my ear.

She hopped back on the barstool and sipped her glass of wine as I left.

"Like I said, we talked for a while. I left..." I began.

Ward held up a hand. "Wait."

The three of us watched as a figure came into the frame. Morgan turned and frowned at him for a minute, then she smiled.

Trav Becker signaled the bartender for a beer.

11

THE TRAV ON the screen took a pull from his beer, and proceeded to "continue" his conversation with Morgan. As they spoke, she grew more and more excited. Finally, in response to something the man said, she nodded vigorously. He tossed a bill on the bar.

We watched as the two left together.

But not before he turned to face the bar and the camera one more time. I had been too much in shock before, but this time, I noticed the ball cap he wore. It bore a sci-fi movie logo.

Jurassic Park.

"You bastard," I whispered.

"What?" Ward asked.

"Nothing."

"So, where did the two of you go?"

"Nowhere."

"You left together."

"It's not what it looks like."

"Well, why don't you explain it to me, Detective?"

"I can't."

"You're not going to deny that's you we just watched leave with a woman who is now missing, are you?"

"That wouldn't do me much good, would it?"

"There has got to be a logical explanation, Trav." Adam's tone was almost pleading. "Just tell us what happened after you left."

"I told you. Nothing. We didn't leave together."

"That's not what I saw," Ward observed.

"I mean, we didn't go anywhere else together."

"Anyone else see you last night?"

Yeah, three other Trav Beckers and Josh Dawson, only not the one who was here today.

And Sam. But I wanted to keep him out this.

I stared at the computer screen. Adam had left the video running after Morgan and Jurassic Trav had walked out of the shot. Someone now crossed in front of the camera's view.

An electric shock ran down my spine.

"Run the tape back," I said.

"What?"

"Run it back. About thirty seconds."

Adam did so. As the figure crossed the screen again, I had Adam freeze the image.

"Can you zoom in on his face?" I asked.

"It's not the most high-res image, it might be blurry. But I'll try."

Adam zoomed in on the face of the man crossing the room.

The image pixelated a little bit, but it was still clear enough that the thing that had puzzled me last night finally clicked into place. It was of a swarthy, middle-aged man. He had dark hair, just beginning to gray at the temples. He was either unshaven, or had a hell of a five o'clock shadow. He wore a long-sleeved shirt, untucked, to disguise a substantial belly.

"Either of you recognize that guy?" I asked

Adam and Ward both shook their heads.

"He was at El Juego yesterday. In the co-working area."

"Are you sure?" Ward asked.

"Yeah. I noticed him at the time because he was about twenty years older than just about everyone else in the room."

"This bar is just around the corner from Clark's building," Ward said. "So, he goes in there for a beer after work."

I tapped the screen. "Still, he doesn't look much like an Internet startup guy to me. Plus, he watched us the whole time we were in there."

"That still doesn't prove anything. Clark said those guys were kind of paranoid."

"I got a feeling about him. Can we check it out?"

Ward examined me. "Mighty convenient that you just *happen*," he made air quotes, "to see something that jogs your memory after what we just saw."

"Humor me. What have you got to lose?"

He glared at me some more, then shrugged. "Sure. But when this turns out to be unconnected, I want to hear again how you left Morgan at that bar when the tape clearly shows her leaving with you."

I started to object again, but he raised a hand. "But, we'll do this first."

He reached for his tablet. "Let's just see if this guy is in the system."

"It normally takes us a week or two to get results back from the NCIC," Adam said to him. "Can you move us up in the queue?" NCIC stood for National Crime Information Center, the FBI's central database for keeping track of crime-related information.

"I can do better than that," Ward replied. "The Bureau has just deployed a mobile system for suspect identification."

"You're telling me there's an app for that?" I asked.

Ward rolled his eyes, holding his tablet in front of the computer screen. From behind him, we could see that he was lining the man's face up with the device's camera. After a minute or two, he seemed satisfied with the orientation, and snapped a picture. He poked at the screen a few more times, and was rewarded with a *whoosh* sound.

"It's on its way to the database," he announced. "If there's a hit, we should know in a few minutes."

"Pretty slick," Adam said.

My phone made the Monty-Python squelching sound.

Can u talk?

"I'll be back in a minute," I said, and slipped out of the room. I found a quiet spot and dialed Sam.

"Trav."

"What's up?"

"Just wanted to give you a progress report."

"Okay."

"I de-mothballed the Cat Box."

"And?"

He hesitated. "And, it's hard to say. I mean, it's only been a few hours, and maybe I'm not remembering it right, but I'm sure that things didn't look like this last year."

"Look like what?"

"Just... messed up. The interface the Cat Box uses to render inter-spatial composition is complicated, but conforms to a very specific structure. Or at least it used to."

The Cat Box was the name Sam had given to the computer software he had designed to view and track the various streams of reality. It took its name from that famous experiment by the physicist Schrödinger, who had postulated that if you sealed a cat up in a box and pumped it full of poison gas, until you opened the box to see if the cat was alive or dead, it somehow was both.

It's like the other old saying, the one about a tree falling in the forest not making a sound if there is no one around to hear it. An observer doesn't just witness the outcome of a given event. Just by being present, he or she also affects the outcome. This idea seemed to be the root of the Traveler science. Somehow, I could simultaneously observe and also direct my awareness to *choose* among many different outcomes. Why I could do this was something neither Sam nor I had ever figured out. And until yesterday, I had been happier not knowing.

"What does it look like now?" I asked.

"Like I said, messed up. Streams intersect, and that *never* happens. Some just seem to end, then start up again. I don't see how that's even possible. It's really weird, Trav."

"And that's a surprise? Last night, three versions of me were holding us at gunpoint."

"There is that. But…"

Even though this wasn't a video call, I knew Sam had pulled out his lower lip, and was now pinching it between his thumb and index finger, something he always did under stress.

"But what?"

"When I went to start up the Cat Box programs again, I noticed that some of the files had been opened recently."

"Not by you?"

"No. I haven't touched any of this stuff in months."

"Can you tell if they were tampered with?"

"I don't think so. Otherwise, the Cat Box wouldn't have launched. But it's still weird."

"Tell me you don't have those files sitting out where anyone can access them."

"Of course not," he snorted. "They were encrypted. Someone would have to know my system as well as me just to find them, let alone decrypt them."

"Or someone would have to *be* you."

"Oh, shit. I hadn't thought of that. Do you think?"

"I don't know. But we do know there are multiple Travs running around with their own agenda. Why not Sams as well?"

"Crap."

We were both silent as we digested this.

"What do we do?" Sam asked after a moment.

"Can you figure when those files were accessed?"

"I don't know. Maybe."

"Try. And keep an eye on the Cat Box. It can't be good that things are this messed up."

"Right."

"Keep in touch."

He assured me he would.

I leaned against the wall and thought about Jurassic Trav. Last year, he had mysteriously appeared on Stream Zero, wounded. He claimed to have been just looking for a quiet place to recuperate, and hung around to help Trav Zero and me complete our mission to rescue a confidential informant from Anton Kaaro. He never told us how he got hurt, but hinted there was some larger conflict going on that he was involved in.

This caused Sam and me to joke later that there was some kind of inter-dimensional Seal Team Six going around fixing breaches in the Multiverse. Was there a covert mission going on around us, involving multiple versions of Sam and me? If there was, and the Trav body count was any indication, it was a dangerous one.

My ruminating was interrupted by Adam, who poked his head out into the hallway.

"We got a hit."

Ward looked up as I walked back into the room.

"I'll be damned," he said. "You were right."

"You thought I was making it up?"

"Honestly? I thought you were trying to distract us from you and Foster. But it appears you called this one."

"I'll take that as an apology," I said.

"Take it any way you like."

"Asshole," Adam muttered.

"He's just doing his job," I whispered.

If Ward overheard us, he gave no sign as he continued working the tablet.

"Does the name Nikodem Bekas mean anything to you?" he asked.

Adam and I shook our heads.

"Polish immigrant, been in the States about nine years. He has some priors. Small-time stuff, but a lot of it. Known associates include one Bilol Grimzyn, and…"

He had been looking at me again while he said this. Now I knew why.

"Let me guess," I said. "Anton Kaaro."

"You know him."

I didn't answer right away. We were back on dangerous ground. Had I in fact recognized him because I had recalled seeing him at Clark's, or had the sight of him also dredged up another, older memory from my short time with Kaaro and his henchmen?

Finally, I shook my head. "I'm not sure. Maybe. I mean, there was something about him that got stuck in the back of my mind. But I don't remember him being one of the inner circle."

"Kaaro and the top guys are in jail," Ward said. "So it's possible that some of the lower ranks have been promoted."

"You think Kaaro is still running his gang from behind bars?" I asked.

"Stranger things have happened. Want to ask him who his boss is?"

"Let's do it," Adam said.

"You guys go ahead," Ward said. "I have some things I need to do here."

Adam and I both looked at the FBI agent, but could read nothing behind his passive expression. Finally, we shrugged and hurried out.

"You mind driving?" I asked Adam.

He frowned. "You always drive. Are you sick or something?"

"No. My car... Uh, I got a check engine light. I don't want to drive it any more than I have to until I can get it looked at."

He shrugged. "Whatever."

The receptionist at El Juego today was a young man wearing a tight plaid shirt buttoned up to his neck and Buddy Holly glasses.

"Can I help you?" he asked brightly.

Adam and I produced our badges. "Please tell Mr. Clark we need to see him."

He slipped the message into a cash railway car and it zipped upstairs. A couple of minutes later, Clark came down.

"What can I do for you? Sanjana isn't here."

"We need to talk to someone in your co-working space," I said.

"Co-working?" he replied with a frown. "What does that have to do with the kidnapping?"

"The name of one of the individuals working there came up in our investigation."

"Wow. That's hard to believe."

"Is there a vetting process your... uh, tenants go through?" Adam asked.

"Not really," Clark said, shrugging. "They usually reserve time online with a credit card. As long as the charge goes through, and they're courteous to others around them, we don't pay that much attention."

"Are most of the reservations long term?"

"It depends. Some come in for just a few hours, but others use the space pretty much as a dedicated office. If you're a freelancer, you spend a lot time by yourself. Sometimes it's nice to get out and work in an environment where there are other people, even if they aren't actually your co-workers. And some of the startups can be here for several months."

We were now upstairs. He reached for the door that led to the co-working space. I put my hand out.

"Wait."

The door had glass on either side of the frame. I waved Adam and Clark away from the direct line of sight of the occupants, and looked inside. Nikodem Bekas was seated at the same workstation he had been when we had been here before. I noticed now this particular desk was positioned so he had a clear view of the door to the El Juego work area.

"There he is. You can stay here, Mr. Clark."

"No. If there's something hinky going on here, I want to know about it."

"Fine. Stay behind us please."

We entered the room. Bekas looked over as soon as he saw movement, and watched us without expression as we walked toward him. There were only five or six other people in the room, and none sat near him.

As we got closer, I noticed that the workspace around him was clear. No papers, notebooks, or anything that would indicate work in progress. A game of solitaire was up on his computer screen.

"Mr. Bekas?" I asked.

"Yes?" It came out sounding like *chess*.

Adam and I badged him. "I'm Detective Becker, this is Detective Yount. We have a few questions to ask you."

He shook his head. "That will not be necessary."

"Excuse me?"

He was wearing a woolen blazer over a dark blue denim shirt, and he put one hand inside. Automatically, Adam and I reached toward our weapons.

He stopped and held up a finger.

"Please."

He slowly reached just two fingers into his inside pocket and withdrew a small envelope, the kind a thank-you card comes in.

It was addressed to me.

"What's this?" I asked.

Bekas shrugged.

I slid a finger under the flap and opened it.

> *Travis,*
>
> *If you are reading this, we need to talk.*
>
> *A.K.*

Even without the clue of the initials, there was only one person other than my mother who called me Travis.

Anton Kaaro.

12

"WHERE DID YOU get this?"

Bekas shrugged again. "Where do you think?"

"How did you know I would be here?"

"I did not," he said calmly. "But I was given that note and told when this man comes to you, give it to him." He gestured toward me.

"Told by who?" Adam demanded.

Bekas didn't answer.

"We saw you here yesterday," I pointed out. "Why didn't you give it to me then?"

"You did not ask."

Adam stepped toward the man. "Maybe you'll be more talkative at the station."

"Wait," I said. "Is there anything else you were supposed to tell us?"

"Only what I was doing here."

Adam and I both raised our eyebrows.

"And that was?" I asked.

"I was to watch."

"And what else?"

"Just watch." He inclined his head toward the door that led to the El Juego space.

"And report to whom?"

Bekas pointed to the note. "He is the one who will answer your questions."

Adam and I backed away, keeping our eyes on Bekas.

"I don't like it," Adam whispered. "What the hell does Kaaro have to do with all this?"

"Something we don't know about." I held up the note. "Which he may be willing to tell us."

"And you trust him?"

"It's the closest thing we have to a lead. We've got to follow it up."

"What about the mailman?" Adam jerked a thumb toward Bekas.

"Call a uniform."

Adam stepped away, groping for his phone. I turned to Bekas. "All right. I'll go talk to Kaaro. But you're going to the station. I would like to know more about who you are supposed to be watching."

He shrugged again, and went back to his solitaire game.

"Man of few words," Adam observed.

"Kaaro encourages it."

"What is going on here?" Christopher Clark asked.

"An officer is on his way to collect Mr. Bekas," I said. "We'll get out of your way in a few minutes."

"You mean he's been here all this time, spying on my employees?" he said. "Does this have something to do with the kidnapping?"

"I don't know, Mr. Clark. But I hope to find out."

"Kaaro… I feel like I should know that name."

"He used to own your building."

"I bought the building from a holding company."

135

"Which was owned by Anton Kaaro. His housing is being handled by the state these days."

"What?"

"He's in prison."

"Prison?" Clark scowled. "How do I know these other people aren't spying on my company, too?" He scanned the room.

"You don't. Maybe you want to do checks on the people you've been renting to."

"Good idea."

"Could you go down and escort our officer up?" Adam asked, taking his phone from his ear. "He'll be here in a minute."

Clark headed downstairs, returning a minute later with two uniformed officers. We turned Bekas over to them, and headed back to Adam's car.

"Oakdale?" Adam asked.

"Oakdale."

I called Ward and updated him as we headed out of town. The FBI agent was surprisingly cheerful, seeing as how just an hour ago he had looked ready to accuse me of being involved in the kidnapping. He agreed that Kaaro was playing some sort of game, but also agreed that we didn't have any other promising leads. He offered to call ahead and tell the warden we were on the way.

"Ask him if he can get together a list of Kaaro's visitors and phone calls," I asked. He said he would.

After I got off the phone, Adam turned on the radio. Morgan's voice was the first thing I heard.

"Shit," Adam exclaimed, looking at me. "What the hell?"

I shrugged, but the mystery was solved a minute later when there was a station break. A male voice announced we were listening to the "Best of *Second Sight*."

"Well, that explains that," I said, turning the radio back off.

"Soooo," Adam said, stretching the word out to sentence-length. "Is everything okay between you and Mary?"

"Yessss," I replied, matching him syllable for syllable.

He waited for me to continue. I didn't.

"Why do I ask, you ask?"

"I didn't."

"You see," he continued, ignoring me, "my friend and partner has been head over heels with his girlfriend since before I knew him. And my friend is kind of an old-fashioned guy. He's certainly not against some regular, good old-fashioned, pre-marital nookie, but his sense of order is going to require him to observe the social niceties, and marry this woman before she wises up. And yet, here I am, walking down the aisle in just a few weeks, while he hasn't even proposed."

He gave a theatrical sigh. "It's a mystery. If only there were a quick-witted, observant investigator who could deduce what was going on."

He straightened in his seat, jerking one finger into the air in an "ah-ha" gesture. "Fortunately, there is. One who is as smart as he is devastatingly handsome. And sure enough, our hero breaks the case wide open."

"What the fuck are you talking about?"

"I'm talking about the psychic. I don't know what you two were talking about at the bar, but it was not our case. Please tell me you haven't been seeing her all this time."

"All what time?"

"Don't bullshit me, Trav. Did you not catch the 'quick-witted and observant investigator' part? I remember the first time I saw her. Last year. She pulled up at the station and you got out of her car. You said she was a witness in that stabbing at the Kremlin, but you never explained what the two of you were doing in her car."

I had forgotten that Adam had seen us together. For the first time, I found myself wishing I had a slightly less skilled partner.

"Yesterday was the first time I saw Morgan Foster since I questioned her last year," I said firmly. "And there is nothing going on between us. Any more questions?"

"Just the original one," he said quietly. "How are things with you and Mary?"

"Things are fine."

With an effort, I kept from gritting my teeth. "Just because you and Kim are on the expressway to matrimony doesn't mean everyone else has to be. Mary and I are happy the way things are. And when it's time…" My voice trailed off.

"When it's time?" he prompted.

"It'll be time," I finished. Lamely.

"Okay," he said. "I'm sure you know what you're doing. But she isn't going to wait around for you forever."

"If I wanted this lecture, I would call my mother," I growled.

"All right, all right, not another word! But when it *is* time, if you need help setting up the proposal, I have it from reliable sources mine was legendary."

"You know, pissing off your best man is a good way to get your bachelor party photos posted to Facebook."

"Why look!" he said. "There's our turnoff."

I rolled my eyes as he pulled in to a frontage road that led to the imposing stone walls of Oakdale Penitentiary.

It never failed to impress me.

In the 1800s, they built prisons to look like prisons.

Located in the small burg of Okaloosa, about thirty minutes from town, the prison was constructed of thousands of tons of limestone, quarried nearby (and probably by prisoners, now that I thought of it) to create a structure that towered over the mature trees which lined the entrance. The walls formed a huge square, encompassing more city blocks than the entire rest of the town.

There was only one gate in the entire complex, and after the guard did a quick check of our IDs, he waved us through.

Adam swung into a parking spot, and we headed up a set of stairs, which from previous visits we knew led to an entrance for law enforcement. True to his word, Ward had called ahead. Our wait was brief, and after having our IDs checked again, we surrendered our weapons and were shown to an interview room.

A few minutes later, the door opened, and a guard brought Kaaro in.

"You can leave him," I said. "We'll call you when we're done."

The guard nodded and withdrew.

Kaaro looked at me. "It's good to see you, Travis."

Like I said, my mother and Anton Kaaro are the only people who call me by my full name. When your mom and an organized crime boss have stuff in common, you really should re-examine your life.

"I would shake hands," Kaaro continued, holding up his manacled wrists, "but..."

He paused, perhaps waiting for one of us to offer to free his hands. But when neither Adam nor I said anything, he hooked an ankle around the leg of the chair, and pulled it out. We did not move to help him, but we did at least wait to make sure he didn't fall on his ass before we sat in the chairs across the table from him.

Anton Kaaro was in his late fifties. His short hair was black as night, with only a touch of gray at the temples. He regarded us with intense green eyes which apparently had no need for glasses.

Kaaro hailed from a Balkan state whose name consisted mainly of K's, U's, and Z's. After emigrating, he had stayed on the right side of the law for years, or at least had appeared to, because he had no problems getting U.S. citizenship. But soon afterward, he had swooped in and consolidated a dozen small to medium-sized gangs, until nothing in the local underworld happened without his approval.

He had also done an excellent job of keeping anything illegal from sticking to him until I had brought him down, with some help from knowledge gained on another stream of reality. Fortunately for him, in this reality I had managed to avoid dropping a burning building on him.

In his pre-prison life, Kaaro had favored tone-on-tone clothing, dressing all in gray or black. Once, I had even seen him dressed head-to-toe in shades of rust. He sported a monochrome look today, too. Orange. But even in his jumpsuit and handcuffs, Kaaro somehow managed to give the air of a businessman entertaining clients in his office. Had he offered me a Scotch, I would not have been surprised.

I tossed the note onto the table. "I got your love note," I said. "I'm here. Now, I want some answers."

"Straight to the point, Travis, as usual. I have always liked that about you."

"We're not here for small talk."

"You were more polite when you were in my employ," Kaaro said reprovingly. His English was nearly perfect, with no discernible accent other than the slightly formal phrasing of someone who learned a language from a non-native teacher.

"I was never in your employ. I was undercover."

Kaaro shrugged. "So you say. But I think part of you enjoyed working with me. If I had had a little more time, who knows? You might have decided to come over for real."

"Not likely." I needed to move this along. Keep going down this path and Kaaro would twig to the holes in my memory.

The fact was, there had always been things about this stream's Trav and his relationship with Kaaro that had bothered me. A bunch of money I had found locked away in "our" apartment, for example.

It wouldn't be the first time an undercover cop was seduced by those he was supposed to bring down. I could not ever imagine doing anything like that, but that's a strange side effect of this whole jumping-between-parallel-realities thing. You get to actually see what happens as a result of your choices. And sometimes it's really surprising.

"We didn't come up here to reminisce," I said. "You knew I would show up and start asking your friend Bekas questions."

"He is not my friend," Kaaro sniffed. "Just a hireling. Someone jailed most of the good help."

"Thanks for the compliment. Now, why are we here? Why was Bekas casing El Juego?"

"He was not casing, Travis. He was *guarding*."

"Guarding? Guarding what?"

"My investment."

I leaned back in my chair. "Your investment? You're an investor in El Juego?"

"That's impossible," Adam interrupted. "Convicted felons are forbidden from having anything to do with a gaming establishment. They check the backgrounds of each and every investor."

Kaaro gave him a withering look. "Rest assured that if I choose to make an investment, Detective, my money will be gladly accepted."

"Even from prison," I said.

"I said *most* of the good help has been jailed, Travis. Not all."

"Spare me the Godfather routine, Kaaro," I said. "Let me tell you what I think. I think you orchestrated the kidnapping of the two missing girls in the first place, and you put Bekas in place to keep tabs on the investigation."

"A passable theory, Travis," he nodded in approval, like I was a student who had given an almost correct answer. "And perhaps the most logical one as well. If I was the kind of man who used the pain of children to further his own ends. But I am not that kind of man."

"Oh, come on," Adam sneered. "We've both seen what kind of man you are. We don't think for a minute you wouldn't stoop to kidnapping if there was profit in it."

Kaaro leapt from his seat and slammed his manacled wrists onto the metal table with a *bang*. Adam and I reared back, hands going to weapons we did not have. Kaaro glared at us, murder in his eyes.

The door swung open, slamming into the wall with a crash almost as loud as the first. The guard stepped quickly into the room, one hand on his baton.

"Everything okay here?"

Kaaro's glare softened, and he looked almost sheepish.

He sat back down. "Everything is fine. I apologize for my outburst."

The guard looked at Adam and me. I nodded, and he withdrew.

"I'm sorry," Kaaro repeated. He fixed Adam with a baleful stare. "But do not think that just because you have read my file that you know anything about me. You know *nothing*."

His voice became a dark, hoarse growl. "Nothing about my business, or my motives. But assuming you have read my file, you know that neither I, nor anyone in my organization, harm children. You may even remember that I dismissed a member of my organization for peddling drugs near a school."

"Dismissed?" I said. "I think the word you're looking for is 'disappeared'. After you bailed him out, no one ever heard from him again."

Kaaro shrugged. "Regardless, he did not again sell drugs to schoolchildren."

"Okay. Let's say that you did call us up here because you want to help. So help. Who took the girls?"

Kaaro leaned back in his seat and gave a long sigh that seemed to actually deflate him. He suddenly looked every inch an old man resigned to spending the rest of his life in prison.

"I don't know," he said quietly. And I could tell the admission unnerved him.

"I will not pretend with you. Even from inside, I have sources. I have people who can ask questions and get answers. I have a vested interest in making sure El Juego has a smooth and profitable beginning. When the child of someone with such a large role in the business is kidnapped, it's logical to wonder if there was a connection. So I asked my... friends, to look into it."

"And?"

He shook his head. "And nothing. None of the competing gaming groups are involved. Neither are any of my competitors. Whoever has done this thing is a new player. Someone who has come, literally, from nowhere. With tactics and motivations that are known only to themselves."

"So in other words, it's a mystery. Not exactly a news flash, Anton."

His eyes grew hard at my casual use of his first name.

"If that's all you have," I said, standing up, "thanks for wasting our time."

He held up a hand. "I did not say that was all I had. Nikodem is a simple man. Not much imagination, but diligent. And he reports that the Patel woman has been acting strangely."

"Of course she's acting strangely!" I snorted. "Her daughter was kidnapped." For just a second, I wondered if the elusive crime boss had gotten senile.

Kaaro shook his head. "She carries two phones, did you know that? On one she talks to her husband and friends. The other, she slips into a pocket. She announces she is going to take a short walk to clear her head. She returns a while later, looking even more distraught than before."

He leaned back in his chair, looking from Adam to me. I exchanged glances with my partner. A second phone? How had we missed that?

"All right," I said slowly, "that is good intel. And you're right. Not something we knew. But Bekas could have told us that himself. Why drag us up here?"

Kaaro's face broke open into a wide smile. I liked it better when he scowled.

"Why, Travis," he said. "I missed our talks. I wanted to make sure the police department was treating you well. That you were happy. A man's legacy is the success of his protégés."

"I am a lot of things, Anton. But I am *not* your protégé. And let me tell you one more thing. You enjoy playing Kingpin of Crime, running your empire from the safety of your jail cell. And your tip is very convincing."

I leaned in, close enough that I could smell the prison lunch still on his breath.

"But if I discover you are playing us, that in fact you are behind the kidnapping, I will personally see to it that they find the mustiest, dankest hole they have around here, and drop you in it."

"Don't make threats, Travis," Kaaro chided. "It spoils your all-American image. I am telling you the truth. You have my word. I am confident this little nudge will help you 'break the case wide open,' as they say on those delightful police shows which seem to be the only programs we are allowed in here."

He stood up. Our audience was over.

"Just one more question," I said.

He inclined his head in a tiny nod.

"Why? What is all this to you that you would put someone in place for surveillance and arrange to get me up here? It can't be just because you're an investor."

"A businessman always looks out for his investments, Travis. I have a very, very significant interest in making sure the El Juego launch goes smoothly. But you are correct. I have another motive as well."

He paused, choosing his next words.

"Let us just say that there is a special hell for those who use the pain and fear of children to accomplish their own ends. And I join you in hoping whoever did this thing sees that hell as soon as possible."

And with that he called for the guard and left without another word.

Adam and I watched him go.

"Well, that was... *unexpected.*" Adam said.

I nodded. We left quickly, and as soon as we were united with our weapons and phones, I updated Ward. He said he would have Sanjana Patel picked up.

As I rode, I thought back over our interview with Kaaro.

Honestly, it didn't really square with anything I knew of him. Either from his record, or the contact I had had with him in the past. Which had mainly been a pitched gun battle ending with Kaaro shooting two people, one of them a police officer, in cold blood. Hearing him indicate there was a line even he wouldn't cross was an admission along the same lines as a TV preacher coming out as a cross-dressing cabaret singer.

But even as I remembered the actions of Kaaro in that other stream, I also recalled other Travs. One on this stream who possessed more cash than I had ever seen. And others who did things that made me shudder.

Was it my right to assume every Anton Kaaro was exactly the same, too?

145

13

THESE CHEERY THOUGHTS kept me company on the ride back to town.

My phone vibrated with an incoming text.

Sam.

Need to talk to you.

As I looked at the screen, I noticed he had also tried to call me while my phone was locked up. Well, I couldn't talk to him with Adam nearby. It would have to wait

Soon, we were pulling up to the station. We hopped out of the car and dashed upstairs.

Ward was in Interview Two. We had no sooner arrived than his phone rang.

"Ward," he said. "Okay. Bring 'em up. She's here. With her husband."

I looked around the small room. It was going to be mighty crowded in here.

"Why don't you watch on the camera?" I said to him.

"The Bureau should be on hand for the interview," he said.

"You will be. *Watching on the monitor.* If half the station is watching her, she'll get spooked."

He gave me a hard look. "Why are you all of a sudden connected to all this, Becker? The psychic, your buddy the math genius. And now Kaaro."

146

"Like I told you. It's a small town."

"Sure it is. And you're connected to all the interesting people."

He let that hang in the air for a moment. "Don't fuck this up," he added softly He turned and left for the observation room.

Footsteps echoed on the stairs, and a moment later a uniform escorted Sanjana and Riswan Patel into the room.

Patel placed himself between us and his wife before we could even offer them a seat. He wore the standard twenty-first century work uniform of a business suit but no tie, along with a look of apprehension.

"What is going on? Do you know something about our girls? Shouldn't Michelle be here?"

"We just have a couple of questions for Mrs. Patel," I said. "Mr. Patel, you can wait outside."

"No," he said firmly. "I will stay with my wife."

Sanjana put a hand on his arm. "It's all right, *mishti*. You don't have to stay."

Patel did not reply. He just planted himself in the chair next to his wife, and laced his fingers through hers.

"Can I see your phone?" Adam asked nonchalantly.

Sanjana frowned but grabbed her purse–aquamarine with jeweled studs decorating its leather sides–and plopped it on the table. She dug into it, produced an iPhone, and slid it toward Adam.

He shook his head. "The other one."

"Other one?" Riswan Patel asked. "What are you talking about? That's her phone."

I caught Sanjana's eye. She held my gaze defiantly for a long moment. But then she turned away.

Riswan's eyes darted between his wife and me. "What is this about?" he demanded.

"Sanjana?" I said gently

"I…" she started. She opened her mouth, but no words came out. Her eyes filled.

"Tell us what is going on. We can help."

She let out the breath she had been holding in a long sigh, and stared down at the table.

"They told me they would kill our little girl," she whispered.

"What?" Patel cried. "You know who took the girls? All this time, and you *knew*?"

"No!" she said quickly. She tried to look at her husband, but turned away with a sob. "Not… at first."

"Have you been contacted by the kidnappers?" I asked.

Sanjana nodded, eyes closed.

"When?"

"A week ago."

"A week!" Patel said. "And you didn't tell me! I didn't know if our Sophie was alive or dead!"

"They told me I could tell no one, or they would kill her," Sanjana replied. She dug back into her purse.

"One morning, when I got in my car, I found this."

She produced a small cell phone. Before Adam or I could touch it, Ward burst in.

"I thought you were going to wait in the observation room," I said.

He didn't reply, but stared me down for a moment before he reached across the table for Sanjana's phone. But before he could grasp it, she snatched it back.

For the moment, he chose not to push the issue. Instead he asked. "How do you know it was the kidnappers?"

"They included a picture." She fiddled with the phone for a minute and showed us.

Sophie and Ella sat next to each other on a bed. They looked pale and frightened, but otherwise healthy. Between them, they each held up one end of a newspaper. It was too small for us to see the date, but the headline and front page picture looked familiar. The previous week seemed about right.

"I need that phone," Ward said. "We can look at the meta-data and discern where the text originated, and where the picture was taken."

"Don't you think I thought of that?" Sanjana said, giving the FBI agent a withering look. "I'm a software engineer, remember? That was the first thing I did. All the meta-data was stripped out. And before you ask, the message was routed through three VPN tunnels to anonymize the source IP. They covered their tracks very well."

"I would still like to see it," Ward said.

This time, Sanjana shrugged and handed it to him. He poked at it for a few moments, and handed it back.

"Well?" Adam asked.

Now it was Ward's turn to shrug. "About what you'd expect. 'We have your daughter. Wait for instructions.' What were the instructions?"

"Why didn't you tell the police?" Patel interrupted. "You had plenty of opportunity."

Sanjana stiffened, her eyes darting from Ward, to me, to Adam, and back again. She didn't answer.

"Mrs. Patel?" Ward asked.

"They said…" She snapped her mouth shut, biting her lip.

"They said what?"

"They said—that they owned the police and would know the minute I said anything." She closed her eyes as she finished, almost as if she was afraid one of us would whip out a pistol and shoot her on the spot.

149

Ward's eyes again darted toward me. I didn't need Morgan Foster to know that he was thinking I was the worm in the department woodpile. I was going to have to figure out a way to defuse this situation soon, or there would be hell to pay.

"I think that's the least of our worries right now," Ward finally said. "But if they didn't ask for money, what did they want?"

"A back door," she said quietly.

"Ah, crap," I said.

You don't room with a computer geek for four years in college and not know what a back door was. And I was pretty sure what the back door was supposed to open.

Ward turned to me. "A back door to what? Do you know?"

"Yeah. A back door to the encryption algorithm for El Juego. Am I right?"

She nodded.

Patel went pale. "What did you do?" he whispered hoarsely.

"I did what I had to do to save our daughter!"

"What were their instructions?" Ward asked.

"I was to rebuild a section of the base code, then provide them an access procedure so they could modify the gaming algorithm at will."

"They could predict or even change the outcome of games whenever they wanted," I said.

She nodded.

"Did you do it?"

"Yes, but it took several days. I just finished it yesterday."

"Then what?"

"After they tested the code and confirmed it worked, they were to text me at four p.m. today with the girls' location."

Ward glanced at his watch. "We have an hour. Will you excuse us?" He motioned Adam and me to step out into the hall.

"What do you think?" Adam asked.

"It's hard to say," he said, shrugging. "I've seen it go both ways. Sometimes your kidnapper lets his victims go when he gets what he wants. But the fact that he's held the girls for this long is not a good sign. Lots more time for him to let them see his face, or absorb details that would help us later. The longer one of these drags out, the more likely it is the kidnapper takes the easy way out."

"I still think we should look downtown near where I lost Dawson's car," I said. "Something wasn't right about that whole thing."

Ward once again looked at me for somewhat longer than my comment warranted. "Maybe," Ward replied, "but let's let this play out. It's three o'clock. We have an hour. If the kidnapper is just a businessman, maybe if he gets what he wants, this gets resolved without any violence."

"And he gets away," Adam said.

"He won't get away," Ward said confidently. "This is what we do. If we can get the girls back, there won't be anyplace he can hide."

Everything he said made sense, but the quick way he shut down my idea led me to think what he really wanted was to keep me where he could see me.

"I would like to call Sam," I said. "My friend who works for El Juego. If all the work he did for them is about to go kablooey, he deserves to know."

"Do you think that's smart? What if they're monitoring the site?"

"Even if they are, Sam knows what he is doing. In fact, he may even be able to see something Sanjana missed."

Ward thought about this for a second. "We have Bureau guys who can do the same thing." He raised a hand to forestall the objection he knew was coming from me. "But it will take them some time to get here. I assume your friend can get here soon?"

I nodded and pulled out my phone. I figured having both Sam and me where he could see us would make him happy.

"About time!" Sam said when he answered. "We gotta talk."

"Save it. This can't wait."

I quickly gave him an overview.

"Shit! You are kidding me," he spat.

"You can get over here?"

"Already out the door."

We went back into the interview room, where Sanjana had more or less collapsed into her husband's arms. While we waited, Adam took orders for coffee and tea. He had just gotten back and was passing the hot beverages around when Sam burst in.

His arrival sent Sanjana back into a convulsion of tears. "Oh, Sam," she sobbed, "I'm sorry."

Sam slid into a seat on her other side, sandwiching the crying woman between him and her husband. He put an arm around her.

"It's okay. The important thing is to get Sophie back." He looked at Adam and me. "So, where do we stand?"

"Still forty minutes until the message is due."

He nodded and disengaged himself from Sanjana. He reached into a messenger bag riding one hip and pulled out a laptop.

"Do you need the Wi-Fi code?" I asked.

"Don't be ridiculous," he snorted. "We'd be here all night. I'll use my own connection."

He turned to Sanjana. "Want to tell me what they made you do?"

I held my breath, thinking this might set off another round of tears, but Sam knew Sanjana better than me. It was the opposite. She sat up a little straighter in her seat, wiped her eyes and pulled the computer toward her. She and Sam were all business for the next twenty-five minutes. The rest of us were treated to an incomprehensible exchange,

152

accompanied by a lot of banging on the keyboard. Chatter that only seemed to be partly in English. I caught *dynamic class, integer factorization,* and *Shor's algorithm.* But once Sanjana started talking about something that sounded like *orthogonality,* I quit even attempting to follow.

At a couple minutes before four, Sanjana pulled her phone out and began staring at it. Sam got up, putting his hands behind his lower back and stretching. He motioned to me, and we huddled in a corner of the room.

"Well?" I asked, keeping my voice low.

"It's a hell of a job," Sam said. "If she hadn't shown me where to look, I might never have noticed it, and I wrote the damn stuff."

"Will it do what she said?"

He nodded. "Pretty much. You can go in and see a list of outcomes for most all of the games. You can also insert a value."

"Whoa."

He nodded grimly. "Yeah, you want the poker app to deal you five aces at precisely eight-thirteen p.m. you can make it happen." Sam paused, looking around the room, before leaning in closer to me.

"But that's not all," he said, his voice dropping to a near-whisper. "The code she used is…"

"What?"

"Coding is like handwriting. She knew I'd be able to tell if she inserted a bunch of stuff that wasn't in my 'style.' So she borrowed from other code I'd written."

"Oh, oh."

"Yeah. She's the one who broke into the Cat Box files."

"I suppose this is better than having another Sam around to worry about."

"Not by much."

153

His expression said he was not as relieved as he should have been.

"What?" I asked.

"It would be nice if this was just industrial espionage," he said, shaking his head. "But it's a weird coincidence that this code gets out at the same time... Well, the same time that your trunk is full."

"You got something you'd like to share with the rest of the class?" said a voice.

Ward stared at us, his innocent tone doing nothing to hide the suspicion in his eyes.

"Nothing important," I said.

Before he could pursue the issue, a soft cry from Sanjana made us all turn toward her.

She stared at her phone, tears again cornering her eyes.

I looked at my watch. 4:08.

"If they were going to follow through on their end of the bargain, they would have by now," I said.

"Maybe the checking they were going to do took longer, or the cell service is slow," Patel said hopefully.

"Anything's possible," I replied, "but I don't want to wait any longer. Adam and I are going to run downtown. I want to look over that area where I lost Dawson's car last night."

I looked at Ward, daring him to object. If he wanted to keep me here, he was going to have to detain me officially.

"Whatever," Ward said. His expression was unreadable. "I'll stay with the Patels. It's still possible the call was just delayed."

"What about you?" I asked Sam.

"I need to dive into this code some more," he said, giving me a sidelong glance. It wasn't the gaming site he was talking about.

"We can't afford to have word get back to El Juego," Ward warned. "For all we know, the kidnappers have someone inside the company. A leak could put the girls into even more danger."

Sam nodded. "I know. I won't go to the office. I can do what I need to do from my own place."

He went over to Sanjana, and gave her a hug. "It'll be okay. We'll find them."

She nodded tightly.

"You should work here," Ward said quickly.

"Why?" Sam asked.

"We can secure your access. Plus, I have a computer forensics team on the way to help."

"I don't need any help."

"Still. There's too much at stake. We need to centralize our efforts."

"Control them, you mean," Sam said. He folded up his laptop, grabbing for his backpack.

"I'm not kidding," Ward said. "You want to help, you stay here."

Sam was trying to stuff his laptop into the backpack, but it seemed stuck on something. He peered inside, and his expression went from obstinate to thoughtful.

"Fine." He turned to me. "Can you set me up someplace?"

"Uh… yeah. Come on."

I escorted him to a small conference room down the hall. "This is as good a place as any, but what the hell? You were ready to walk."

"I was, but I wanted to talk to you before you headed out, and that Agent Ward has radar or something. Every time I tried to talk to you, he was watching. I figured this was the best way to get a couple of minutes. I was trying to get hold of you before I knew about Sanjana, remember? We need to talk about the other stuff."

"Okay. But I don't have much time. Whaddya got?"

"I just wanted you to know that whatever is causing all the chaos that is showing up in the Cat Box is getting worse. The program is almost unusable."

"That can't be good."

"No. But now I'm wondering if what Sanjana did might have something to do with it. My Cat Box algorithms were only to be used for that one specific purpose. Who knows what could happen if they got out in the wild?"

"Wait. If that's true, and the weird readings are Sanjana's doing, these issues are related to things that have been done on this stream by people from this stream."

"Yeah…" He wasn't following.

"Then what is the deal with all the dead and wounded Travs?"

"I don't know," Sam replied. "All I can do is try and backtrack through the code now that I know it's out there on the site, and see if I can find a connection."

I turned to leave, but Sam said, "Oh, wait. I figured out what this is."

I turned around. He held the silver bracelet Jurassic Trav had tossed to me.

"So, what is it?"

"You're not going to believe it."

"I'll believe about anything at this point."

"It's a watch."

"Really?" I turned it over in my hand. "It doesn't look like any watch I've seen. Where's the clock face?"

"Put it on."

I did so. "Now what?"

"Wait."

I stared at my wrist, feeling pretty stupid. But after a few seconds, a three-dimensional, holographic image of a watch face came into view, slightly above the surface of the bracelet. It spilled over a half-inch or so on either side of the bracelet.

I touched the image with the finger of my other hand, and it went right through it.

"Whoa."

"Cool, huh?"

"Not really my style, but, yeah. So, it's just a watch?"

"Oh, much more than a watch. Ok now, here's the weird part."

"We're way past weird."

"Well, wait till you hear this. I was taking a break, and I had slipped it onto my wrist so I didn't lose it. A lab rat saw and completely lost her shit."

"A lab rat?"

"Well, that's what they call themselves. It's a little department that's housed in the basement of the Physics building. They keep a really, *really* low profile. It's kind of a skunk works. Different teams working on some pretty wild stuff. All applied sciences. Biology, engineering. They call themselves the lab rats. I go down to their area sometimes. They have the only Coke machine on campus."

The university had entered into one of those exclusive marketing deals a few years previously, and had gone all Pepsi. The change had been very hard on Sam, a total Coke-aholic.

"I thought Coke machines were *verboten*."

He shrugged. "They got around it somehow. Something to do with government contractors not being able to have an exclusive supplier. One of the bio-researchers I have lunch with sometimes saw it on my wrist and went berserk.

"Melody—that's her name—gets real pale, grabs my arm in a death grip, and says 'Where the hell did you get *that?*' She thought I swiped it from one of their labs. Fortunately, once she got a good look, she was able to tell it wasn't one of theirs. But there is some guy down there working on a device that looks almost just like it."

"You are kidding me."

"I know." Sam shook his head. "I couldn't believe it either. But it looks just like a prototype they're working on for the military. It reads pulse and galvanic skin temperature to help a soldier use biofeedback techniques to relax during the downtime of long deployments."

"All that?" I regarded it doubtfully.

"And a music player."

"A music player?"

"Yeah, they're trying to cram a bunch of different functions into it. The brass is not happy about all the smartphones and tablets out in the field. They're worried about terrorists hacking in and using GPS and stuff to target soldiers. It uses biometrics and some kind of bone conduction for the sound. The user can hear it without headphones. It originally was designed to relay announcements and instructions from a commanding officer, but they found that it could also store and play music. The testers loved that function, so they figured it would help in adoption."

"Quite the gadget. Does it do anything else?"

He shrugged. "Apparently they're working on ways to link it to things like video players, game consoles, even interact with sensors *inside* the body."

"Inside the body?"

Sam nodded. "The idea is that soldiers could swallow capsules with antibiotics, antidotes to chemical weapons, stuff like that, which would remain inert until they were needed. A device like the bracelet could send a signal activating the meds remotely."

"Whoa."

"I know. But it's all experimental right now."

"On *this* stream."

"Right. Somebody else has gotten quite a bit farther."

I took the bracelet off. The clock face vanished.

"And each of the other Travs had one," I mused, turning it over in my hand. "Why is this standard equipment for them?"

Then it hit me.

"What songs are on it?"

He shrugged. "I don't know. Biometrics, remember? It's 'tuned' to one person. I can't make it do anything. Which was fortunate, because if it had started doing stuff, I probably would have found myself in an NSA prison in Poland."

"And you think it's tuned to me?"

"Who else? You think multiple versions of you are carrying around someone else's iPod?"

"Good point."

I put my index finger on the top of the bracelet, right under the ghostly time display.

I could feel the metal get warm at my touch. A moment later, music began to play.

It was very strange. Perfectly balanced stereo, even though I wasn't wearing headphones. I looked at Sam.

"You don't hear that?"

"Hear what?"

His voice came through perfectly, not drowned out by the music at all.

"Hear what?" Sam repeated.

"It's playing music."

"What kind?"

"Weather Report."

"Who?"

"It's jazz. You wouldn't understand."

"Well, that settles it," he snorted, "as if there was any doubt. It might as well have your name inscribed on it."

I wasn't paying him much attention, busy learning the controls of the strange device. It was quite intuitive. Stroke up or down along the bracelet's face to control volume. Long press right in the middle to turn it on or off. Satisfied I had figured out its basic operation, I looked at Sam.

"Anything else I should know right now?"

He shook his head.

"Okay, then. I gotta go."

"And I gotta see if I can fix what Sanjana did to my work. I do not want to tell Chris his site is compromised."

"Before I go," I said.

"What?"

"About Ward."

"Yeah. What is his problem?"

"He's suspicious of me."

"Of you?" he snorted. "How dumb is that? Compared to you, Captain America is subversive. What is he, high?"

"He's smart, is what he is. And he knows there is something going on with me that I'm not telling him. He's suspicious of me, and anyone close to me."

"Like me."

I nodded.

"So what do we do?"

"Just be careful around him."

"I'm careful around everyone who carries guns and probably knows how to break me in two."

"I just wanted you to know. Now, I gotta go, before he figures out a reason to keep me under his thumb. Good luck."

"You, too."

We bumped fists, and I left the interview room. Adam waited at his desk.

"You ready?"

He nodded. "Where are we going?"

"Tell you in the car."

"I'm low on gas," Adam said, as we threaded our way to the stairs. "If you want me to drive, we'll have to stop."

The Universe seemed to be conspiring to make sure I drove around with a car full of both cops and corpses. As soon as this was over, I was going to have to take care of my cargo. Not only was it making me change my behavior, it would soon start to smell.

"It's fine," I sighed. "I can drive."

We piled into the Mustang.

"So, what is this mysterious lead I don't know anything about?" Adam asked. I didn't reply, just closed my eyes for a second, and tried to center myself.

When I opened my eyes, a translucent, red-lined duplicate of the rear end of my car shimmered into view, pulling in to traffic.

Yes.

I followed Red Trav down the street. I was happy to have a guide, but I had an idea where we were going.

"Did you ever look up Josh Dawson?" I asked.

"Of course. Nothing."

"Well, I Googled him this morning."

"Well, aren't you the President of the Internet. I assume you found something."

161

"Yeah. The paper did a feature on him about ten years ago. Seems that when he was a kid, his mom worked at Siemans Furniture. When she had a Saturday shift, he came with her."

"So?"

"One day he was poking around in the basement and found an old steam tunnel. Apparently, there are miles of them linking just about every building in the downtown. Over the years, he found all kinds of interesting stuff. That's what the article was about. After all the retail stores left downtown, they were writing features on the history of some of the buildings. Dawson took a reporter on a tour. One of the things they found was a boarded-up room in the back of the old Montrose Hotel. There had always been stories about Mr. Montrose running a speakeasy, but no one had ever found it."

"Until Dawson."

"Right. He'd spent hours playing in the room as a kid. There were still old liquor bottles, pictures on the wall, newspapers. Even money in the cash register. The Historical Society took it all and made an exhibit of it in the museum."

"Now that you mention it, I saw that exhibit in school. I remember wondering why they would put a dusty room filled with junk behind glass. When the teacher told me we were going to the museum, I thought we'd see dinosaurs. Instead, we got my grandma's basement."

"Culture is lost on some people."

"Bite me. You think that's how he got away from you last night? Hid his car in a secret room?"

"It's the only logical explanation."

After you eliminated *shifted to another stream of reality*, of course.

It would be really nice if this mystery had a more mundane solution.

Following the red-lined version of my Mustang, I retraced my route from the night before. Brooklyn Avenue is one of the main arteries headed into downtown, and as we approached the blind turn where I'd lost Dawson, Red Trav's car halted.

I did the same.

As Adam and I got out of the car, I noticed one of those giant dumpsters, the kind they park in front of a big remodeling project, taking up two parking spots right in front of a narrow alley.

"Son of a bitch," I muttered.

"What?" Adam asked.

"Kooj was parked about halfway up the next block," I replied, pointing. "I lost Dawson when he turned the corner. Kooj should have picked him up. But if he turned down this alley…"

"Kooj's view would be blocked by the dumpster," Adam finished. He squinted at the narrow space between buildings. "Tight fit."

"And the Superbird is not a small car," I said.

But as we walked down the alley, we got a surprise.

The alley entrance was quite narrow, but just a few yards in, it spread out into a wider space that had room to park four, maybe five cars, before narrowing again and opening into the next street.

"Is that how he got away? Through this alley and over?" Adam asked.

"Maybe." But I didn't think so.

And neither did Red Trav. My translucent, scarlet-lined twin had walked over toward one of the buildings, and stopped in front of what looked like a wooden wall.

"What?" Adam followed my gaze.

"That's a brick building," I said, "But the area in front of us is wood."

We walked closer, and my suspicions were confirmed.

163

It wasn't a wood wall. It was a big door, mounted on a track that ran along its upper edge. The door was secured with an old-fashioned hasp, in which rested a very modern padlock.

"A loading dock?" I wondered.

Adam shook his head. "Not many loading docks at ground level. They're always raised up a few feet."

He squinted at the door with an expression I knew meant he was searching his memory.

"Wasn't one of these buildings a car dealership back when you had things like that downtown? You know, storefront with two or three cars inside, before all the dealers moved out to where they could have a huge showroom and parking lot?"

I shrugged. "No idea. At least, that's not what the front of this building looks like now. But Dawson is a car guy. And an old dealership might be just the kind of place he went looking for when he was a kid."

While I spoke, I examined the wall.

"What are you looking at?" Adam asked.

I put a finger to my lips. Adam could not know, of course, that I was watching Red Trav, who had leaned up against the wooden door, one ear pressed right against the wall.

Adam closed his mouth, and watched as I matched Red Trav's pose. I closed my eyes and listened. My eyes popped open and I looked at Adam.

"What?"

I crooked a finger, motioning for him to join me.

"Listen."

He pressed his own ear to the door, the opposite one, so that he was facing me. An instant later, his eyes got wide as mine at what we heard.

The soft sobs of a crying child.

14

ADAM AND I looked at each other. Even though there was no reason to think anyone knew we were out there, we began to whisper.

"Do you think Dawson is in there with them?" Adam asked.

"I don't know."

"We need backup."

I nodded. "But I don't want to wait around. Why don't you call it in while I try to figure out a way in?"

He nodded and turned away, whipping his phone out.

I reluctantly pulled my head away from the door. Some irrational part of me did not want to lose contact, however tenuous, with the girls.

At least I hoped it was the girls. If the voice belonged to some half-crazed homeless woman, I would get to add embarrassing fuckup to my list of accomplishments for the day.

I looked at the hasp and padlock. It wouldn't be too hard to knock the hasp off, but if Dawson was in there, the noise would warn him. I looked around, hoping that Red Trav might show me the way, but he had disappeared.

Typical. Never any help around when the real work needed to be done.

There had to be another way in. If Adam was right, and this was the way they brought cars into the showroom, there had to be another door nearby. They wouldn't have wanted to wrestle with the big loading door whenever someone just wanted to come into the building.

Normally, you'd expect an entry door to the right or left of the large one. But the right and left sides of the sliding door were both featureless brick. There was no entrance door.

Or was there?

I studied the center of the wooden door again. It was weathered, and over the years the wood had warped and split. It was no longer a set of tongue-and-groove panels snugged tightly together. The gaps were not so big that you could see through them. But the lines created a kind of mosaic, a crazy quilt of cracks and joinings that masked a subset of gaps that were more regular.

I backed away a few feet from the door, so that I could see the big picture.

Yes.

What at first glance appeared to be just another bunch of lines and cracks was actually a rectangle the size of an entry door. All the other cracks in the door camouflaged it quite effectively.

It was like that picture that is either a vase or two people kissing, depending on how it struck you.

Now that I knew what to look for, however, I noticed a round hole right where a doorknob should be.

When I was little, my cousins and I played in an old barn on my uncle's farm. Most of the doors to the building were secured with a bent nail that you hooked an eyebolt to. But some of them had knobs.

Not doorknobs like I had at home, though. These were just a hunk of metal attached to a long, four-sided rod, with a similar hunk on the opposite side. The rod ran through a square bracket, fitting snugly.

Turn the knob, the rod turns the bracket, which pulled the latch out of the way, door opens.

One time, we had slammed the door extra hard, and the knob on our side had fallen off. In trying to reattach it, we'd succeeded in pushing the rod out the other side. We'd had to yell and yell until my aunt came out of the house to rescue us.

Could it really be that simple?

As my panicked cousins and I had discovered, sometimes the simplest door lock was merely the lack of a handle.

If Dawson was hiding the girls in there, removing the doorknob not only made it nearly impossible to open the door without tools, but actually hid the fact that there was a door here at all.

I bent down and studied the hole. Now that I looked at it carefully, it did not look like the knothole it first appeared to be. It was perfectly round, obviously drilled, maybe three-quarters of an inch in diameter.

I reached for the Swiss Army knife that always resided in my left pocket. Flipping open the knife blade, I studied it.

Might be too wide, but worth a try.

I slid it into the hole.

Sure enough, it stopped maybe an inch inside. Had the gap simply been a knothole, my knife would have gone all the way through.

I applied pressure. There wasn't any give in whatever was blocking the way, making it more likely to be metal rather than wood.

I pushed harder, and turned the blade. It caught on something, and I was rewarded with a *click*.

A gap about two inches wide appeared as the door swung inward.

I looked back at Adam. His back was to me, and he was waving his hands in the direction where the little alley opened onto the street, giving directions.

I put a foot in front of the door so it didn't latch again. Backup should be here in less than five minutes. I turned to Adam to signal that

I had found a way in, when Standard Entry Procedure went out the window.

"Is... is someone there?" a small voice quivered out of the darkness.

I looked over at Adam. His back was still turned.

Crap.

I knew I should wait. Wait till backup arrived, or at least until Adam turned around. But as I held my ear close to the crack in the doorway, I heard the soft sobbing start again.

Screw it.

I pushed the door open just far enough to squeeze in. With my foot, I scraped some gravel into a small pile against the door frame so it wouldn't shut behind me.

I quickly moved to the side, so I wouldn't be silhouetted against the light. It sounded like the girls were alone, but no sense taking any more chances than I already was.

"Is someone there?" repeated the voice.

"Yeah, honey," I replied softly. "I'm with the police. Can you see me?"

A wet sniff. "A little."

"Is there anyone else here?"

"Just Ella."

"Okay. Sophie, I'm going to come over to you."

"How do you know my name?"

"A lot of people have been looking for you, hon."

My eyes were now adjusting to the gloom, and I realized the room wasn't totally dark. There was light, maybe from a small lamp, emanating from a space at my ten o'clock. I carefully moved in that direction, sliding each foot forward a little before taking a step so I wouldn't trip.

As I got closer, the layout of the room became clearer. It was a big space, lending credence to Adam's idea that this building had once housed a car dealership. The light was coming from behind some old crates or boxes, stacked up perpendicular and parallel to one wall, to create an enclosed space.

I turned the corner, and saw that the space had been furnished, after a fashion. There was a bed, and the lamp casting the light sat on a box which was stood up on its end to make a sort of nightstand.

Sophie Patel and Ella Day sat on the bed.

"Boy, am I glad to see you two," I said.

The girls looked at me as I came into the light.

"Hi," I said. "My name is Trav."

The girls' eyes grew wide. Sophie grabbed Ella, pushing her protectively behind her. The younger girl shrieked in terror.

"Girls, it's okay," I said. "I'm a police officer."

"Help!" screamed Sophie. "*It's him! He's here! Help us!*"

"Girls!" I hissed. "It's okay!" I took a step forward.

Big mistake.

I wouldn't have thought it possible, but Ella's screaming got even louder, and now Sophie joined in. Their shrieks bounced off the concrete walls and metal joists of the big space, echoing and creating a cacophony four little lungs should not have been able to make.

I continued trying to shush them, but before I had time to do more than feel a little ridiculous, a door to my left swung open.

Josh Dawson stormed into the room.

"Girls!" he exclaimed. "What the hell?"

Then he saw me.

"You!"

He leapt at me, arms outstretched.

I tried to swing my gun hand around, but he closed too fast, crashing into me. I hit the ground, hard, Dawson on top. Air *whooshed* out of my lungs. I thrashed from side to side, trying to breathe and also keep Dawson's hands from scrabbling at my weapon.

The girls continued their screeching as Dawson and I rolled around on the concrete floor.

He was focused on going for my gun, and I took advantage, keeping it out of his reach while working one leg between us. Finally, I got enough leverage to cock my leg and push as hard as I could, knocking us apart.

I was also lucky at placement, as my kick had the double benefit of being right in his balls.

His shriek outshone the girls'.

I leapt to my feet, covering Dawson with my Glock.

"Stay down," I wheezed, still trying to get my breath back.

He glared at me, hands automatically, if tardily, covering his privates.

My breathing finally returned to normal. I chanced a look at the girls. They sat stock-still, wide-eyed and frozen in terror. I looked away quickly, not wanting my examination of them to set off another round of screaming.

"On your knees," I said softly to Dawson. "Hands on your head."

He obeyed, still scowling.

"You won't get away with this," he said.

"Get away with what? Sending these girls back to their parents?"

That stopped him. His frown changed from one of anger to confusion.

"It can't be," he muttered, more to himself than me.

"What can't be?"

"Shit. You don't know, do you? You aren't..."

"Aren't what?"

"You poor son of a bitch. You have no idea."

He shook his head as he looked up at me, his eyes widening.

"Why didn't you tell me?" he demanded.

"Tell you what?" I responded. But I realized an instant too late that he was looking past me.

Before I could turn, two gunshots blasted, filling the building once again with deafening echoes.

Dawson jerked as holes appeared in his chest. He fell forward, still looking confused.

I whipped around, but not fast enough.

The butt of a pistol smacked me hard across the cheek, I staggered backwards, trying to keep to my feet as stars cartwheeled in front of my eyes.

But my vision was clear enough to see who had pistol-whipped me.

It was Trav Becker.

He looked at me and shook his head.

"You guys just don't quit, do you?" he asked.

I started toward him.

He rolled his eyes and smashed the pistol across my face again, this time from the other direction. I lost the battle to stay standing and sank slowly to my knees. Tears from the blow to my nose, more stars and yellow streaks shot across my sight, and the room began to sway and shimmer.

As I fought to stay conscious, I heard the new Trav say, "Come on, girls."

He tossed his gun at my feet.

A wave of dizziness swept over me, and I could only watch blearily as Trav, Sophie, and Ella winked out of existence.

Ten seconds later, Adam and half the squad arrived to find me kneeling beside a dead body, right next to the murder weapon.

Which was covered with my own fingerprints, of course.

15

T RAV, WHAT THE hell?" Adam exclaimed.

"It's not what it looks like..." I began.

"Step away from the suspect, Detective," Ward cut in. He was leading a phalanx of suits who had entered right behind Adam.

"Suspect? Trav's not..."

"I said, step away. I won't say it again."

Suddenly, we were both looking at the business end of Ward's weapon, backed by several more. I raised my hands.

"Trav..." Adam looked at me helplessly.

"Do what he says, Adam. It'll be okay."

Adam stepped back. The Feebs pushed our guys aside and secured the scene, bagging the weapons, searching the makeshift bedroom area, all that investigative stuff.

Oh yeah, along with searching and handcuffing me.

I was hustled outside, where the tiny parking lot was now choked with black-and-whites and nondescript Fed sedans. Ward stood by my car. The Feeb who had collected my personal effects tossed him my keys.

"I'm going to need to see a warrant, Agent Ward," I said.

"Funny man," Ward replied. "Oh, I think any judge would agree that finding you standing over a body with the murder weapon in your hand..."

"Not my gun, wasn't in my hand," I interrupted.

He waved my objections aside. "Save it. But since you brought it up, I just happen to have a warrant."

He chuckled again at the look of astonishment that burst onto my face. "Weren't expecting that, were you?"

"Wait," I said, trying to recover. "What is your probable cause?"

He leaned in close to me. "There is something fishy about this whole mess, Becker," he said softly. "Nearly three weeks have gone by since the girls disappeared, and the investigation you are leading can't generate a single clue. The mother of the kidnapped girls works for your friend, who is always pulling you away for secret confabs. You claim you chased and lost a suspect, but the officer on the scene can't find a trace of him. And this suspect has a hundred witnesses who saw him miles away at the exact same time. You say you don't know Morgan Foster, but her cat acts like you're its best friend. And the kidnappers told Sanjana Patel they owned a cop. Gee, I wonder who that could be?"

"You got a warrant based on that shit?" Adam asked, incredulous.

Ward grinned like a shark. "We've had our eye on you for some time, Becker. You came out of that mess with Anton Kaaro just a little too clean. Then you end up as lead on this kidnapping investigation that goes nowhere. So, Special Agent Kelly tasked me to look into it."

"You weren't here to help out with the investigation at all," I said. "Your boss put you here to spy on us," I said. "Without informing Captain Martin."

"I don't answer to Captain Martin. And neither does the judge who agreed to provide a warrant should I need one. I'm only sorry I waited as long as I did. Maybe Joshua Dawson wouldn't be cooling to room temperature."

Of course, the Josh Dawson who had come to the station might not be cooling to room temperature at all, and wouldn't it be funny if he showed up there again. But I was more concerned about the FBI agent's second point.

"You can't think Sam has anything to do with this."

"On the contrary, I think he's your accomplice. Along with Morgan Foster. Of course, it could be the other way around. Although you are probably funded by a third party. Care to tell me what you and Anton Kaaro really talked about?"

"I can tell you," Adam said, pushing past the Feebs.

"Stand down, Detective," Ward warned. "Don't worry, I'll get to you later."

"Don't make this any worse," I muttered to Adam. "There is no use in us both being in handcuffs."

Ward tossed my keys to one of the other Feebs.

"Search the car."

"What?" I yelped. "You can't do that!"

"I can and I will. What's the matter? Think I will find something there that will surprise me?"

"You don't know the half of it," I muttered.

Ward frowned, but was enjoying his moment too much to get sidetracked.

"Travis Becker," he intoned, "you are under arrest for the murder of Joshua Dawson. Agent Shaw, please read Mr. Becker his rights."

Agent Shaw, a beefy guy whose suit was not tailored quite well enough to handle his muscular physique, Mirandized me.

One of the Feebs motioned Ward over. "Matt, you want to take a look at this?"

Ward made a little show of slowly taking a pair of surgical gloves from his pocket and working his hands into them. He walked around to the rear of the car and peered in.

"Detective Yount, you'll want to see this, too."

Adam frowned at me, and rounded the car. I followed.

Ward leaned in the back door. He straightened up so we could see what he was looking at. It was my gym towel. Even wadded up as it was, there was no mistaking the bloodstains all over it. Sam must have tossed it into the back seat when I had handed it to him during our body shuffling.

Ward and Adam looked at the macabre mosaic for another moment. In almost perfect synchronization, they swung their heads slowly round to look at me.

Ward's face was expressionless, but there was no missing the triumphant glint in his eyes. Adam just looked sick.

"So? That's *my* blood," I said.

"Bullshit," Ward snorted. "That towel is covered with it. If you'd lost this much blood, we'd be picking you up off the floor."

"It's not fresh."

"Care to show me the wound?" Ward asked dryly. "Must have been a doozy."

"It wasn't that bad," I replied. "It just bled a lot."

Even I knew how ridiculous that sounded.

"Pop the trunk," Ward ordered.

"Oh, I don't think you want to do that," I said.

"Oh, I think I do."

"Suit yourself. Don't say I didn't warn you."

"Warn me about what?"

"That your worldview is about to get expanded."

He and the other Feeb searching my car exchanged looks that were almost pity, and moved to the rear of the car.

I heard the trunk lid open with a dull thunk, followed by a long silence.

Too long. Adam had been watching me curiously, and followed when I rounded the back fender.

"Keep him back," Ward said.

The other Feeb put a hand on my chest and nudged me backward, but not before I could see what Ward was looking at.

Nothing.

The trunk was empty.

"What the hell?" I said, pushing against the agent charged with keeping me back.

"I said keep him back," Ward snarled. A second Feeb appeared to assist in restraining me.

"Trav, what's the matter?" Adam asked, looking from the trunk back to me in confusion. "What's in there?"

"More blood," Ward said. "And..."

He was feeling along the side panels of the trunk with one blue-gloved hand. He pulled a section of the liner aside. He grunted with satisfaction.

"Well, well, well."

Ward held a sawed-off shotgun.

"I believe the barrel of this gun is a little shorter than is legal, Detective. Care to tell me where you got it?"

I looked past him, into the trunk, even though I knew it was silly. If there were two bodies in there, they would have spilled out as soon as he had popped the lid. Where the hell had two Dead Travs gone?

Ward slammed the trunk shut. He turned to the agent who had discovered it.

"No one touches anything until our Mobile Crime Lab arrives."

"The city CSU team is on the way. They can process the scene a lot quicker," Adam said.

"No," Ward replied firmly. "We do this by the book. No coworkers."

I finally found my voice. "I'm telling you. That's my blood."

"R-i-i-i-ght. And I'm sure Yount here will make sure your CSU sticks with that story."

Adam started toward Ward, but I got between him and Ward just in time. "It's okay, Adam. Do what he says. This is all a mistake. It's my blood, I promise. If the Feeb's lab can process it quicker, all the better."

I smiled at Ward. You never called an FBI agent a Feeb to his face. Would have been a terrible *faux pax,* except I'd done it on purpose.

"I'll come quietly, Special Agent," I said.

And I took off for his car at the fastest walk I could, forcing him to run to catch up with me. In my head, we looked like two diplomats from The Ministry of Silly Walks.

"You're baiting Adam for no reason," I said when he had caught up.

"I don't waste diplomacy on dirty cops."

"We're not dirty cops. You haven't even given me time to explain. Those girls are still in danger, and I'm the only one who can help them!"

"Spare me the drama, Becker," he said. "You've done a great job of deflecting suspicion from yourself up to now, but your house of cards just came tumbling down. I don't know how Morgan Foster, your buddy Markus, and Yount are involved in all this, but they are. And I'm going to figure it out. It's just a matter of time."

He leaned in closer to me.

"Why don't you make it easy on yourself? Tell me where the girls are. You know it will go easier for you if you do."

"Believe me," I sighed. "Nothing about this is easy for anybody."

"Okay. Don't say I didn't give you a chance," he said. "Have it your way."

And with that, he pushed me into the car and I was transported to the station.

I'll spare you the description of what came next. You've seen the routine on TV a million times, and the reality is pretty close.

When they make a movie of my life, this scene will be a fast-moving montage of handcuffs, fingerprints, mug shots, all against the tight faces of my shocked and disappointed co-workers. Suffice it to say, after an hour or so, I was inside a holding cell, minus my shoes and belt. The orange jumpsuit would come later, when I was transferred over to County, awaiting the pleasure of a judge.

At least they gave me some ice for my bruised face, wrapped in a too-short-to-strangle-myself-with washcloth.

But the ice barely had time to melt before I was on the move once more. I'd been in the cell maybe ten minutes when the door opened, and a stone-faced Adam escorted me out and down the hall.

To Interview Two, of course. Agent Shaw stood by the door. He opened it for us then took up station in the hall.

I spent a few minutes staring at the tiny TV camera in the corner. Its red light was taped over, but I knew the camera was running.

Standard procedure. Suspects had been known to bang their heads against the corner of the table until they concussed themselves and later claim police brutality.

The door opened while I was considering if doing likewise was preferable to being questioned.

I was expecting Ward, so imagine my surprise when Mary swept into the room.

I jumped to my feet and she rushed into my arms. She wore an emerald-green shirtwaist dress with a men's style collar which she wore turned up, accenting her long neck. Her sandals were black, with thin straps that crisscrossed her feet in a complex diamond pattern.

She kissed me, before pulling back. A frown creased her smooth forehead.

"Trav, what's going on?"

"It's nothing. Just a misunderstanding. We're getting it cleared up."

The frown stayed in place, not letting me out so easily.

"Trav, they told me you were under arrest. That doesn't sound like a misunderstanding. And who is that man outside the door? Where is Adam?"

"Agent Shaw is just doing his job, trying to keep this investigation moving forward, which is more difficult than you would think in a police station," said Ward, entering the room.

"Ms. Logan, correct?" he continued.

Mary nodded. Ward looked at me expectantly.

"This is Agent Ward of the FBI," I finally said.

"Well then, Agent Ward, maybe you can tell me why Trav is being held here in his own office."

Ward ignored her question. "When was the last time you saw Mr. Becker?"

"Yesterday morning," Mary answered automatically.

"Not last night?"

"No. He had to work."

"That what you told her?" Ward asked me, raising an eyebrow.

"That's what I told her. Because it was the truth."

Ward consulted his tablet. "Now was this before or after you left the bar with Morgan Foster?" he asked innocently.

"Who?" Mary asked.

"Detective Becker never mentioned his friend Morgan Foster to you?"

"Morgan Foster? From the radio?"

"That's enough!"

I stepped between Mary and the FBI agent. "You are out of line, Ward. Mary is not here to provide me an alibi. You want to question her, call her in and she'll bring her attorney."

"Why would Ms. Logan need an attorney?"

"I said that's enough. You come in here, you talk to me. Mary is off limits."

"I'll bear that in mind. I just came in to tell you our team is back from your apartment."

He emptied the contents of the garbage bag he had brought in onto the table. I recognized the bag even before he opened it.

"Care to explain this?"

Bloody towels, sheets, and bits of gauze spilled out.

Mary gasped and leapt back, the color draining from her face.

"What the hell is your problem, Ward?" I snarled.

"Well, you've been telling me all along this blood is yours," Ward said evenly. "I just thought Ms. Logan here would appreciate the chance to back up your story. Ma'am, you see Detective Becker often. Have you noticed any wounds that would cause him to lose, oh, about a quarter of his blood supply?"

"I'm not Trav's mommy," Mary retorted. "He doesn't come running to me to kiss his boo-boos. If he says the blood is his, it's his."

"Loyal," Ward said. "Very nice. We'll see if Ms. Logan is so supportive when she finds out everything you've been doing."

"That's it," I replied. "We're done here."

"I have some questions."

"You have questions *for me,* I'll answer them. Mary is not involved."

He looked from me to Mary, who glared at him, arms folded across her chest. He picked up the bag.

"I'll just check this in. Be right back."

"Nice guy," Mary said after the door closed.

"Yeah. Our relationship has turned a little rocky. Thanks for not letting him rattle you."

She smiled. "I watch TV. I know the bad cop routine when I see it. But Trav, what the hell is going on? What's this about blood in your apartment? And what does that radio psychic have to do with it?"

"The mom of one of the girls hired her. I ran into her last night."

"In a bar. You did tell me you were working."

"I was. It's…"

"Don't tell me. Complicated. And you can't talk about it."

I gave her a rueful smile. "Got it in one. Sorry."

"I'm used to it," she replied tightly.

"Ward is just trying to rattle me by upsetting you. I'm sure that's why he let you in here in the first place. It's not exactly SOP for detainees to have unsupervised visits."

She brought her face very close to mine. In her heels, she was a little taller than me. This would bother some guys, but I liked being able to look directly into her eyes.

"It's going to take more than him to rattle me," she said. She grabbed my chin and pulled my face into line with hers. "As long as you're being honest with me. Are you?"

"Lie to you? What, you think I have a death wish?"

"Good," she said, giving me a hard stare. "As long as you understand the stakes." Then using my chin as a handle, she pulled me in and gave me a kiss that curled my toes.

"But," she said when we came up for air, "this is weird even by your standards."

"It is. But I swear, once they start to look at the actual evidence, it's not going to point to me. And I'm not quite out of tricks yet."

She looked at me uncertainly. "Are you sure you don't need an attorney?"

"If I do, I'll call one."

"Promise me you will," she said. "You don't have to do this all by yourself."

"I know."

Which was a lie. Few suspects had ever been more alone than I was at this moment.

"Look, Mary…"

She frowned at me once again, worry lines crinkling her forehead. "What?"

I took her hands. "If I don't succeed in clearing my name, you have to promise to stay out of it."

"But you just said it was all a misunderstanding. That the evidence will clear you."

"And it should. But you saw how Ward has it in for me. He can make things rough."

"Then, we'll make things rough right back for him!"

"NO!"

I took her by the shoulders. "That's exactly what I'm talking about. If things go bad, you have to stay away. Don't get involved."

"Now you're being ridiculous. I will never desert you."

"Even if they accuse me of taking the girls?"

"So what? They can accuse you all they want. *You didn't do it.*"

"You're right. I didn't. But that might not keep them from saying I did. You know what the media is like. If it gets out, you'll be the monster's girlfriend. They'll be relentless. They'll show up at your apartment, at work. It could cost you your job. Life as you know it will be *over.*"

"Trav, you're scaring me."

"You should be scared."

She shook her head. "Not about the media, you dope. Listen to yourself. You're talking like you've already been charged. Hell, like you've already been found guilty. Like you're not going to put up a fight."

I let go of her and turned away. "I'm just saying, that if I'm not around to defend myself, don't waste your time trying to do it for me."

She grabbed me with more strength than you might imagine she would have, and swung me back around to face her. "What do you mean, if you're not around?"

I closed my eyes. "Never mind. I'm just being stupid. You're right."

I opened my eyes and smiled at her, loving her more in that instant than I ever had before. She would fight for me, no matter what I said and no matter what it cost her. And woe betide Ward or anyone else who got in the way of the force of nature that was my girlfriend.

"You're right," I repeated, folding her into my arms. "We'll fight the bastards. And we'll win. It'll be fine."

She clung to me, holding me so tight I had trouble getting a breath.

"That's the Trav I know," she whispered.

She was about to say something more, but the door opened, and Ward re-entered.

"I hate to break up this tender scene," he said without an ounce of sincerity, "but I have more questions for Mr. Becker."

Mary glared at him, but he refused to burst into flames, so she turned her back to him and gave me another kiss. It went quite a bit longer than jailhouse decorum should have allowed.

"I will see you when this whole thing gets straightened out," she said firmly. "Which will be *soon*."

And with one more final glower at Ward, she stalked out of the room.

A hand caught the door before it shut. Leon and Adam came in. Both looked grim.

"Have a seat, Detective," Ward said.

Instead, I leaned one haunch on the edge of the table and folded my arms.

I turned to my boss.

"Leon, I'll be lodging a complaint against Agent Ward here. He let Mary in here, specifically to shake her up."

"You'll have to get in line, Detective Becker," Leon replied smoothly. "I have already started a complaint to Agent Ward and Agent Kelly's bosses. It appears they have been using the pretense of assisting us as an excuse to run their own investigation into my department."

He turned to Ward.

"No one spies on my officers." Leon's voice was soft, but his tone was steel. "When I am through with you and Kelly, you'll be lucky to get a job cleaning toilets in your Bismarck field office."

"We can talk about that later," Ward cut in. If Leon's threats bothered him, he gave no sign. He produced the evidence bag again. "You never answered my original question. Care to explain this?"

"I already did."

"You expect us to believe these towels and sheets, covered in blood and what appears to be abdominal fluid, is from the same wound that produced the blood in your car?"

"Yes."

"The wound you can't show us."

"The blood is mine."

"You realize if all the blood we found was yours, you'd be in the hospital?"

I didn't reply.

"All right. Let's talk about your car. Which also yielded massive amounts of blood that you claim is yours. And just for now, I won't even ask what you were doing that caused you to bleed copiously in your own trunk. So why were you so reluctant for us to look in your trunk? Granted, you'll need to answer for the shotgun, which does not appear to be registered. But you didn't even spare the gun a glance. What were you were afraid I would find, Detective?"

"You wouldn't believe me if I told you."

"Ward, you're fishing." Leon interrupted. "For those of us coming into this in the middle, why don't you run down the evidence you actually do have?"

"We are still gathering the evidence, Captain. But why don't I run down what has been going on?"

Leon waved a hand for him to continue.

"First off, I do apologize. I'm sure it seems to you that I came here under false pretenses. But please understand that my primary objective was in fact to help find the kidnapped girls."

"Investigating my officers was just a fortunate by-product."

"No. A possible connection," Ward corrected. "Last year, I was tasked by our Organized Crime Division to profile Anton Kaaro and several members of his gang."

I leapt up. "Wait a minute. I was never a member of Kaaro's gang."

Ward ignored me. "May I finish?" he said to Leon.

"Let him go, Trav," Leon said to me. "The sooner we hear his wild theories, the sooner we can shoot them down"

"Thank you. As I said, we profiled all the men in Kaaro's inner circle, which included two undercover cops. Detective Becker, and..." He consulted his tablet. "...Amy Harper."

186

"Who actually *was* a bent cop," Leon finished. "Do you have any facts I don't already know?"

"Well, there is this," Ward continued mildly. "Our analysis revealed that of the two, it was actually Detective Becker who had the higher probability of going on the take."

"Now, wait just a goddamn minute!" I snapped.

"Captain, I am trying to explain this all calmly," Ward said. "But if Detective Becker is going to keep interrupting, we'll be here all day."

"Keep going," Leon said. "But we better start getting to some facts pretty soon. All I've heard up to now is conjecture."

"We have plenty of facts," Ward said. "An investigation into Kaaro's organization, which like this kidnapping, went many months with little or no progress. Large amounts of cash that were never fully accounted for. Plus, I have had the chance to review the recording of the interview Detectives Becker and Yount did this afternoon with Anton Kaaro. You'll want to see it. Kaaro certainly did not treat Detective Becker like the officer who arrested him."

I pulled out a chair and sat down. "Can I get some popcorn and a Coke?" I asked. "Sounds like this story is going to go on a while."

"Not helping, Trav," Leon said quietly. He turned to Ward. "Detective Becker took down Kaaro's organization almost single-handedly, despite the fact that in Officer Harper, Kaaro actually did have a source in our department."

"Personally, I think Becker and Harper were both crooked all along," Ward continued. "I think Becker got cold feet and sold Harper and Kaaro out. But even if he was straight at the time, something changed. Because we are now certain that Detective Becker, Sam Markus, and a third subject, unknown at this time, engineered the kidnapping for the purpose of hacking El Juego Grande."

"Wait," Adam interrupted. "Didn't Sam Markus write that code? Why would he force someone else to hack into it?"

187

"To divert suspicion," Ward said. "At some point, they enlisted the help of Joshua Dawson and Morgan Foster. It was obvious that despite his claim of not knowing Ms. Foster, Detective Becker had been at her house at some previous time."

"Based on the fact he petted her cat," Adam snorted.

"That's enough, Adam." Leon said. "Keep going."

"We think Morgan Foster wanted out, and she was silenced. Hence the blood in Detective Becker's car…"

"Wait just a goddamn minute," I leapt out of my chair.

"Same story with Dawson. He and Becker had an argument, but Dawson escaped."

"Only to walk back into the station under his own power the next morning," Adam pointed out.

"We think that was a cry for help," Ward said. "Dawson was hoping to get some protection, but fled when Becker showed up."

Leon looked skeptical. "Assuming all this is true, why did Trav take Adam downtown? If he was going to shoot Dawson, he could have gone there by himself."

Ward shrugged. "We're still putting some of the pieces together."

"Then who took the girls?"

"The third member of the group, who is unknown at this time. But there is someone right here in this room who knows where that person and the girls are."

He turned to me. "Detective, I would like to think this was just about the money, and that you never intended anyone to get hurt. But Josh Dawson is dead, Morgan Foster probably is too, and the girls can't be far behind. Don't get their blood on your hands, too—"

He was interrupted by a chirp from his tablet. He glanced at it.

"Speaking of blood, that's the lab. Last chance, Becker. Once we know for sure whose blood is all over your car and house, your bargaining power goes way down. Got anything to say?"

"I'm just as anxious to see the lab report as you are."

He swiped at the screen.

And stared at it for a very long time. We watched as he thumbed the screen up and down several times, frowning.

"That's not possible," he muttered.

"Well?" Leon growled.

"Were they able to identify the blood?" I asked innocently.

"Laugh it up, Becker," Ward stabbed his finger at me. "Even without the blood, there is plenty here to indict you. I still don't know what game you're playing, but I will get to the bottom of it. Captain, may I have a word?"

Leon looked at me sadly and left with the FBI agent.

"So," said Adam. "Is it just me or has there been somewhat of a cooling in the friendship between you and agent Ward?"

"Oh, shut up."

"Seriously, Trav." He swung his leg over the chair opposite me and sat down. "He's right. There is plenty to indict you. If you go to trial, your career is over."

"I know."

"What happened in there?"

"I didn't shoot him, if that's what you're asking."

"Hey, I believe you. But what we need is some proof."

"Stay out of it, man. Ward is out for blood, and he is not going to care who he brings down with me. I'm sure both you and Leon are at the top of his list. Exposing a PD full of crooked cops is the kind of thing that gets Feds promotions."

"Whatever. You didn't do this, and you're not going down for it. There is evidence out there that will clear you, and I'm going to find it."

I reached across the table and clapped him on the shoulder. "You're right. Thanks." I paused, thinking. "Do you think you can get into the kidnapping scene and take a look around?"

"I can try."

"That's as good a place as any to start."

"I'm on it. We'll beat this, Trav. I promise."

He practically ran out the door, and I felt bad sending him on a wild goose chase. He wouldn't find anything at the scene that would help. But it would get him out of the building and away from Ward for a while.

Adam was right. Ward wouldn't stop until he brought down a department he thought was full of dirty cops. I was sure he would be able to indict me, and he might even be able to dredge up enough evidence to make a murder charge stick.

And speaking of evidence, what the hell had happened to the two bodies in my trunk? I started trying to tally up the times the car had been out of my sight. Much of the time it had been sitting in the station parking lot, which was covered by surveillance cameras. It would be interesting to get a look at that footage, but I didn't dare suggest it. Anything I said or did now would eventually find its way back to Ward, and I certainly did not want him to come into possession of a tape that might have Trav Becker hauling bodies out of his trunk.

And speaking of extra Trav Beckers, Ward's comments about profiling me caused me to think of Trav One, the original Trav from this stream, for the first time in a year. Ward had no idea, of course, that much of the data he had gathered was not on me at all. Was it possible he was right? Had Kaaro subverted Trav One like he had Amy Harper? If I hadn't happened along, would my analogue from this reality now be sitting in a cell across from Kaaro, or would the kingpin have ever even been arrested at all?

And what did all this have to do with the kidnapping?

I was mulling all these questions over when the door opened and Leon strode back in. He sat down across from me. He carried a manila folder, which he placed unopened on the table between us.

Ah. This was the formal suspect interview. The folder gave it away.

"Ward was right about one thing," he began.

He slid a picture out of the folder. It showed the bloodstained sheets and towels Ward had found in my apartment, now tagged and dated.

"This is a lot of blood. And I've seen you in your Speedo three times a week for the last two months. There's not a mark on you. Where did all this come from?"

"Does it matter, Leon? Just because I bled a little, you think I was in on it?"

"I don't know what to think. I've known you since you were fourteen. Your dad was my partner. But..."

"But?"

"No leads on the girls for months, then last night you get into a chase with a man who could not possibly have been where you said he was. Not to mention that whole mess with the psychic. And today we find you where the girls had been kept, with a dead body for company. What the hell am I supposed to think?"

"Do you believe him? That Kaaro bought me months ago?"

"I don't know what to believe. But that doesn't matter now. Where are the girls, Trav?"

"I have no idea."

He nodded, not surprised by my answer. "We can come back to that, I guess."

He reached once again into the manila folder and spread several pictures out on the tabletop. They were photos of Josh Dawson's corpse.

He gestured at the pictures. "Want to tell me what happened?"

"I didn't kill him, Leon."

"Then what?" he demanded. "Obviously, there was a struggle." He pointed to my bruised face. "Did he draw on you?"

"Would you believe me if I said he did?"

"If you could also give me a logical explanation why the M.E. says Dawson was at least eight feet from the gun when he was shot."

"Doesn't much sound like we were struggling and it went off, does it?"

Leon shook his head. "No, it doesn't. And your fingerprints are all over the gun. Dammit, Trav! I want to help, but you've got to give me something to work with."

I had to tread carefully here. The story I had come up with fit the evidence, but was pretty thin.

"I didn't shoot him. There was someone else in the room. He clipped me with the pistol and shot Dawson."

"You get a look at him?"

I shook my head. "It happened too fast. He hit me, fired, and smacked me a couple more times. I was barely conscious. He put the gun in my hand, and slipped out."

"Why didn't you tell this to Ward?"

"Ward has already convicted me, Leon. And now we know why. He's had me in his sights practically since the beginning."

"I know," Leon replied. "But what about the girls? Forensics says they had been there for some time. Who moved them? Dawson? Your mystery man? And when? There was a sandwich on the bed that had a bite taken out of it maybe thirty minutes before the FBI's mobile lab got there. How'd you miss them?"

"This other guy, Dawson's... partner, must have taken them," I ventured.

Leon raised an eyebrow. "In broad daylight? On a street half the force drove down to answer your squeal?"

"Well, he took them somewhere."

That at least was the truth.

"I'd like to believe you, Trav. And the presence of a third individual does explain your wounds. The contusions on Dawson's hands don't match up. But we went over the room with every instrument we have. The girls were there. Dawson was there. You were there."

"And no one else," I finished.

Leon nodded. "And no one else. No trace of this third person."

"Yeah. About that."

My jaw hurt like hell. And I was tired of trying to make up believable explanations for unbelievable acts. I wanted nothing more than to spill my guts right now. Leon Martin had been my dad's best friend, and a father figure to me even before Dad had died. I wanted to tell him everything, unburden myself completely, and beg him to help me find a way to fix it. But even as the thoughts took form in my head, I knew I could never do it. Even if he believed my fantastic story, what would the cost be to him?

I'd let Morgan in, and look what had happened to her. If Ward had his way, Sam might very well be sharing a cell with me. Every time someone tried to help me, they got hurt. Mary, I thought, should be safe. Leon could be, too.

He was watching me expectantly.

"I can't say any more," I said slowly. "Until I talk to my attorney."

That surprised him. He just stared at me, unspeaking for almost ten seconds.

"Really? You're going to play it that way? You pull the trigger on an attorney and I can't do anything to help you, Trav. You go into the system just like anybody else."

"I appreciate what you're trying to do, Leon. But there are things at play here you don't know about."

He slammed his hand on the table. "Then tell me, *God damn it!*" His tone turned pleading. "Trav. *Please.* Don't do this. If you don't come clean, the Feebs are going to hang Dawson's murder *and* the kidnapping on you."

I didn't reply. After a few seconds of silence hung in the air, Leon finally just shook his head.

"Very well," he sighed. "Mr. Becker, we will transfer you to County for processing. You may have a phone call when you get there. Is there anyone you would like *me* to call?"

I shook my head. Leon continued to look at me. Searching, I was sure, for the Trav he thought he knew.

He held my gaze again for what seemed like a long time. I looked away after just a few seconds.

"Someone will be in to transport you in a few minutes," he finally said. The disappointment in his tone was almost physical. "Don't go anywhere."

He stood up, but before he could say anything else, Ward came back in. He pushed some papers he was carrying at Leon.

"Before you go, Captain, I need you to sign off on the special procedures for Mr. Becker's detention."

"Special procedures?" Leon asked, searching Ward's face for an explanation. The FBI agent didn't say anything further, so Leon looked at the papers.

"Suicide watch? You think Trav is going to kill himself?"

Instead of answering, Ward produced his tablet and pressed on it.

My voice came out of the device's little speaker.

"I'm just saying, that if I'm not around to defend myself, don't waste your time trying to do it for me."

194

"That's not what I meant, Leon!" I said desperately, "Don't let him do this."

He sighed. "Sorry, Trav, you had your chance. Do whatever you need to do, Agent." He looked at me sadly one more time. "Lucky for me I don't have to tell your dad about this. Lucky for you he'll never know."

He signed the paper, and left with Ward.

I took off my clothes under the watchful eye of a uniformed officer, who gave me some hospital scrubs. No drawstring on the waist, of course.

The station had one cell designed to house prisoners who might be a danger to themselves. Padded walls, no furniture. I curled up in one corner of the small room and surrendered myself to a few moments of glorious self-pity.

But just a few. If I didn't get my ass in gear, everything Leon had said would come true. His parting words about my dad really stung, but I couldn't afford to think about that. And who knew what Ward had planned for me next? He could be asking for permission to sedate and restrain me right now. I had one move left, and I couldn't make it while drugged.

In the movies, parallel reality stories are about how the entire world would be different if some key action was changed. What if the dinosaurs hadn't died out? What if Germany had won World War II? What if Yoko had been shot instead of John?

However, in my little corner of the Multiverse, the different streams only had minor distinctions. Well, minor in the grand scheme of things. The one where I woke up drunk and out of a job may have been major to me, but it wasn't exactly Russia beating America to the moon.

Sam had once said reality was like the Mississippi Delta. The main channel of the river spreads out, sending smaller streams filtering through the land on their way to the ocean. Each stream might take a slightly different route, or flow faster or slower than another, but the final destination was the same.

Jumping streams wasn't time travel, but if you were lucky, sometimes you could get to one where events were playing out slower, or even in a slightly different order.

That's what I was counting on.

The girls were the key. Somehow, this was all about them. I was pretty sure they were gone from this stream, but it was possible they, or a version of them, were still in the warehouse on another.

I didn't have much time before Ward came in and dropped something else on me, so I needed to get cracking.

I took a deep, calming breath. What I was about to do would require a special kind of mental focus I hadn't practiced in a long time.

Music was the focus tool I had used to move between the different reality streams. I associate favorite songs with important events and people in my life. Bringing a particular song to mind helped me visualize the different streams and move to the one of my desire.

I still didn't know why Sophie had a forty-year-old Billy Joel song on her computer, but it would now provide me with the exact tool I needed to search for her.

I played "Miami 2017" on the stereo in my head and stared at the door to the padded cell. For the longest time, there was nothing. I took another deep breath, trying to stay calm. Like a basketball player at the free throw line, tightening up and second-guessing myself was a sure path to disaster.

Sweat broke out on my forehead, even though the room was quite cool.

I pushed the doubt and uncertainty that kept trying to insert itself into my thoughts aside, and focused completely on the door.

After an eternity, just as my eyes began to burn from staring so long at a fixed point, a second version of the door appeared behind the real one. Then another. And another, and more and more, until my entire field of vision was taken up by an endless line of lookalike doors, arcing off into infinity. All were lined lightly in blue, except one, maybe a dozen down the line.

It pulsed in scarlet.

I focused on that one, and wished it forward. The intervening doors flew past at cartoon-like speed, until the red-lined one stood in front of me. The red outline faded as the door gained solidity, and a moment later, the vision of the endless line of doors also vanished, and I faced a door that seemingly hadn't changed in any way–except I knew I was now in a different stream of reality, one where the girls could still be found.

And therefore, one where I had not yet been arrested. And hopefully also one where this cell was unlocked. I tried the doorknob, the first acid test.

It turned easily. I cracked it open, looking up and down the short hallway before I stepped out.

The coast was clear. Trying to affect a normal pose, I headed for my desk. Alex Monroe, a genial, wide-bodied detective I often worked with, was the room's only occupant. He pecked at his keyboard with two fingers, looking up as I entered.

I inclined my head, and he nodded back, but not before frowning and glancing toward the restroom door.

That look meant I probably didn't have much time.

First order of business was shoes. I don't know about you, but the thing I have always found the most unbelievable about the movie *Die Hard* is not that John McLane crawled through eight city blocks of furnace ductwork, or wrapped a fire hose around himself and jumped off the edge of a skyscraper.

It was that he did it all barefoot.

I wasn't going to get very far without shoes, and there was no handy dead terrorist to swipe a pair from.

But fortunately, I kept a pair of old running shoes in my desk, in case I wanted to go out for a jog in the middle of a long shift. I slipped them on. There were some sweats in there too, but I didn't dare take the time to grab them. The scrubs would have to do.

Of course, I'd been relieved of my shield and gun when I'd been processed, not to mention the contents of my pockets, including car keys. But I kept an extra set in my desk. I grabbed them and stood back up.

Nodding again at Monroe, I scooted out of the room, passing the rest room door just as it opened. I put a hand up on the side of my face, pretending to scratch an itch as I passed Trav Becker.

Seeing myself confirmed my hope that the Mustang would be in the parking lot, the first in a rather long chain of things that would have to break just right for my loose plan to be successful. I hoped it was a good omen.

As I left the building, I tried to convince myself I wasn't running away.

In particular, I hated myself for leaving Sam behind. With me gone, the full weight of Ward's displeasure was likely to fall on him. But he was still probably safer in custody than where I was going.

My disappearance was going to look pretty bad for Leon, too.

And Mary. My chest ached as I thought of leaving her with no explanation for my inexplicable behavior. I swore to myself that if I got through this, and despite the dangers that had led me to keep the truth from Leon, that someday I would tell her everything, no matter how crazy it sounded.

If I ever got the chance.

But for now, there was nothing to do but find the girls. Leon did not know it, but I was following the lessons he had taught me. Work the case. There are a thousand things in a cop's life that will shake his concentration. Don't lose focus. Every step, every clue, brings you closer to resolution. Trust your instincts and the evidence. Do the work and everything else will fall into place.

It was all I had left now.

Once in the car, it only took a few minutes to reach downtown. I parked in the same hidden lot Adam and I had found before.

I was unarmed, of course. My service weapon was five miles and a couple of realities away. The sawed-off shotgun Ward had found in my trunk, believe it or not, was an heirloom.

Along with some magic props and his album collection, the gun was pretty much the sum total of my inheritance from Dad. Don't get the wrong idea. As a cop, Mike Becker was straight as an arrow. Two beers and he handed the car keys to Mom. But the shotgun was the one not-quite-legal item he allowed himself, a last-ditch resource in case of emergency. I kept it around for the same reason.

Fortunately, in this stream it had not been confiscated by the FBI. But that was no guarantee the trunk was empty. I popped the trunk open, half convinced two dead bodies had somehow followed me across the streams.

It was empty. I let out the breath I hadn't even realized I'd been holding. I quickly freed the shotgun from its hiding place, jacked a couple of shells in and headed toward the building.

The door was slightly ajar. Saved me picking the lock again, but the change amped my nerves up about ten notches. I quietly nudged it open just far enough that I could slip in.

I'd gotten this far pretty much on automatic pilot, but now had to regroup. I couldn't approach the girls–they would start screaming bloody murder like last time. I had some vague idea of hiding in the warehouse until the stream-traveling Trav showed up, and somehow trying to follow him when he grabbed the girls.

If I could keep him from shooting Dawson and save the Trav of this branch from a murder rap in the process, all the better.

Listening for any hint of sound from the girls, I slid along the wall, moving away from the kidnapper's alcove. I only got about six feet when the foot I silently extended to make sure the next few inches was clear met an obstruction.

"Watch it," a voice hissed.

16

"**W**HY AREN'T YOU in position?" the voice demanded in fierce whisper. "He's almost here!"

"Wha…?"

But I had no chance to finish my question. Suddenly every light in the warehouse flashed on.

The instant brilliance revealed a row of black-clad figures, at least eight, ringing the walls of the girls' sheltered alcove.

"Now!" called another voice.

"Come on!"

The black-clad man nearest to me nudged me toward the girls, as each of the others moved forward as well. I stumbled ahead, falling into step with the rest. As I did, I got a good look at my neighbor.

He wore a now-familiar pair of black fatigue pants, long-sleeved t-shirt, and vest. A black ball cap was pulled low over his eyes. It partially obscured his face, but what I could see was enough.

I quickly glanced around at the other figures.

Yep. All Travs.

The now brightly-lit scene revealed the two girls perched on the bed. But no screaming this time. They sat, frozen in terror, as the Trav platoon descended on them.

The door on the side swung open, but this time, Josh Dawson did not emerge alone.

Trav Becker was with him. This Trav was identical to the ones near me in every way, except his ball cap was bare of any insignia. He and Dawson immediately reached behind their backs.

"Freeze!" yelled one of us.

Trav and Dawson did so, staring into the barrels of eight shotguns. Nine if you counted mine, which I swung, somewhat belatedly, in their direction.

The Trav nearest them, who I now identified by his cap as my pal Jurassic Park Trav, jerked his head. Two of the others relieved Dawson and his Trav of the pistols each had stuffed into the back of his pants. Two more peeled off and went over to the girls.

Jurassic turned toward the Trav next to me.

"O'Connor..." he began. But his eyes narrowed as he took in my puke-green scrubs and lack of ball cap.

"Wait a minute...Who the hell are you?"

The Trav nearest me, the one he had called O'Connor, looked me up and down, now realizing I was not wearing the Trav Platoon uniform.

He swung his weapon over to cover me. Facing him directly for the first time, I noticed the *Lord of the Rings* logo on his cap.

"Where'd he come from?" asked Jurassic.

O'Connor shook his head. "He bumped into me when it was dark. I thought he was just out of position."

"All right," Jurassic responded with a sigh. "Bring him. Val, give O'Connor a hand."

A Trav wearing a *Star Wars* cap nodded and started toward us.

But before Jurassic could give the move out command, Generic-Cap Trav took advantage.

He snapped around and shoved Dawson, hard. The other man careened into the two Travs sent to guard them. They in turn fell into

Jurassic. All four went down in a heap. Generic leapt for the girls, who still sat petrified on the bed.

Before any of the rest of us could move, he'd gathered them up in his arms, and hurtled around the corner.

"Get him!" howled Jurassic, from the bottom of the Trav pile.

The rest of us took off after him. We rounded the corner, trying to stay out of each other's way.

But as we turned, the Trav in the lead suddenly braked, nearly causing another pileup. As the rest of us skidded to a stop and peered around him, we saw why.

Generic had produced another gun from someplace and was holding it to the head of little Ella. Her lips trembled, too frightened to even sob.

His other arm encircled Sophie, over her shoulder and under her opposite elbow, like the cross-chest carry they teach in lifesaving.

He looked up at us, smiled, waggling his eyebrows, and disappeared.

Jurassic Park Trav arrived an instant later with the others. They had Dawson in tow.

Jurassic rounded on Dawson. "Where did he go?"

Dawson shrugged. "He didn't fill me in."

"You're lucky he didn't fill you with bullets," I muttered.

Which reminded Jurassic of my existence.

"And what the fuck are you doing here?"

"Same thing as you. Looking for the girls."

"Yeah," he snorted. "Nice work. If you hadn't blundered in, we would have had them, *and* the Collector."

"Collector?"

He shook his head. "Later." He walked away from me, stopping in front of Dawson. He looked the man up and down for a long moment and sighed quietly.

"Bring 'em."

O'Connor and another Trav, this one wearing a *Babylon 5* cap, grabbed me by the elbows and held me tightly between them.

I don't know if it was the bracelets they wore, or maybe they were just a lot better at this shifting thing than me, but when these guys jumped to another stream, there was none of the red and blue images I used.

In the time it took for them to push me forward one step, we were simply somewhere else.

And not only that, we had changed physical location as well. I had no idea how they did that. When I shifted streams, I appeared in the closest analogue to the location I had just left. We were no longer in the former car dealership.

We had stepped into Central Station.

And if you didn't look closely, you might not think anything about the room was unusual. There were papers strewn across the worn desks. Men sat at several of them. Some stared into computer screens, a couple fiddled with their phones.

But unlike the station I knew, staffed by Leon, Adam, Monroe, and a host of other officers, each of these men at these desks wore my face.

As I looked over the room filled with Trav after Trav, my vision started to swim.

"I..." I tried to say. Suddenly, standing was something that was simply too complicated to continue doing. I started to sway, and would have collapsed if Lord of the Rings Trav, the one they called O'Connor, hadn't caught me.

"Ah, geez," he said. "Get him some water."

A moment later, a glass was pressed into my hand. I took a drink, and my stomach settled down. After the dizziness passed, I straightened up.

"Thanks," I said.

"De nada," O'Connor replied. "Happens to a lot of us the first time we get here."

"So, you going to live?" Parker asked.

"I'll be fine," I said hoarsely.

"Then maybe you can tell us what the hell you were trying to do."

But before I could answer, O'Connor interrupted. "Jesus, P. Give him a break. He just got here."

"After busting up an operation we'd been planning for weeks."

"And saving YaYa's life."

"YaYa?" I asked.

"You're pretty confused, I'm sure," said O'Connor. "I've been there. We've all been there."

There were a couple of nods from the group.

"Let me introduce you around," he continued. "There'll be time for questions after you get your bearings."

Jurassic shrugged. "Whatever."

He sat down heavily at a desk, which in my stream was normally occupied by an African-American detective named Stevens.

"This is the weird part," O'Connor said.

"I thought I'd already seen the weird part," I replied.

"Not even close," Jurassic said from his seat.

"Little Mary Sunshine there is Trav Parker," O'Connor continued, pointing at Jurassic. He turned to a Trav sitting in what I thought of as Adam's desk.

"Trav Gomez." He gave me a one-finger salute, touching the brim of his *Firefly* cap.

"Trav Emdall." His cap was from *The Matrix*.

"Trav Gant." *Babylon 5*.

"Trav Valuk." *Star Wars*.

"Trav Cooper." *Speed Racer*.

"Trav Omar." *Terminator*.

"And I'm…"

"O'Connor," I finished for him. He nodded and looked at me expectantly. The others were watching me, too.

You ever been in a situation where everybody was in on the joke except you? Well, when they all *are* you, you feel extra stupid.

I frowned. There was something about these names that was familiar, and everyone was obviously waiting for me to get it. Which I finally did, but it took a few minutes.

When we were college roommates, Sam introduced me to geek culture. Every day when I came home from class, he was studying with the TV on, watching *Star Trek*–the original one from the Sixties. I ignored it for a while, but eventually I got sucked in.

The original *Star Trek* led to *Star Trek: The Next Generation*; which led to *Deep Space Nine, Voyager, Enterprise*.

Then we branched out. *Babylon 5, Stargate SG-1*.

Yeah, I didn't date much in college.

Movies were next. I'd seen *Star Wars* and the Marvel stuff, of course, but soon found myself sitting through beer and pizza-fueled binges of *The Matrix, Blade Runner, Dark Star, Shaun of the Dead…*

And *Buckaroo Banzai: Adventures Across the Eighth Dimension*.

I won't bore you with the synopsis, but suffice it to say, a bunch of the characters were aliens masquerading as humans, but they didn't

206

understand human naming conventions. They knew to take different last names, but all took the same first name, John.

You can see where this is going.

John Parker, John Gomez, John O'Connor, John Gant, John Valuk. Even John YaYa.

I looked at Trav O'Connor. "You are fucking kidding me."

"Shit."

Trav Emdall reached into his pocket, pulled out a five dollar bill, and handed it to Trav Gomez.

"He had 'freaking' in the pool," O'Connor explained. "It's almost exactly a fifty-fifty split whenever a newbie shows up."

"That's what you guys do for fun?"

O'Connor shrugged. "Not a lot to talk about in this group. We get our entertainment where we can. We call ourselves the Rangers."

In spite of the surreal environment I found myself in, I chuckled. "*Lord of the Rings* Rangers or *Babylon 5* Rangers?"

"That's something else that's about fifty-fifty." O'Connor turned to Firefly Trav. "Gomez. I think it's your turn for the Sorting."

"The Sorting?" I asked.

"Yeah. Just like Harry Potter. Only you get to keep the hat."

Gomez crossed the room, heading toward a cardboard box sitting on a table. Without looking, he reached inside. When he withdrew his hand, he was holding a black ball cap. He tossed it to me. It bore the Stargate SG-1 logo.

"What's the next name on the list?" O'Connor asked.

A Trav in the back of the room, whose cap logo I could not see, had pulled out a piece of paper. He seemed to be consulting a list, and after a minute, looked up and smiled.

"Nice," he said. "Gentlemen, say hello to Trav BigBootie."

Everyone laughed, looking at me expectantly.

I knew immediately what I was expected to say.

"It's Big Boot-TAY."

Another round of laughter.

Trav Parker had ducked out during the Sorting, and now reappeared.

"Glad you're all having fun, but the orientation can come later. Buck needs to see him."

"Who's Buck?" I asked.

"He'll explain."

I followed Parker down the hall. To be honest, I thought we would head to Leon's office. I couldn't imagine where else the leader of this weird group would be.

But instead we headed toward Interview Two, and when Parker opened the door I could see why.

Leon's office was small, and could not possibly have contained the piles of documents and folders that littered the conference table, not to mention the big sheets of flip-chart paper that lined all four walls.

Two men stood in front of a wall covered with big white sheets of paper. Row after row of cramped handwriting covered each of them.

One of the men turned as we walked in.

I was just two steps into the room, but I stopped dead. A cold trickle slithered down my spine as I examined him.

My dad had been dead for more than two years, but last year I had encountered him on a stream where his death had not yet occurred. For just a second, I thought that was happening again. But I quickly realized that was just a family resemblance. I was not looking at Mike Becker.

I was looking at yet another Trav Becker. But while every other Trav I had met had looked virtually identical, this one had lines on his face none of the rest of us had, and the light reflected off the gray streaks in his hair.

He was me, all right. But older.

He studied me from under the bill of his cap, which had a *Buckaroo Banzai* logo.

Of course.

He stretched a hand forward. I took it automatically.

"What do I call you?" he asked.

"Big Booté, apparently."

He chuckled. "I wondered when someone would end up with that one. Sit."

He turned to his companion. "Gear. Company."

Since the other man was several inches shorter than Buck, I was somewhat prepared when he turned around.

It was Sam, also older. He wore a pair of glasses so large they almost qualified as goggles, with thick black frames half-again as thick as conventional ones.

Like all the Travs, including Buck, he wore one of the silver bracelets on his wrist, but a half-dozen other gadgets poked out of the pockets of the khaki vest that shielded his pot belly. It was one of those tech vests they advertise as having twenty-some pockets. Combined with the crown of fuzzy red hair that ringed an otherwise bald head, he looked like a steampunk Bozo the Clown.

Gear turned, and a bushy orange eyebrow went up as he noticed me for the first time. He put a finger on the side of his glasses, and looked me slowly up and down.

"Are you feeling better?" he asked.

"What?"

He turned back toward the paper on the wall. Which turned out to be not paper at all, but a screen of some kind, because the handwriting that had adorned the center section suddenly erased itself, and was replaced by the silhouette of a human body. The picture was colored in splotches of red and blue.

"Involuntary displacement often results in some physical discomfort, as the body and mind adjust to being pulled out of a stream, rather than shifting naturally. On the screen, we see the adjustment lag indicated by the red and blue areas. Once fully habituated, the red and blue areas fade."

Gear continued rubbing the right temple of his glasses, and I realized that was how he was manipulating the image.

"What he's trying to say is, give it a few minutes and your aura will settle down," said a feminine voice behind us.

By now, I was not surprised at all to see the voice belonged to a mature version of Morgan Foster. Like the Travs, she was dressed in utilitarian, quasi-military fashion, black cargo pants and a long-sleeved top. But she dressed it up with a shawl or long scarf, almost a cape. It swirled around her hips as she swept into the room.

Of the three, the years had changed Morgan the least. Her long blond hair showed only a few silvery glints. It was gathered behind her head, kept in place by a thick golden clip.

She stood for a moment, hands on her hips, looking from Buck to Gear to Parker.

"You haven't told him anything, have you?"

"He just got here," Buck replied mildly.

"And it's about damn time," Gear added.

Morgan shook her head in exasperation. "I'm sure you have a lot of questions," she said to me.

"You think?"

"Where would you like to start?"

"At the beginning. If there *is* a beginning."

"Can we at least sit down before you get into this?" Morgan asked.

Buck nodded, and the five of us arranged our chairs around the table.

"In a sense," Buck began, "this story has been going on for hundreds of years, but our portion begins not quite ten years ago. Subjective time for us, at least." He spread his hands in a gesture to include Gear and Morgan.

"By now you know, and have used to your advantage, that while moving from one stream to another is not time-travel in the strictest sense, not all streams move at exactly the same pace. And that you can sometimes travel to a stream where a given event that has already happened in another stream has not yet occurred."

I nodded. "We're all headed to the same place, some are just traveling a little faster than others."

"That sounds like something I would say," Gear piped up.

"You have," Morgan said. "More times than I can count."

"Fay," Buck said.

"Sorry," Morgan, or apparently Fay, replied. But before I could ask about the Morgan naming convention, Buck went on.

"Our story, and the story of every other Trav who is here, started much like I imagine yours did. Sam discovered the existence of the streams at virtually the same time my ability to move between them manifested itself. I met Fay—Morgan, at just about the same time."

Buck looked at Gear out of the corner of his eye. "Confirming the existence of parallel universes was not...good... for Sam. He became convinced that all those branching streams weakened the very structure of reality itself, and that the only way to fix things was to eliminate what he thought was the catalyst behind the damage."

"Don't tell me," I interrupted. "You."

Buck nodded. "And any other Trav Becker he could locate."

"This sounds familiar."

"I'm sure it does. And I guess that means I don't have to go through the whole story of trying to learn how to master this power at the same time you're trying to track down a madman."

"Hey!" Gear exclaimed with a hurt look.

"Sorry. Long story short, once Sam realized I was not only on to him, but could move between streams with enough skill to head him off before he could cause more trouble, he disappeared."

"Wait," I said. "Disappeared? You mean..." I turned to Gear. "You're not...?"

"God, no!" Behind his thick glasses, Gear's eyes were huge, and his face started to turn red. "That wasn't me! Do I *look* insane?" He turned to Buck. "They *always* think it's me! Why do they always think it's me?"

"Calm down, buddy," Buck said. "No. It's a common mistake. Gear came in the next chapter of the story. Any other questions so far?"

I shook my head.

"I came up dry searching for Sam. But when I starting poking around in the different streams, I sometimes would find a set of circumstances beginning that would set off the same chain of events. I couldn't save Sam. But I could try to keep other versions of him from making the same mistake."

"So, you just started going around saving Sams?"

"It wasn't that easy. At first I didn't have any luck. If anything, I made it worse."

Fay smiled tenderly up at him, and covered his hand with hers. "But then he got some help."

Buck smiled at her, and for just a second, some of the fatigue lifted from his face. "It took a lot of work," he continued, "but eventually we were able to get to a Sam before he went over the edge. Which brought some much-needed technical expertise to the team."

Buck inclined his head toward Gear, who had found something on the wall screen to study.

"Speaking of the team," I said. "How many of... us are there?"

"Thirteen Travs," Gear supplied, without looking up. "Well, twelve now. Eight Sams, nine Morgans."

"That's a lot more Travs than Sams."

"Our success rate is about fifty-fifty," Buck admitted.

"And the percentages are getting worse," Gear added. "Last year was really bad. We lost two Sams in one incident alone."

"Uh, I guess that was me," I said. "But I did save one Sam."

Who was either in jail, or at the very least answering some very uncomfortable questions about the kidnapping right now. But at least he was alive.

"That was actually our one bright spot in the past year," Buck said. "It was nice work."

"I had a lot of help," I said. I couldn't bring myself to look at Fay as I spoke.

"But you quit," Parker said, speaking for the first time.

"Inter-Dimensional Cop was not a job I wanted."

"That's about fifty-fifty as well," Buck said. "Half of us are just happy to survive, *when* we survive. And half want to keep fighting."

"Fortunately," Parker continued, "there are *some* of us who can think about someone other than themselves."

I whirled around to face him. "What is your problem?"

"My problem is we gave you a chance to help. You turned us down, but then you blundered in anyway and ruined an op we'd been planning for weeks."

"Maybe," I replied slowly, "if you had explained to me what was going on instead of kidnapping Morgan, I would have stayed out of your way."

"I don't answer to you," he growled.

"Speaking of Morgan, where is she?"

"She's safe," Parker replied.

"I want to see her."

"You're not the boss here, Junior."

"Boys!" Fay said sharply. "Enough. That does no one any good. Morgan is fine. You have my word."

She pointed a slender finger at Parker. "You should know as well as any of us that everyone finds their own way to this place. No one can be forced to take this burden up."

Now she turned back to me.

"But I will be the first to admit we were disappointed last year when you didn't continue down the path that would have led you to us."

"Wait. You were watching me?"

Gear waved his arm and the whiteboard suddenly displayed a mosaic of hundreds of small pictures. Dark figures moved around in each one. I was too far away to see any of them clearly, but I was able to make out a very familiar Cardinals jacket in almost every one.

Dozens of Travs.

"How…?"

"One of the first things Sam does when he discovers a Trav that can jump streams is give him a nano-tracer," Gear explained.

I remembered that. A long time ago, in literally another world, Sam had given me a pill and told me it was a hangover cure.

"I programmed my version of the Cat Box to alert me any time a new tracer came on line. After that, it's just a matter of tapping into laptop and cell phone cameras, traffic cams, and the like to keep tabs on you."

"You can hack into webcams in a parallel universe?"

Gear shrugged modestly. "What can I say? It's a gift."

I turned back to Buck and Fay. "But if your mission is to save Sams, where were you when one was laying waste to my stream?"

214

Buck's lips tightened. "It's not that simple. If there is one thing we've learned, it's that there is a nuance to how we can influence events. What we're doing, even though necessary, also goes against the very manner in which reality itself is organized. We can't just go charging in."

"Tell that to the Travs and Sams who died."

"Believe me, I did what I could." Buck looked over at Parker, who rubbed the scar on his forehead.

"You were there on purpose?"

"You thought it was a coincidence that I happened along into the middle of your trans-dimensional mess, just in time to save the day?" he asked with a smirk.

"I don't remember you doing much saving."

"Even so, without me there, you would have failed."

"Right."

"Hey, you don't have to believe me." He jerked a thumb at Gear. "It's all in the math."

Gear nodded.

"Let's not get sidetracked," Fay said. "You did fine with the amount of help we were able to give."

"You consider losing all those Travs and Sams 'fine'?"

She laid a hand on my arm. "We understand. You're still grieving the wasted lives. We do, too. Every day. But you got through it. That's the important thing. And now you're here. You don't have to fight alone anymore."

This was all too much. I sat back down, rubbed a hand up and down my face, and decided to change the subject.

"Where is 'here,' by the way?" I waved a hand. "This room. This building. This world. Don't the regular cops wonder why everyone running around is wearing the same three faces?"

"We call it the Treehouse. It's a reminder," Buck said quietly.

"A reminder. Of what?"

"The stakes. Gear, you want to take over?"

"I can assume you've had the same explanation from Sam about the structure of reality that everybody gets when they start Traveling?" He sounded a little bored.

"I guess. The different realities are like the Mississippi Delta. A big river filtering into smaller streams that run more or less parallel to each other, seeking a shorter path to the ocean."

Gear nodded. "Ever wonder what happens when one of those streams gets blocked from heading to the ocean?"

"Sam said something about it kind of pooling. That time would slow down, even stop?"

"Pool is pretty close. I usually think of it as more like a bubble in space-time. Time doesn't run here like it does other places."

"But where are all the people?"

He shrugged. "They're here. We just can't see them because they're... well, *out of phase* with us. We're running on different clocks. Theirs is so much slower than ours we can't even perceive them. Or they us."

"Well, that's not weird at all."

"Is there anything about this that isn't weird?"

"Good point. How did it get like this?"

"This is what happens if the Opposition wins."

17

"THE OPPOSITION. WHAT'S that?"

Buck suddenly looked very old. Fay put an arm around him and rubbed his neck. Gear had gone back to scribbling on the wall.

"Just as I formed the Rangers to help me," Buck said with a heavy sigh, "Sam... the one from my stream, the one I've been trying to find for all these years... has done the same thing. He's recruited other Sams, and even some Travs, to help him achieve his goal."

"His goal is to make other streams like this?" I asked. "That doesn't make sense."

"Not all streams," Buck said. "Sam thinks that Traveling between streams weakens the barriers in between the different realities."

"Does it?"

Gear looked uncomfortable. "We're very careful. And we follow the EKG."

"The what?" I must have sounded confused and exasperated, because Morgan laid a hand on Gear's arm.

"When Gear first arrived," she explained, "he developed a way to use his software to send echoes back along the time stream to look for anomalies, in the same way an echocardiogram uses sound waves to create a picture of the heart. So we called it the EKG."

"We wanted to know if anyone else had ever tried to repair things the way we wanted to," Buck put in.

"And?"

"All we've ever found is some slight traces of extra-dimensional activity about fifty years ago."

"If you let me work on it more," Gear complained, "I could get you better data."

"We don't have that luxury right now," Buck reminded him. He turned back to me.

"But what the EKG gave us was a framework to follow. Whatever happened back then created... well, call it a patch. A patch that we can measure. When we go out to help a Sam and Trav on another stream, Gear uses the EKG to monitor our effect on that stream. We work until we get a patch that looks similar to the original one. After all that one has held for fifty years."

"But Sam..." I looked at Gear, adding quickly, "the original one. He doesn't agree?"

Buck shook his head. "He thinks the only way to fix it is a full reset. Collapse all the streams back to one. There wouldn't be any others."

"He can do that?"

Buck shrugged. "I've learned never to bet against him."

"But how?"

"We're not sure," Gear put in. "My team has been working on it. All we know for sure is that it has something to do with the girls."

"Sophie and Ella? What could two little girls have to do with Sam trying to reboot the universe?"

"That's why we're trying to find them."

At that moment, the door opened, and another Sam poked his head in. Like Gear, he wore a pair of Clark Kent glasses. But before he could speak, he was shoved out of the way.

Morgan Foster burst into the room and flung her arms around me.

218

"They told me you were here, but wouldn't tell me where. Are you all right? Where's Sam? Have they told you what's going on? Are you going to help them?"

"Whoa, slow down!" Buck said, putting up his hands. "We're just getting there."

"Wait," I said to him. I gently disengaged Morgan's arms but, keeping hold of her shoulders, looked her up and down. I can't tell you how I knew, but there was no doubt in my mind this was the Morgan from my stream.

"Are *you* all right?" I asked.

She nodded. "Oh, Trav, you wouldn't believe it. It is so weird, but so wonderful."

"I've seen the weird part."

At that moment, someone else joined our little party. Noah the cat hopped up on the table and bumped his head against my hand.

"How'd you get here?" I asked him, giving his ears a thorough scratch. "Like you didn't cause me enough trouble back home?"

"He comes and goes," Fay said.

"Wait." I turned to Gear. "I thought you said we were out of phase with the local residents."

"Not him. It's a real mystery," Gear said. "It's like every version of him is connected somehow, in a way the different versions of people are not. Noah exists on just about every stream. And on every one, even if the local Trav and Morgan haven't ever met, when he sees Trav he's on him like he has a pocket full of tuna."

"Now you've lost me. How could he know us on streams where we've never met?"

"I wish I knew."

"And this isn't something you've ever researched?"

"Oh, I've tried," the little man replied. "But short of anesthetizing him and opening his skull so I can examine his brain…"

"Which I forbid," Fay put in.

Gear shrugged. "You've met him before, I trust?"

"Oh, yes. In fact, it was one of the things that made the FBI think I kidnapped the girls."

"Nice," Buck said.

"And he's the only animal that's visible to us?"

"Him and bugs," Parker said. He pointed to a fly buzzing around the room.

"Sorry to interrupt." The Sam who had come in with Morgan had been hopping from one foot to the other while I was getting my orientation into Treehouse physics. "But I think we've got something."

Gear's gaze snapped to his twin. "What is it?"

"Look for yourself."

Gear stared into space, making *hmming* noises.

"They do this a lot," Morgan said softly to me. "The glasses project images on to your corneas."

"Why doesn't everyone have them?"

"Apparently, they give the rest of us headaches."

Gear was making swiping motions in the air, like he was going through pictures on his phone.

"That one?" he asked.

"Yeah," New Sam replied.

"Uh huh, that just might do it."

"Want to share with the rest of us?" Buck asked.

Gear waved his hand at the white board, and it changed to a scene of a man in one of the other interview rooms. It was Josh Dawson, and he'd been stripped down to a pair of boxer briefs. Two Travs stood nearby. What we were seeing was a live video feed, because the Travs were moving, arranging Dawson's clothes and personal articles on the table.

"Where does all the tech come from?" I asked Morgan out of the side of my mouth.

She jerked her head at the older of the two Sams. "That's why they call him Gear. All he does is tinker, working on new detectors and weapons. He and his wife, that is. She's just as smart as he is."

"Wait, what? His wife?"

"Yeah. Her name is Melody."

"Oh my God."

Morgan arched her eyebrows at my stricken look. "Why, do you know her?"

"No. But Sam mentioned a friend named Melody just today. It's obviously more serious than I thought."

"Or will be."

I swept my eyes up and down her once again. "You know an awful lot about this place, considering you've only been here a few hours."

She smiled. "A few hours for you, two weeks for me. That's the other reason they use this stream as their headquarters. Time runs faster here. They have more time to get ready for their next move."

I opened my mouth to why, if time itself ran slower, stuff like the electricity worked, but Sam started talking before I could.

"There."

New Sam pointed at a corner of the table displayed on the screen. Gear did something that zoomed in. It was the gun Gomez had knocked out of Dawson's hand right before taking him down. As the gun came into focus, it suddenly displayed the red outline I associated with the "right" direction to go in shifting from stream to stream.

"Yep. That's exactly what we need. Good work," Gear said. He and New Sam exchanged fist bumps.

"Whaddya got?" Buck asked.

"This," Gear pointed at the scarlet-lined gun, "did not originate from the same stream as Dawson."

"Is it Arkham?"

"I don't know." Gear rubbed his chin. "But it's the closest we've ever come."

"Arkham?" I whispered to Morgan.

"It's what they call where the Opposition is based. The anti-Treehouse. It's from–"

"I know what it's from. Freaking nerd-fest."

"What?"

"Nothing."

Buck turned to Parker. "Get 'em ready." Then to Gear, "How long till you can get a lock on it?"

"A couple of hours."

"You in?" Buck asked me.

"For what?"

"For years now, we've been in something of a Cold War with the Opposition. We keep a Sam from going bad, they recruit a Trav to put his Traveling powers to work for them. And as you've heard, their team of Sams seems to be ahead of us in tech. But not anymore."

Buck smiled as he held up a tablet, not unlike Ward's.

I looked around at the others, hating being the only one who didn't know what the hell was going on. "Okay," I said, "I'll bite. What is it?"

Buck looked at Gear, who cleared his throat. "As you know, while people make small shifts from stream to stream all the time, our minds smooth over any discontinuity caused by those shifts."

I nodded. "When you find your car keys in your coat pocket, even though you're sure you already looked there. What you think is a senior moment is actually a shift to a reality where the keys were in your pocket all along."

"Just so," Gear agreed. "But one of the first things we Sams learned when we discovered our respective Travs were moving from stream to stream was that we could track them by introducing a pill with nano machines into their system."

"Nano machines?" Morgan whispered, tilting her head toward mine.

"Tiny little robots," I whispered back.

"Once these nano machines had gathered data from several streams, we could release the suppressed memories and give Trav the full knowledge of his travels."

I remembered when Sam had done that for me. It literally had felt like someone split my head open and poured memories into it. And the headache that came with it was legendary.

Gear was still talking. "I've finally figured out a way to reverse the effects." He pointed to the tablet. "Run the app on this tablet in the presence of a Trav with the nano machines in his system, and they'll be deactivated."

"So?" I asked.

"His brain will once again suppress the memories of Traveling to different streams. He'll just be a normal human again."

"How long will it take?"

"Normally, it would take hours or days for the memories to fade," Gear said. "But I just caught a lucky break. The tracking program that allows the nano machines to be followed is a two-way street. We can also push information back through the link. Eventually, memories could be inserted the same way they are revealed now. We might even be able to push—."

He stopped, looking over at Buck.

"Push what?" I asked.

"Above your pay grade," Buck said.

"Anyway," Gear said quickly, "at the very least, the immediate effects will be significant confusion and disorientation."

"Depriving Sam of his soldiers," Buck finished. "With any kind of luck, mopping up will be pretty easy."

"Wait a second," interrupted Parker. "If all you need is to be in proximity to that thing to have your nano machines erased, what's to keep mine from getting scrambled?"

"We've pushed an update to all of our wrist units," New Sam said. "As long as you're wearing one, you'll be fine. Plus, you have to be within a few feet of the device for it to work."

Parker nodded.

Buck turned to me. "So, you in?"

I returned his gaze. "Honestly, I'm still not sure this is my fight."

"Oh, for God's sake," Parker said in disgust. Buck held up a hand, silencing him.

"I understand. You only just got here. And besides, we haven't done much to endear ourselves to you. But there's one more thing."

"What's that?"

"I'm pretty sure that's where Sam is keeping the little girls."

Of course. A part of me was feeling just a wee bit manipulated, but this was the reason I had started Traveling again to begin with.

I nodded. "Then I'm in. But that does not mean I am signing up with the Rangers. I am not volunteering to keep this Cold War going. Once the girls are safe, I'm out."

"Fair enough," he said with a smile. "Who knows? Maybe we'll change your mind. Now, it will be a while before we're ready. Igraine, why don't you show him around?"

My stomach growled.

"Come on," Morgan giggled. "Sounds like you could use a snack. You can't save the universe on an empty stomach."

I looked over at Buck, who waved us off. "Go ahead. We won't leave without you."

He turned away, looking at the whiteboard with Gear.

"Igraine?" I asked, when Morgan and I were in the hallway.

She shrugged. "We all have nicknames, you know. Hard to keep everyone straight otherwise."

"Yeah."

"What one did they give you?"

"Big Booté."

"Where the hell did they get *that?*"

"Long story. You said there was food?"

She grabbed my hand and led me down the hall to the building's small kitchen, which looked pretty much exactly like it did in my stream.

Except for the amount of food in the refrigerator. I was used to seeing some soda cans, a couple of takeout containers, and maybe the desiccated remains of someone's pizza, but this version was full of fresh food.

Morgan began pulling meats, cheeses, and cut vegetables from the fridge, and we made ourselves sandwiches.

"So, if you've been here two weeks," I said in between bites, "you've had a pretty good chance to get to know everyone."

"I guess," she said uncertainly.

"So, run the situation down for me."

"Well, to start with, the biggest thing is how different everyone is."

"Who is?"

She pointed a mustard-covered finger at me. "You. The Travs. You're all fundamentally the same person, right?"

I nodded.

"But you all couldn't be more different. Buck tries to keep up a good front, but when he thinks you're not looking, you can tell he carries the weight of the world on his shoulders."

"Not world. *Worlds*."

"Yeah," she agreed. "Parker functions as second-in-command. You probably figured that out. And he takes it so seriously, all business all the time. I don't think I've ever seen him smile. Of them all, O'Connor is the most like you, or at least what I know about you. The rest of them try to keep it light, with their hats and their bets and their Sorting, but..."

"But?"

"They've lost so many, Trav." Her voice turned hollow. "They've lost Sams, and Morgans, and so many Travs. They never talk about the ones who are gone."

"I never served in the military," I said, "but black humor, bonding rituals, not talking about the ones who didn't make it–those are all pretty common to units seeing significant action. And the Rangers seem to function like a military unit."

"I guess, but no one can live under that much pressure forever."

"I think Buck knows what he's doing. And if you've thought of this, you know Fay probably has, years ago. And from what I know of Morgan Foster, she's pretty smart."

Morgan blushed, and refused to meet my eyes. She suddenly became very interested in her food.

"Igraine, huh?" I said, to break the silence that had suddenly become rather uncomfortable.

She nodded. "Guinevere was already taken."

I chewed and thought about that for a minute before the penny dropped. "King Arthur?"

"Yes. I suppose with a name like Morgan, it was natural to name us after the other witches in his story. The Travs' names are pretty crazy. Yours especially."

"They're from a movie called *Buckaroo Banzai*."

"Never heard of it."

"If we get out of this, I'll loan you my copy."

That made her frown. "What do you mean, if we get out of this?"

I explained the mess I had left on our home stream.

"You escaped from jail?"

"I didn't have much choice. I figure the only way to clean this up is to produce the girls. Maybe if I can do that and come up with a story that sounds halfway plausible, everyone will ignore the inconsistencies."

"That could be a tall order."

We finished our sandwiches.

"So, you're going to go with them to rescue the girls?" Morgan said, daintily wiping her lips with a napkin that said "Casey's" on it.

"I don't see what else I can do."

She frowned. "Why so reluctant?"

"I'm still worried that all of this stamping around between streams is causing damage."

"Damage?"

I told her about Sam's concerns and also how Sanjana had hijacked his equations.

"And he thinks her using his files could have something to do with all this?"

I shrugged. "The girls, El Juego, this inter-dimensional war between Buck and the Sam who is his arch enemy. It all has to be connected somehow."

"Wait," she said, frowning in thought. "If this mess among the streams is so obvious to Sam, why hasn't Gear, or any of the other Sams here, noticed it?"

"I think they have, and this is how they're trying to fix it."

"It sounds like you think the Opposition Sam may be right."

"If he is, I don't condone his methods. And like you said, Gear and his team are just as smart. Who's to say they aren't right?"

"Then, what do we do?"

"I don't know. I just wish I could talk to our Sam about it. But I can't go back without the girls."

"And you can't rescue the girls without 'stamping around between streams.'"

"You got it."

We silently tidied up our mess. "What now?" I asked when we had finished.

"Let's go see what the others are up to," she said.

"Others?"

"Other Morgans."

"Oh. Sure, why not?"

She led me back out into the hall.

"You know, I should be mad at you. Really mad."

"I'm sorry. I didn't mean to get you involved in this."

Stopping so fast I nearly ran right into her, she whirled around and whacked me on the shoulder, hard. Her fist was tiny, but there was quite a bit of muscle behind it.

"Ow!"

"Not that, you moron. For not being honest with me in the first place!"

"I don't know what you mean."

"Don't you give me 'I don't know what you mean,' Trav Becker," she hissed. "Fay isn't here because she got drafted, or just happened to be in the wrong place at the wrong time. She's here to be with the man she loves. And so is Gwen, and Elaine. And all the others. Why didn't you tell me?"

She looked at me expectantly. My mouth opened and closed a couple of times, but nothing came out.

"Well?" She arched an eyebrow.

"Look," I finally said. "I did know that on at least one stream, it appeared that we were, you know, together."

"Appeared? Trav, Guinevere is *pregnant*."

"I… whoa. That's weird."

"Seems like you use that word a lot."

I leaned against the wall, trying to find the right words. "What was I supposed to tell you? 'Hi, I haven't talked to you in a year, but we're married in a parallel universe. Want to get a drink?' Besides…" My voice trailed off.

"I know," she said. "You've got a girlfriend."

I nodded. "She's a good woman. Better than I deserve. And I should have asked her to marry me a long time ago."

"But you haven't."

I shook my head.

"Because of me?"

"I don't want there to be any doubt, you know? When I ask her to marry me, I want to be sure. It was… really weird to see Trav Zero and his Morgan together. And even more so when I see Buck and Fay."

229

She smiled. "There's that word again. But they're good together, aren't they? Who wouldn't want that? Well, without the having to fight the crazy guy trying to destroy the universe part."

I wanted to chuckle, but just couldn't make it happen. "That's what I thought I had with Mary. But after everything I've seen... I just don't want to hurt her."

"Wait just a second, mister," she snapped. "It takes two to tango. Don't think that I'm just waiting around. I have a life, too, you know. And besides, what makes you think I'd go out with you even if you asked? Until today, you haven't spoken to me in a year."

And with that, she turned and marched off down the hall.

I hurried to catch up to her, feeling like I should apologize, and not knowing what to apologize for.

So in short, pretty much like any man's relationship with the women in his life.

Morgan stopped at the open door to a small conference room.

In my stream, it was a pretty featureless square, with walls painted the same puke green that decorated most of the station. The sole piece of furniture was a conference table with six beat-up chairs.

Not this version. Multi-colored cloths and tapestries covered nearly every square inch of the wall space. The fluorescent lights had been left off. A couple of floor lamps had been brought in, but most of the illumination was provided by candlelight.

The smoke alarm had been jerked out of the ceiling. I hoped the fire sprinkler had been disconnected, too.

The conference table was still there, but it was also covered with rich cloths that shimmered in the muted glow.

Three women sat around the table. They held hands, eyes closed.

They were all Morgans, of course.

One was Fay. My finely-honed deductive powers informed me the pregnant one was probably Guinevere. A third sat cross-legged on top of the table.

Morgan stopped short as we crossed the threshold of the door, and I almost crashed into her again.

Fay opened her eyes and smiled.

"Good. You're here."

"You were expecting us?" I asked.

She smiled mischievously. "Well, I generally have a one-in-three chance of guessing right whenever the door opens."

"Point taken."

"Gwen, Elaine, this is Big Booté."

I sighed. "How about we just go with Big? And, um, nice to meet you both."

Gwen smiled pleasantly, shifting in her chair to find a more comfortable position. She looked about seven months along.

Elaine giggled. "Igg and Big. Cute."

Morgan stiffened. I tried to find someplace else to look. Fay skillfully re-directed the conversation.

"Please sit down. We were just about to spread the cards."

"Cards?" But as I sat, I was able to answer my own question. "Tarot cards. Really?"

"You haven't seen this before?" Fay asked, with a questioning look at Morgan.

Morgan shook her head. "It's something I want to incorporate into my practice, but I haven't ever gotten around to it."

Fay nodded. "Then this is the perfect time to introduce you." She motioned again to the chairs. Morgan sat next to Fay and I took the chair by Elaine, which put me directly across from the senior Morgan.

I looked down at the cards. They were oversized, nearly half again as big as regular cards. Automatically, I began thinking how I would have to adjust in order to pull off any of my favorite card tricks.

"These cards are a little big for card tricks," Fay said with a pointed look at me. She turned to Morgan. "But that will not keep him from appropriating them to do sleight of hand. Keep them locked up. Otherwise, they will keep disappearing on you."

My mouth fell open, and her eyes flashed in delight. Gwen and Elaine made no attempt to stifle their chuckles.

"Buck doesn't get away with *anything,* does he?" I asked.

"He finds ways to keep the mystery in our relationship," she said.

Morgan cleared her throat. "So, show us," she said tightly.

Fay's smile became a frown as she studied her counterpart, but she continued.

"Yes. Well, as you know, practitioners have used Tarot for hundreds of years. But now, with what we know about the structure of reality and the literal ability of our thoughts, Trav's in particular, to manipulate that reality, a whole new aspect of their utility becomes available to us. With proper concentration, the cards can help focus on the pitfalls possible in a given course of action, and give us some ideas on how to avoid them."

She must have been able to read the doubt in my face. Or hell, maybe she actually *was* reading my mind, because with a sharp look she continued, "It is at least as logical as using a Billy Joel song as a focus object."

I didn't say anything, trying to keep from looking like a kid caught coloring on the living room wall. After a beat, she dealt five cards facedown, clockwise, in an arch, with the third card in the twelve o'clock position.

"This is a simple Tarot spread called the Horseshoe," she explained. "Buck calls it 'The Arch'."

Of course he did.

"The first card shows where you are now." She turned it over, revealing a short man wearing curly-toed shoes, and a hat with floppy points that ended in bells.

"The Fool," Fay pronounced.

"You're kidding, right?" I asked.

She smiled. "It's not what you think. The Fool represents Potential, either positive or negative. The X Factor. New Beginnings. That is definitely you. The Fool is almost always pictured walking toward the edge of a cliff."

I looked at the card and saw this was so.

"Because with any new experience, there is also risk." She paused and looked at me. When I didn't say anything, she touched the next card.

"The second card tells you your next step." She turned it over. It showed a hand holding a sword.

"The Ace of Swords. The Ace shows that you are at the beginning of a situation whose potential is double edged. Things can go well, or they can go ill."

"So, pretty much like any situation," I remarked.

Morgan kicked me under the table.

"Ow!"

"I would have kicked you, too," Elaine said. "Hush and let her work."

"The third card represents obstacles you will encounter."

Fay turned over the card at the top of the horseshoe. It was a skeleton riding a horse. I did not need to look at the legend on the card's bottom to know its name.

"Death," she pronounced.

"Oh for—"

Morgan's eyes flashed.

"—Uh... I mean, isn't Death always an obstacle?"

"You're being too literal," Fay said. "The Death card simply indicates a time of transformation is upon you. Or that a former perspective will no longer be useful to you. Ask yourself what you are carrying that may no longer be of use."

"Okay."

"Strengths and resources," she said as she turned over the fourth card. It depicted a woman with red hair that flowed from under a gold crown. She held a shining blade aloft.

"The Queen of Swords represents a person of insight, not necessarily a woman."

Fay paused, looking around the room, and a smile once again played across her lips.

"Although noting the company you keep, it's likely."

Gwen stifled a giggle. Morgan, staring at the cards, didn't look up.

Fay turned up the final card. It was a single-turreted building on a summit.

"The Tower."

"Well, that's good, right?" I said. "I have to travel to the Tower, or wherever it is Dr. Evil and the Opposition are." I pointed to the Queen of Swords. "And a person of insight will give me good advice."

I looked up hopefully into the faces of the women.

Their mouths were each set in the exact grim line.

"No?"

Fay sighed. "At its best, the Tower signifies the need to move past former ideals or beliefs."

234

"At its worst?"

"Crisis," said Gwen.

"Downfall," Elaine added.

I looked at Morgan. She bit her lip.

"Ruin," she finally said.

"Great." I looked at the spread of cards. "So, what do we have?"

Fay studied the cards. After a moment, she looked up at Gwen and Elaine. Something seemed to pass between them.

"What?" I asked. I looked at Morgan. "What?"

She shrugged, looking just as confused as I felt.

"It's... complicated," Fay finally said. "The cards show a time of transition, but also hope."

"But the Swords," Elaine said. "That's weird."

"Why?" I asked.

Elaine shook her head. "With a spread like this, I would expect to see something in the Cups, or Wands."

I frowned at Morgan, who supplied, "Those are other suits in the Tarot deck."

"What's the matter with Spades and Hearts?"

She rolled her eyes.

"Well, if this was supposed to give me some clarity, it hasn't," I said.

"It's not what I had hoped for, either," Fay admitted. "Sometimes we get an inspiration, other times it's only after the fact that the message becomes clear."

"So, I guess I'll keep my eye out for a Tower."

A shadow fell across the table.

"There you are." Trav Gomez stood at the door. He made a windup motion with his finger. "Saddle up. Time to go."

18

I NODDED AND stood. So did the three Morgans. Gwen took Gomez's arm and led him down the hall. The other two followed.

Left alone, Morgan and I looked at each other uncertainly.

"Well, you heard the man," she said. "Let's go. They have an armory set up. We can stop there first."

"Wait. *We* can stop there?"

"Of course. Did you think the women folk stay behind and roll up bandages? This is an equal opportunity outfit."

"Wait a minute. You're coming?"

"We all are. Well, not Gwen."

"I would hope not."

"I think if she wasn't quite so far along, she probably would. That raid you stumbled into, just Travs, was unusual. The Rangers usually deploy in Trav-Morgan teams."

"Wow."

"What's the matter? Don't you think we can handle it?"

"No, no, not at all."

"I'll have you know, I'm certified to teach self-defense *and* I have a concealed-carry permit for my own..."

"Desert Eagle." I finished.

She did a small double-take before realization dawned. "Right. That Morgan you met on the other stream. Trav Becker, I swear. When we get out of this you are going to give me a complete, blow-by-blow of every word you exchanged with other versions of me. You cannot believe how irritating this is! How would you like it if I knew things about you I had no business knowing?"

"Keep hanging around with Fay. That seems to be her gift."

That made her smile. "Yeah, it kind of is, isn't it?"

A noise from down the hall reminded us of the business at hand.

"Crap. We gotta get moving," Morgan said. "Come on."

I followed her to a room that was used for file storage on my stream. Here, it was an NRA member's wet dream. The walls were lined with racks on which rifles and shotguns were mounted. A steady stream of Travs and Morgans filed in and out, emerging with armloads of gear.

Morgan and I joined the queue. "Where does all this stuff come from?" I whispered.

"I don't know. Pretty impressive, though."

When it was our turn, I surveyed the selection. And realized I knew exactly where the weapons came from.

This wasn't just a storage room for weaponry. It was a storage room full of exact duplicates of the *same* weapons. I took two pistols, both of which looked just like my service weapon, right down to the scratches on the grips, along with a short-barreled shotgun, twin to the one I had carried when I stumbled on to the other raid. I wondered how many Travs had carried these weapons before me. And what had happened to them.

The only new items were some flash grenades and a rack of clothing. I grabbed some pants and a shirt, grateful to finally get out of the scrubs I was still wearing. I grabbed a utility vest, and seeing that it had pockets that would accommodate flash-bangs, I added some of those, as well as ammunition for the shotgun and my Glocks.

Morgan also grabbed a vest, along with a Desert Eagle, of course. She checked the giant pistol over expertly.

237

I started to head for the bathroom to change, but realizing that was silly given the company I was keeping, just undressed quickly and slipped into my new clothes. No one paid me any notice.

The clothes fit perfectly, of course.

Buck, Fay, Gear, and a Sam who I assumed was the same one who had joined us in Interview Two appeared just as we finished gearing up. In all, I counted eight couples besides Morgan and me.

"Everybody ready?" Buck asked. "Gear, Dick, what can you tell us?"

The younger Sam, who apparently went by Dick, pointed at the wall. An image of Dawson's gun appeared.

"This weapon did not originate on the same stream as we found it. There is chrono-residue on it that we've been able to trace to a point of origin."

"How do we know the residue isn't from someplace else?" someone asked.

"It points to an area that I can't penetrate with any of our instruments," Gear said. "Which means it's a pan-dimensional zone similar to the Treehouse, one where time flows so slowly we're out of phase with the natural inhabitants. So the good news is, you should not have to worry about noncombatants. If it moves, chances are it's a part of the Opposition."

"That all?" Parker asked.

Dick looked uncertain. "Well, there's something else. The Boss has managed to place some extra layer of... something, beyond what we've done to disguise the Treehouse."

"The Boss?" I whispered to Morgan.

"That's what they call the original Sam, the one who started with Buck. For some reason, he doesn't call himself Dr. Evil."

"Right."

"An extra layer of what?" O'Connor asked.

238

Dick shook his head. "I can't tell. But be extra careful when you start to shift streams. If it was me, and I had the capability, I would do something that would make it harder for you to get to me."

"Any idea how he's doing this?" Buck asked.

Gear shook his head.

"He's always a few moves ahead of us," Buck muttered. "Maybe we can stop that today. Parker, you want to orient the newbies?"

His expression said he'd rather do just about anything else, but Parker's tone stayed civil. "It's your responsibility to bring Igraine across. Your bracelets are tuned to each other. Try not to get separated, but if you do, it's your job to find her."

"How?"

"When the time comes, you'll know."

"Some orientation," I muttered. Morgan elbowed me in the ribs.

"Like Gear says, Arkham is hidden," Parker continued. "We won't know much about the layout till we get there. But we can assume it probably is a place that feels familiar and safe to Sam, like Central Station is for us. And they're expecting us, so we go in hot. Gant, you and I will take point and figure out a way in. Everyone else, keep us covered as best you can."

"*I'll* be on point with you," Buck interrupted.

"What?" Fay said.

"Are you sure?" Parker asked. "It's been a while since you've been in the field."

Buck raised an eyebrow. "You calling me *old*, Junior?"

"No," Parker said quickly. "It's just…"

"Just that you can't let your desire to find Sam override good sense," Fay warned.

"I'm not. You've each risked your lives time and time again, trying to make right a mistake I made. Not today."

"Then I'm going, too," Fay said. "Parker, would you kindly fetch my gun?"

Buck opened his mouth to object, but her look stopped him.

Parker looked at Buck, shrugged and went into the armory, returning a moment later with a Desert Eagle and shoulder holster. He helped Fay shrug into it.

"Gomez, you'll coordinate here," Buck said.

"Wait...what?" Gomez sputtered. "Why?"

Buck looked at Gwen. "In all our years, this is our first pregnancy. And just because we're all biologically the same person does not mean I intend to risk your child growing up without his or her actual father. It will be easier on me if I don't have to worry about putting a dad in the line of fire. Everyone else okay with that?"

There were nods all around.

"Good. Any questions?"

I raised my hand. "I, uh... know this is a newbie question, but can I assume we will be fighting other versions of ourselves?"

Buck nodded.

"So, how do we tell them apart?"

"No movie logos on their hats," he replied. "Other than that, if they're shooting at you, they're probably the Opposition."

"And of course, any Sam you see is part of the Opposition," Parker added. It was only then I realized that it was by design that none of the Sams had suited up.

"Okay," I said.

"Anything else?" Buck asked, making eye contact with each of us. The room was quiet, and after a moment, he nodded.

"Let's roll."

He moved over to stand by Fay and took her hand. Each of the other Travs and Morgans did the same. Gear made the picture of the gun reappear on the wall, and the Travs focused on it. A moment later, they winked out of sight.

Taking my hand, Morgan stood on her tiptoes and kissed me.

"For luck," she whispered.

"Wait…" I began.

"Hey, I said I've been here two weeks," she said, not looking at me. "And go figure, the only movies around here are your favorites. Now quit gawping and let's go. You don't want to miss the fun, do you?"

"Whatever this is going to be, it's not going to be fun."

I pushed aside the distraction of Morgan's body next to mine and, turned toward the wall, focusing on the image of Dawson's gun.

Immediately, a line of duplicate images of the weapon sprang into view behind it, curving off into infinity. I focused not on the gun, or guns, but on its surroundings. Some versions of the gun were held in hands, others were holstered. In others it just rested on a dark surface. It was one of these that attracted my attention.

It felt "right." That's the only way I can explain it. It was the same as when I jumped from one stream to another. Something in my subconscious, or maybe some connection to the other Travs, directed me to my desired goal. That was what I felt now.

Within my perception, the stream I needed to get to took the form of a light at the end of a long dark tunnel. I stretched my hand out, calling it to me.

But even as I did this it seemed to pull away. The light got smaller and dim.

What the hell?

I reached for it again. And away it skittered once more. I took a deep, calming breath and tried a third time, but much more slowly. Perspiration ran down the back of my neck, and also made my grip on Morgan's hand slippery.

It was like walking through Jell-O. Something resisted each mental "step" I took. And just when I thought I was making progress, the literal light at the end of the tunnel remained out of reach.

If this was Boss Sam's doing, he had an understanding of how to manipulate the streams that was far beyond anything I had ever seen before.

After what seemed like hours, I had closed the gap maybe halfway. I cursed under my breath and redoubled my effort. I subjectively progressed a foot, and the light receded again, but this time only by six inches. I pressed forward again, making two feet. The light seemed a foot closer.

I wanted to tell Morgan what was going on, but if I lost my concentration, we might get kicked out of alignment with our goal entirely, ending up who knew where. And I wasn't even sure if I could carry on a conversation while Traveling. It had never come up before.

Six inches.

Eighteen.

A yard.

I had a splitting headache, and my arms felt like I was trying to bench press a Buick.

Two feet.

Five feet.

I had closed maybe half the remaining distance. What was that brain teaser? If you closed half the distance toward your goal with every step, how long would it take you to get there?

The answer, of course, was never. You would just slice ever-decreasing slivers of the remaining distance without ever arriving.

That was exactly what this felt like. After another eternity, and just as it seemed I had come up against a rubbery wall that resisted every effort I had, Morgan squeezed my hand. Taking energy from her presence, I pushed again.

242

Six feet.

The light now filled nearly my entire field of vision, and I again stretched out my free hand. I had a sensation of trying to hold something that was trying to wriggle away.

Oh, no you don't.

The light expanded and I lunged forward. With a sensation like bursting out of a bubble, I stumbled forward.

Right into a war zone.

The first thing I saw as my vision cleared was the barrel of a rifle pointed in my direction. I hit the deck, pulling Morgan with me, twisting as I went down and wrapping my arms around her as we rolled. I covered her with my body.

Our faces were very close.

"Are you okay?" I asked. She was pale, and perspiration had caused her hair to form little ringlets which were plastered to her forehead.

She nodded. "I think so. What happened? It seemed to take forever."

"Something definitely did not want us to get here. Must have been that something Dick was talking about."

I lifted my head. We were in front of a large building that took up pretty much the entire block. I knew it immediately.

It was Building 231, which housed the university's Math and Physics departments. It had been Sam's home away from home since he was an undergrad. In retrospect, we should have known. When Buck needed an HQ, he picked Central Station, a place he knew as well as the house he grew up in. It made sense Sam would do the same thing.

But he'd remodeled.

The city and the university had grown up together. Many of the college buildings were in the central business district. In fact, Building 231 was only a few blocks from Central Station.

In my stream, there was a row of angled parking in the front, and about forty yards of green space between the wide sidewalk and the building.

But here there were no cars parked in front, because they had all been moved to the very front of the building. There were about twelve vehicles of varying ages and models, parked nose-to-rear, and forming a protective wall of metal. Men with guns crouched behind the cars.

Our roll had taken Morgan and me behind a statue of some famous science professor— I couldn't remember his name— so we were somewhat shielded.

This was not true of the remainder of our team.

Buck was crouched behind three recycling containers chained together about twenty feet to our left. He was trying to wrap a bandage, one-handed, around Fay's arm. Blood pulsed from an ugly wound in her shoulder.

Between us, a body lay unmoving on the sidewalk.

As I watched, O'Connor and Elaine winked into existence.

The gunmen picked them off before they even had time to get their bearings.

"Aw, crap."

"What?" Morgan asked.

I let her up, making sure she stayed shielded by the statue. She saw the bodies and turned her head away with a gulp.

I pointed toward where Buck and Fay were, and told her to get ready to move.

"Go!" I hissed, and popped up, firing. Trying to keep my body between her and the shooters, I kept up a barrage of fire as we scuttled across. Buck saw what I was doing and started firing as well. We slid in behind the garbage cans like we were stealing home.

"They were expecting us," I said, when we had caught our breath.

"You think?" Buck replied.

"Is Fay all right?"

"I'll be fine," she gasped.

Morgan took the bandage from Buck and continued wrapping her wound.

"How many more got through?" I asked.

"We're it."

"What? How?"

"I don't know. Fay and I got here first, even though Parker, Gant, and Valuk started ahead of us. You saw what happened to O'Connor and Elaine."

"We gotta get out of here."

"I know. I've been trying to open a path back, but something is blocking me."

"How about if we tried together?"

"Worth a shot."

"Can you two hold them off while we try?" I asked the women.

Morgan nodded immediately. Fay said, "Help me get turned around."

Moving carefully to keep her wound from starting to bleed again, we got her into a position where she could rest the hand holding her Desert Eagle on top of one of the containers. Morgan put an arm around her and sighted her own weapon. I put my pistol down where she could reach it if she ran out of ammo, and turned to Buck.

He put a hand on my shoulder and closed his eyes. I did too. Morgan squeezed off a couple of shots. I put our plight out of my mind, trusting her and Fay to keep us safe while we made with the magic.

Piece by piece, I put together a mental image of the bullpen back at the Treehouse. First the institutional green of the walls, then the furniture. I put Gear and Dick in there, too.

It was exhausting. No matter how hard I focused, the image stayed fuzzy, like trying to recall a dream. I opened my eyes. Buck remained crouched in front of me, still as a stone. His lips pressed in a thin line, and sweat rolled down his temples. Suddenly, he gasped, and his eyes flew open.

"Got it!" he crowed.

Immediately, I could feel the Treehouse as well. But before I could grab the girls, Morgan let out a loud curse, and I could hear the hammer of her Desert Eagle make a futile click.

She dropped the big handgun, fumbling for my Glock, and snatched it up.

Six men had popped up from behind the cars and were now approaching us. Like us, they were dressed all in black. They held the sights of short-barreled machine pistols to their faces, blocking their features.

Fay tried to continue firing, but her gun was empty as well. Morgan aimed my Glock at the oncoming figures.

Nothing happened.

"Shit!"

She banged the gun with the heel of her other hand and tried again, with no effect.

I jerked my shotgun loose from its strap on my shoulder. I brought it up and squeezed the trigger.

My gun was jammed, too.

I watched in disbelief as the Opposition figures approaching us dropped their guns.

And drew swords.

"We gotta go!" Buck cried.

The Opposition crew was almost on us. There was no way we would have time to grab the girls and maintain enough focus to make the transition.

Before I could think about what I was going to do, I grabbed the Morgans by their collars and shoved them bodily into Buck.

"Go!" I screamed. Grabbing my useless shotgun like a club, I charged.

The Trav on point saw me coming, but holding my shotgun at each end, like a quarterstaff, I was able to catch his blade on the trigger guard and deflect his blow. He was off-balance just long enough for me to swing for his head, connecting with a dull *thunk*.

He went down right in front of one of his compatriots, who tripped and fell over him. I swung my shotgun wildly again, causing the others to back off slightly. I chanced a glance back at the recycling station.

No one was there. Buck had managed to get the girls out. I turned back to the fight, but my moment of inattention cost me.

I whipped around just in time to see the pommel of a sword arcing toward my head.

And then I saw nothing at all.

19

I T'S NOT GETTING knocked out that hurts.

It's waking up.

As I slowly became aware again, it was actually my stomach which hurt worse than my head. I locked my jaws to keep from vomiting, but that caused my head to start pounding like I was coming off a two-week bender.

I lay very still, keeping my eyes closed. After a minute, I remembered how I had gotten the headache. Someone had hit me with the handle of a freaking sword.

Swords. Dead Trav Two had been wearing a sword. And there were pictures of swords. Where had I seen those?

Oh, yeah. On the Tarot cards. Right before Fay said sometimes you didn't understand what the cards were telling you until later.

No shit.

Good thing she hadn't drawn the Ace of Wands. I probably would have found myself in a smack down with Harry Potter.

I slowly opened my eyes. It took an effort to focus, but I could do it, which I hoped meant good news on the concussion front. I pushed myself up on my elbows.

I lay on an army cot. It looked like one Sam used when pulling all-nighters in his lab. A bunch of classroom chairs, the kind with the little writing desk attached, were pushed haphazardly against a wall across from me. That meant I was probably in a classroom. Which was confirmed as I turned my head to take in the rest of my surroundings. Moving did not make me feel worse, so I took that as progress.

The door opened, and Trav Becker walked in.

"You're awake. Good. How's your head?"

"How do you think?"

"I think you're lucky you got the handle rather than the point."

"Yeah. Why was that?"

He shrugged. "The Boss wanted you still breathing."

I sat up, a little slower than I absolutely needed to. No reason to let him know the full state of my recovery.

He carried a glass of water and three tablets. Here. These'll help," he said.

Remembering Sam's tracking pills, I said, "No, thanks."

"Relax. It's just Advil. I promise."

My head really hurt, so hoping he was telling the truth, I downed the pills and the water. Everything stayed down.

As I did, I examined the man standing in front of me. He was dressed in what I was beginning to think of as the standard Traveler uniform. Black military-style cargo pants tucked into work boots, black long-sleeved t-shirt, and vest. A pistol hung from one hip, a sword from the other. He wore a ball cap, but it was white, not black. It sported the logo of the Oakland A's.

He saw me looking at his head.

"Movies were taken."

"What do I call you?"

He tapped the brim of his cap. "Oakland will do."

As he took the empty glass from me, there was a knock. Sam Markus poked his head around the half-open door.

"Can I come in?"

"It's your universe."

249

He chuckled. "If your sense of humor is back, you didn't get hit too hard."

He dragged a chair from the pile, turned it backwards and perched on the desk part, with his feet on the seat.

Meeting Gear had prepared me for the sight of an older Sam, but there were differences. Boss Sam was wearing Traveler Black, not khakis, and while his hair had also receded, it was short nearly to the point of being shaved, a ginger dust that circled his temples. He also was missing the pot belly of the other middle-aged Sam I had met. In fact, he carried himself with the rangy confidence of someone who knew his way around a fight.

He leaned forward and rested his elbows on his knees.

"Look, Trav. I know what you've been told, and I want you to hear the other side of the story."

"The other side of the story?"

"Yes. It's important that you know what is really going on."

"Why?"

"Because you're important."

"I'm important."

"Yes. I mean, all of you... all of us, are important..."

"What about the Travs you gunned down outside? Were they important?"

He sighed, and looked much older. "I'm not going to bullshit you, Trav. People have died. Good people. On both sides. And I get to live with the knowledge that I started it all. But I'm trying to end it."

"End it how?"

"Have you ever done any research into the history of Traveling?"

"I didn't know there was any."

250

"Good point. There are no textbooks on parallel universes. But if you look hard enough, and read between the lines, you can start to see some patterns."

"Patterns."

"Yeah. Throughout history, there have been people who have an awareness of things beyond conventional reality. Witches, fortune tellers, prophets. Most of them are fakes, of course. But some aren't. Some actually are able to see…"

"The future?"

"A future," he corrected. "I mean, isn't that what you do, when you Travel? See an assortment of probable outcomes and go to the one you want?"

I shrugged. "I suppose."

"But not everyone can see perfectly, which is how you end up with prophecies that don't come true. Whoever it was saw the wrong one."

"I don't know what this has to do with what's going on between you and Buck."

Sam chewed on the inside of his lip. "Like I said, no one's ever written down any rules for parallel universes. Have you ever wondered why not?"

Maybe it was getting conked on the head, but I was having trouble following this odd conversation.

"What do you mean?" I asked.

"We've already established that hundreds, maybe thousands of people through the ages have had this talent like you guys do. But you can't be *that* special."

"I never thought we were. Like you said, there had to have been others."

"Then why have we never heard about other Travelers?"

"Because anyone who talked about it would get locked up."

"Maybe. But we can prove it. I could take you to a science conference and demonstrate the reality of Traveling in front of hundreds of impeachable witnesses. But no one ever has. No one has ever accidentally appeared on a busy street, or disappeared in front of a crowd. Don't you think that if people had been shifting between streams of reality as much as we have, it would have gotten out?"

"Have *you* told anyone?"

He grinned. "You got me there. No. But remember what Ben Franklin said. 'Two people can keep a secret. If one of them is dead.' Somebody, sometime would have spilled it."

"I don't understand what you're getting at."

We were interrupted by Oakland Trav, who stood up and stretched, yawning.

"Sorry," he said, "not my first time hearing this story. Do you want anything?"

"I'll take some coffee," Sam said. "Want anything?" he asked me.

"Coffee's fine."

"You going to be okay here by yourself?" he asked Sam.

Sam looked at me and smiled. "I don't think I'm in any danger. Am I?"

Still thinking it was a good idea to reinforce the idea I was weak, I said, "I'm in no shape to make a run for it, if that's what you mean."

"We'll be fine," Sam said.

Oakland turned to go.

"Don't you want to know how I take it?" I asked.

"Funny," he smirked, before sliding out the door.

"All right. Where were we?" Sam asked.

"Why there aren't a bunch of Travelers."

"Right. And here's why. There aren't any others."

252

"What? I don't follow."

"Seers, yes. Prophets, yes. Maybe even the occasional person who somehow slipped into a world just a little different than the one they knew. But I think you... all of you, all of us, are the first to actually control our movements between the dimensions. I think that the combination of my research, your latent abilities, and some other related events caused this."

"What about that evidence Buck and Gear found that indicated someone had found and fixed a breach in the main stream some years ago?"

He waved a hand. "I'm not convinced that's what they actually discovered. I've been studying this longer than anyone and I've never seen any other footprints in the time stream."

He leaned forward in his chair. "But even if someone did, it was one isolated event. Traveling is not a natural thing that's been going on throughout history. It's *wrong*. In fact, it is seriously fucking up the natural order of the universe."

His voice dropped to an intense whisper.

"We have to stop it."

20

M Y HEAD, WHICH had been feeling better as the ibuprofen took effect, began to pound again.

"If you think about it, you'll know I'm right," Sam continued. "The more you Travel, the easier it gets, yeah?"

I nodded.

"But that's not because you're getting better at it. It's because the barriers between the streams are wearing down."

"And no one on Buck's team, even though they know the same stuff as you, has figured this out?"

Oakland Trav returned with two cups of coffee. I took a grateful drink. Sam held his cup with both hands and stared into it.

"It's more about *who* figured it out," he said quietly. "When Buck and I first discovered the streams, I went a little nuts. I became convinced the only way to maintain the integrity of the different realities was to eliminate the Traveler."

"So, you started hunting Trav Beckers," I finished. "I've heard this story before."

"Of course, you have. But unlike the Sam you tangled with, I realized that trying to solve the problem by myself with violence was never going to work."

"Hence the guns, swords, and wall of cars outside. Oh yeah, and the bodies. Thank God you decided to forego violence."

"Do you think I want it to be this way?" he hissed. "I don't have a choice! I've tried to communicate with Buck, but whatever credibility I had with him was destroyed years ago. He is convinced this is all just part of my evil plan to rule the universe. But his solution of running around putting Band-Aids on the tears in the timeline is about as effective as putting an ice pack on a severed limb. The bottom line is I'm right, Buck's wrong. I know what needs to be done. If Buck gets in the way, I don't have any choice. We go over him."

Throughout this speech, Sam's eyes had gotten a little wild, and he punctuated his sentences by stabbing the air. He stopped, and his cheeks turned pink.

He cleared his throat. "Sorry. I got carried away. Although that's what the villain does, right? Monologue? And according to Buck, I'm the villain. Isn't that what you think?"

"I think it's complicated."

"You're right about that, my friend."

Something had been nagging in the back of my mind through this, and I finally realized what it was.

"What does all of this have to do with the girls?"

"The girls?" Sam looked blank. Then understanding flowed across his face. "Oh, yeah. Sophie and Ella. That's all about you."

"Me?"

"You still haven't really figured out your role in all of this, have you? Buck didn't tell you, of course. I have yet to meet a Trav Becker who was a sharer."

"I don't understand."

Sam turned to Oakland. "Oak, tell uh—" He looked at my cap, which lay on the floor next to my cot, "—Stargate here, how you and I met."

"Adam was killed responding to a call," Oakland said without expression. "I left him watching a suspect who we thought was down, but the son of a bitch had a second gun and neither of us were fast enough. It was my fault. I was so hot to go after the other guy, I didn't make sure the first one was fully out of commission. I got fired. When the Boss found me, I'd crawled pretty far into a bottle. He offered me a way out. A way to do something that had some meaning."

"Sound familiar?" Sam asked.

I nodded.

"You see, Buck recruits the versions of you that are successful and well-adjusted. I have to look a little farther afield. No offense," he added with a look at Oakland.

The other man shrugged.

"Anyway, I have to go to those streams where the breaks didn't fall Trav Becker's way."

He held up a finger. "Except for one that got away. You see, there was this one Trav who started out in the shit pile, but somehow managed to find a solution to his local version of the Trav-Sam conflict that did not result in two armed camps and a Cold War. Needless to say, this attracted the attention of both Buck and me."

"Should I be flattered?"

"Well, it was pretty impressive for your first try. It's like…"

He stopped, searching for the words.

"Okay… multiverse, infinite number of realities, differing from each other only in small ways, right?"

I nodded.

"But all the streams aren't created equal. Streams that are similar to each other tend to group together. Like a tree. Some branches are big. Other, smaller ones sprout off them. Buck's original stream is one of those big, prime lines of causality. The set where Trav Becker loses his job and descends into alcoholism is another.

"But you, with your original solution to the program, introduced a whole new wrinkle. A brand new, main branch. But there were consequences."

"Consequences."

"Oh, yes. When you 'fixed' the problems in your little corner of the Multiverse, you also created a pretty significant new timeline. One where there was peace between you and Sam."

He leaned forward in his chair, his eyes intense, mouth tight.

"But also one where a new risk suddenly presented itself." He stopped and took a sip of coffee, waiting for me to put it together.

I'll blame the time it took on the fact that my head still felt pretty scrambled. But finally I saw where he was going.

"Quantum computing,"

"Got it in one. In this new timeline, instead of being killed, or recruited to either Buck or my groups, your Sam went back to work. Unfortunately, this created a situation where Sam's formulas get out of the lab."

"You're talking about El Juego. But what does that have to do with anything? Sam didn't invent quantum computing."

"But he did invent an entirely new way to design the underlying structure of the site's games. And here's the problem: It attracts attention. Other sites pick it up and reverse engineer. Next thing you know, the same algorithms that powered the Cat Box start showing up all over the world. Pair this with the weakening of the barriers between the streams, and the catastrophe we've been working to prevent gets accelerated."

"Wait." I saw a hole in his argument. "You said we created a new timeline. That means there aren't any other streams where time ran faster for you to see all this. You don't know for sure that things are this dire."

"Trav, what the hell do you think I do around here all day?" he exploded. "I don't go out and track down Sams and Travs just to come hang out in the clubhouse. I have a *team* of Sam Markuses who have done *nothing* but model this problem for months. It will happen, take my word for it."

"You still haven't explained about the girls."

"That was just to get *you* here. Well, not totally. Our software models also said that the girls' disappearance slowed down the launch of El Juego by a few weeks. I looked around and located a Josh Dawson who could be recruited to our cause. Since he was dating Sophie's mom on your stream, the girls thought nothing of getting into his car. And the native Dawson knew nothing about it. It was perfect. Later, I sent a team in to sabotage the web site, but Buck had men on the ground, too. There was a fight."

Which finally explained the dead and wounded Travs who kept showing up at my house.

"But you got on the girls' track," Sam continued. "My Dawson just barely shook you. I knew it wouldn't be long before you found them, and I still needed to buy time. So we brought them here."

"But it happened more than once. You took the girls on another stream as well."

"You can't do something like that on one stream and not have it echo on neighboring ones. Our target was the girls on your stream. The others were…"

"Collateral damage?"

Sam looked shocked. "What do you take me for, Trav? I would never hurt little girls. On any other stream where a kidnapping occurred, they've been returned to their parents."

"But your empathy obviously doesn't extend to a grownup like Josh Dawson."

"I told you," he said tightly, "I'm trying to stop the killing."

258

"I can tell. Look, can we cut to the chase, Sam? Just exactly what is it you want from me?"

He looked perplexed. "I thought it was obvious. I need you to go back. Tell Sam to pull all the Cat Box algorithms out of El Juego. Crash the site if he has to. In short, I need you to join the team."

"And if I don't?"

He looked away.

"Then I have to make a hard decision," he said softly. He looked back at me, and his tone became pleading. "Don't make me do that, Trav. We can do good together. We can fix it."

"What about Buck and his team?"

Sam shook his head. "They made their choice."

"I see."

His phone beeped. He glanced at the screen.

"I gotta go. Think about what I've told you, Trav. I know it's a lot to take in, but if you give it some consideration, I think you'll see I'm right."

"In the meantime, I'm a prisoner here?"

"Oakland will be right outside if you need anything."

And he left.

Oakland Trav went over to the door.

"One question," I said.

He looked at me for a second. "Okay."

"What's the deal with the swords?"

"Your gun misfired, right?" he asked.

I nodded.

"And yours wasn't the only one."

I nodded again.

He patted the blade that rode on his hip. "When the shit hits the fan, and there are a bunch of us in one place, shifting in and out, probability goes all to hell. The chances of a gun misfiring goes up about a thousand percent. It's good to have a backup.

"Besides," he added with a crooked grin, "swords are cool."

"Damn right," said a female voice behind him. "And pointy, too."

Morgan illustrated this by poking him in the back with the blade she held.

"And if you make a sound," she continued calmly, "you'll find out just how pointy this one is. Hands where I can see them, please."

Oakland raised his hands. Morgan, who had slipped in the door which Sam had left ajar, kicked it shut with her foot.

"What the hell are you doing here?" I demanded.

"We're a team. Did you think I was just going to leave you?" She prodded Oakland forward. "Take his gun and sword," she said to me.

"Buck and Fay?"

"They got out, I think. At least they disappeared."

I disarmed Oakland. "Sit down on the bed," I ordered. "No sudden moves."

Morgan and I took up station between him and the door.

"I thought that whack-job would never leave," Morgan said.

"You mean Boss Sam?"

"Can you believe that load of crap?" She put a hand to her forehead. "Oh, Trav," she said dramatically, "I need you on the team to help me kill everyone who doesn't agree with me."

"You have no idea what the hell you're talking about," Oakland snarled.

"Shut up," she said. She looked at me. "Can you get us out of here?"

I frowned, and extended my senses. After a minute, I realized the dizzy and off-kilter way I'd been feeling since I had awakened was not due entirely to head trauma. I hadn't really noticed before, but the subtle swirlings of the various reality streams had been in the background of my awareness for months, maybe years. It was like the hum of traffic outside a window. I didn't notice it until it was gone. Now I realized I felt like there was a layer of cotton between me and the outside world.

"Has the Boss done something to keep us from shifting out?" I asked Oakland.

He shrugged.

"I think there's some sort of dampening field," I told Morgan. "We'll need to get clear of the building."

"Then let's go."

I held up one hand. "Wait. Where are they keeping the girls?" I said to Oakland.

He just glared at me.

"I'm not leaving them here," I told Morgan. "We'll have to go looking."

She nodded and jerked her head at Oakland. "What are we going to do with Mr. Baseball?"

I looked around the room. "Any chance there is something in here we can use to tie him up?"

Her face brightened. "No, but I have something. Watch him."

I kept the sword pointed at him while she undid something from her wrist. I hadn't noticed it before, but she wore a green and yellow fiber bracelet, in addition to the silver one I had come to think of as her Traveling bracelet. As I watched, she picked at it, and began unraveling several feet of cord.

"Paracord bracelet," she said in answer to my questioning look. "Didn't you ever weave one in summer camp?"

"No."

"It was a way to pass the time in the Treehouse."

Once undone, her bracelet yielded at least ten feet of lightweight rope. Using her blade, she hacked off several lengths. Soon, Oakland Trav was firmly secured to a table that was itself bolted to the floor.

I sliced off a section of the sheet that covered the army cot for a gag, and approached Oakland. He glared at me, jaw locked.

Morgan put the point of her sword to his throat.

"The people lying in the street outside were friends of mine," she murmured. "Now, Trav is a well-trained professional. He would never harm a defenseless person. I, on the other hand, am an emotional amateur."

She began applying pressure. The point of her blade began to sink into his soft tissue. She leaned in closer, until her lips were next to his ear.

"I'm unpredictable when I'm upset," she whispered. "Trav will be really pissed at me if I hurt you, but he'll get over it."

"Morgan," I said.

"Shut up," she hissed. "You're not the boss of me." She pressed a little harder, twisting the blade's point slightly, and stared unblinking into Oakland's eyes. "What's it going to be?"

He relaxed his jaw.

"Good boy," she cooed, patting him on the head. A moment later, he was securely gagged. She stood up, and turned to me.

"Ready to go?"

I just stared at her.

"What?"

"You can be a very disturbing person."

She reached up and patted my cheek. "You have no idea. Now, let's move. Sam will be back soon. We gotta get out of here before he takes your mom hostage or comes up with some other new wrinkle to get you to enlist with him."

"Don't even say that."

I grabbed Oakland's weapons belt and buckled the gun and sword to my waist. Morgan plucked his hat from his head and put it on me. She peered from him to me, frowning critically.

"You'll do," she finally pronounced.

"I'll do? In the history of changing places with your guard to break out of jail, this is as close to a slam-dunk as you'll ever get."

She rolled her eyes. "Let's find Sophie and Ella."

I opened the door and peered out. I groaned softly, quickly pushing Morgan back inside. I leapt out and had just closed the door, leaning against it, when Trav Becker rounded the corner.

Our eyes met as he passed me. I raised an eyebrow and gave him the bored look that is universal in any organized force for *Why do I always get the chicken-shit duty?*

He nodded sympathetically and kept on walking. After he had passed from sight, I opened the door. Morgan leaned out.

"That was close."

"Yeah."

"Where to?"

I screwed up my face, summoning up my memories of this building. It had been a decade since I'd sat in one of these classrooms, of course, but because Sam worked here, I'd been in and out with some regularity. The structure dated to the fifties, but had been added on to just after I'd graduated. The labs were in the new part. We were in the original structure, where most of the classrooms and lecture halls were.

I looked down the hallway. About five doors down, a laundry basket sat outside one of the classrooms.

Could it be that easy?

Hoping that maybe just this once, there were no ugly surprises waiting, I motioned to Morgan, and we crept down the hall, alert for any familiar faces to show themselves.

I put one ear to the classroom door. I didn't hear anything. I looked at Morgan and shrugged.

"What should we do?" she whispered.

"I can't go in there. The last time the girls saw me, they screamed bloody murder."

"Then I guess it's up to me."

"What if there are a couple of Travs in there standing guard?"

"I'll try and keep them off balance until you can leap in and save the day. But no pressure or anything."

I looked into her eyes, which were dancing with mirth despite our predicament.

"You're enjoying this, aren't you?"

She shrugged. "Like I said, it beats guessing the sex of the caller's baby. I'll yell if there's trouble."

I nodded and squeezed her shoulder. She opened the door and slipped in. I put my back against the door and resumed my bored guard persona. My brilliant acting was wasted, however, since no one came by.

Morgan did not yell for help, so I waited, trying to look calm. But inside it was like thousands of ants were running around just under my skin. *What was she doing in there?* I was about ready to burst in when I felt the door handle move in the small of my back. It opened, just a crack.

"Come in," Morgan said quietly.

I did. This classroom was much like the one I had awakened in. Big room, most of the chairs pushed to one side to create some space in the center. But there were two army cots instead of one, and a sleeping bag laid neatly on each.

Sophie Patel and Ella Day stood in the center of the room. Each girl wore a small backpack, and just like the last time I had seen them, Sophie had one arm curled protectively around Ella. Sophie looked right at me, chin held high and doing her best to look unafraid. Ella's eyes were wide, doe-like as if she wanted to bolt as soon as I entered the room.

Morgan stood behind the girls, and put her arms around their shoulders.

"I know he looks just like the other men, but I promise, he's going to get us out of here and take us home."

I smiled and tried to look non-threatening. "Hi, girls. I have been looking very hard for the two of you."

"Why didn't you just ask your twin brothers?" Ella asked.

I smiled. "That's a good question, Ella. Let's just say sometimes my brothers and I don't get along. You know what that's like, right?"

She nodded seriously. I crossed the room, and squatted down in front of them. I was gratified that they didn't shrink back.

"Morgan and I came here to take you back to your families," I continued. "But you have to trust us, and do exactly what we say. If I tell you to be quiet, you have to be still like statues. If I tell you to run, you peel out as fast as you can. Whatever Morgan or I tell you, you have to do it, no questions, or we're all going to be stuck here. Do you think you can do that?"

Ella nodded again, so vigorously I could almost hear her eyeballs rattle. Sophie joined her, but still watched me warily.

"Okay," I said. "Do you have everything you need?"

They nodded again.

"Great. I'll go fir–"

Before I could finish, the door swung open.

21

W E WATCHED SILENTLY as a woman nudged the door open
with her hip and backed into the room, carrying a cafeteria tray.

"Okay, girls," she said, still with her back to us. "Lunchtime."

Sophie and Ella looked at Morgan and me, eyes wide. We moved
forward, completely in sync. I drew my weapon while Morgan glided
up next to her and smoothly lifted the tray from her hands.

I snaked a hand around to cover her mouth and put the barrel of
my gun against the back of her neck at the same moment I softly said,
"Shh."

She went stiff as I pulled her close to me, but nodded.

Morgan set the lunch tray down and I maneuvered our new
captive to a chair, sat her down and moved around front where I could
see her.

Morgan was already there, head tilted at a comical angle,
studying our captive.

"I don't know her," she said. "Why don't I know her?"

But I did. "Hi, Amy."

Amy Harper glared at me. She opened her mouth, looking like
she was going to yell, but I brought my gun up, and Morgan lifted the
sword she still held.

"Amy?" Morgan asked.

"Amy Harper," I explained. "Late of the police force. She sold
out to Anton Kaaro, and got swept up in the arrests last year. In our
stream, she's in jail."

266

"Jail?" Amy said, speaking for the first time.

"Oh, yeah. But you were better off there than in another stream where I met you. Kaaro shot you in that one."

"What are you talking about?"

"Never mind. How did you get mixed up with Sam?"

"Sam?" she said, her tone mocking. "I'm not here with Sam. I'm here with you, lover boy."

She took the opportunity to rake Morgan up and down with her eyes.

"So, this is the great Morgan. To hear the Boss talk, she's one part Batgirl and one part Sabrina the Teenage Witch. I'm not impressed."

"*I'm* not the one who is a prisoner," Morgan said, eyes flashing as she prodded the other woman with her blade.

"Don't," I cautioned, not taking my eyes off Amy. "She's just trying to get a rise out of you. Get us both off our guard."

"Not much chance of that."

"Doesn't matter," Amy sneered. "It's just a matter of time before they find you. Do you think the Boss doesn't know everything that goes on? He's like Santa Claus. Knows when you're sleeping, knows when you're awake. I don't know how you got in here, but believe me, you're not getting out."

"She's right," I said, still watching Amy carefully. "If Sam doesn't already know we're loose, he will soon."

"What do you want to do?" Morgan asked.

"Got any of that paracord left?"

She did, and a few minutes later, Amy was trussed securely to the chair. I watched both women as Morgan tied her up. I tried not to think about the inter-dimensional edition of *The Dating Game* that seemed to pair me with different women in each set of realities. It was bizarre enough seeing the tender moments between the Rangers and their respective Morgans. But Amy Harper?

"What?" Morgan asked, seeing me shaking my head. She'd finished, and was watching me in that knowing way I still hadn't gotten used to.

"Nothing. Just wool gathering."

"Gather on your own time, *lover boy*. I want to get out of here."

"Me, too."

With one last look at Amy to make sure she couldn't raise an alarm, Morgan gathered up the girls, who had watched the entire exchange with Amy in shocked silence. When we were all ready, I cracked open the door and peeked out into the hall.

The way seemed clear. I waved the girls and Morgan out, and quietly closed the door behind us. I led our little party a few steps, before halting. I turned around to see Morgan looking at me. A small smile played about her lips.

"You don't know which way to go, do you?"

"Well, I was kind of unconscious." I made an *after you* gesture. "Would you like to lead us?"

"I thought you'd never ask."

And she started off down the hall in the opposite direction as I shook my head. She was having way too much fun.

The next hallway was long. It stretched the entire length of the building, nearly a city block. When we had almost reached the other end, Morgan stopped in front of a door. The glass was frosted, so I couldn't see through it.

"There's a loading dock down these stairs." She pushed the door open.

"Hey!" a cry came from the direction we'd just come. "Stop!"

"Crap," I muttered. I shoved Morgan through the door, and hustled the girls after her. "GO!"

Two Travs raced down the hall toward me. I slid through the door and pulled it shut behind me, looking around frantically for something to block it with. There was nothing on the small landing, but an empty fire extinguisher bracket was mounted on the wall.

"Paracord!" I yelled to Morgan.

She was halfway down the stairs, but turned and tossed me what was left of her original bracelet.

There was just enough. I wound the cord several times around the door handle and the bracket, quickly knotting it. I gave it a test pull, then took off down the stairs.

Morgan and Sophie tripped lightly down the staircase, graceful as dancers. Little Ella, however, needed two steps on each tread, and had fallen behind. When I caught up, I scooped her up and carried her. There was banging and cursing behind me, followed by a big crash as they got the door free.

Ella and I joined Morgan and Sophie at the bottom of the stairs.

"That paracord?" I said to Morgan. "Best stuff ever."

We were in a receiving area. Some garbage and recycling containers were against one wall, along with some pallets. There was a garage door used for loading with an entry door beside it. Morgan grabbed Sophie's hand and ran toward it. Ella and I were right behind her. We burst outside and ran down another, shorter flight of stairs to street level.

"Where to?" Morgan said.

"That way," I said, pointing toward the north. There was a small residential area in that direction, mainly older houses, most of which had been broken up into student apartments. We dashed across the street and crashed through a hedge that separated two houses.

"There they are!" The two men chasing us spilled out onto the loading dock, where they were joined by another half-dozen who apparently had been patrolling the rear of the building.

I put Ella down, and pushed her toward Morgan and Sophie. Once she was clear, I pulled Oakland's pistol from my waistband and squeezed the trigger. I was rewarded with a loud retort. The horde of Travs in pursuit scattered, diving behind whatever shelter was near them.

"Guns work!" I shouted to Morgan. "Take the girls to the back yard! I'll cover you." She tossed her sword aside, whipped her Desert Eagle from its holster, and disappeared around the corner with the girls.

I got off a few more shots to make our pursuers think twice before charging out into the open, then took off in the direction I'd sent Morgan.

I rounded the corner of the house and stopped short.

Boss Sam held a dagger to Sophie's throat.

"Stay where you are, Trav," he warned. I did so, raising my hands as I assessed the situation. Morgan stood just to my right, arms wrapped around Ella. Sophie must have been just a couple of steps ahead of them, and run right into Sam's arms.

"Drop the gun and kick it this way," Sam said.

I hesitated.

It's not going to surprise you when I say that real life policing is not like you see on cop shows. But one area where reality is wildly different from fiction is that a police officer is trained to never, never lay down his or her weapon.

That "Here, I'm putting down my gun so we can talk," thing? Strictly a TV convention to build drama. I mean, think about it. If you put down your gun, what is the bad guy going to do? Shoot you, that's what.

But I didn't have many options. And there wasn't much time. Sam's reinforcements would come storming around the corner any minute now.

"How'd you find us?" I asked. "Did your algorithms predict what I'd do?"

He snorted. "We have security cameras."

"That's actually kind of disappointing."

"Sorry, I'll try to whip up something more magical next time. Come on, Trav. Put down the gun, and let's go back inside, crack open a couple of beers, and talk this out."

"I don't think so, Sam."

He shrugged. "Have it your way. But give me the gun."

I stood there, bringing my gun arm down slowly, slowly, as slowly as I possibly could, buying every last second, desperately trying to think of a way out.

In situations like this, time sometimes seems to slow down, and your senses become hyper-aware. I could see the sweat trickling down Sam's temple, the faint tremble of the arm he had locked around Sophie. I heard the buzz of an insect as it zipped past my ear.

My eyes locked onto a wasp as it buzzed away, long legs dangling from its thorax.

Not a wasp, a yellow jacket.

A yellow jacket is a kind of wasp, of course. But not the kind that build those nests of mud or paper that stick to your house. Yellow jackets nest in the ground. I'd run over a yellow jacket nest once when mowing the lawn, and collected a hell of a sting.

Ignorant of the fact that it was one of the few creatures in phase with we Travelers, the wasp swung through the air. But rather than flying up and away, it descended toward Sam's legs.

A couple of times, when my back was against the wall, I found that instead of traveling *to* a stream, I could cast my awareness out in search of a tiny change, and *bring it to me.*

I looked over at Morgan. If there was ever any moment for her to be able to read my mind, this was it.

Be ready, I thought at her.

Sweat ran down my temple as I concentrated on the wasp's nest that *had to be* near Sam's right foot.

My arm was now below my waist. I kept moving it lower toward the ground, my eyes on Sam but my mind reaching out, searching for one particular possible chain of circumstances.

When Sam grabbed Sophie, he dragged one foot over a little hole. As he shifted his balance, he stepped on it, blocking it. Now, as he watches me lower my gun, he leans forward, moving that foot a tiny, tiny bit. But just enough to...

"OWW!"

Sam jerked his leg up and away from the yellow jacket nest. Involuntarily, he swatted the air near his ankle with the hand holding the knife.

The instant the blade was no longer against the girl's neck, Morgan whipped her Desert Eagle up, firing in the same motion.

BLAM!

The slug caught Sam in the shoulder, and he spun away from Sophie. She sprinted to me, and I threw an arm around her.

Sam clutched at his wound, glaring at us, while shouts and scuffing sounds came from around the corner of the house.

"C'mere!" I called to Morgan. With Ella in tow, she hurtled toward me. I dangled my gun with one finger in the trigger guard, reaching for her.

She grabbed my hand, I squeezed it tight and pulled her toward me, jerking Sophie close with the other hand.

A half dozen Travs bounded around the corner. They saw me, and raised their weapons.

I had no time to visualize the streams, carefully choosing the one I needed, with the mental melody of a song to help me focus. As the platoon of Trav Beckers brought their guns up, all I could do was gather

Morgan and the girls into my arms, and concentrate with every filament of my awareness on three words.

Bring them home.

22

FORTUNATELY, WE APPEARED in a version of the yard that did not have a bunch of Trav clones pointing guns at us.

Unfortunately, we appeared in a version of the yard that had two coeds sunbathing topless in it. And we blinked into existence standing right on top of their discarded bikini tops.

The girls screamed, snatching beach towels to their chests, and pulled futilely for the scraps of cloth trapped underneath our feet.

"Watch out for the wasps!" I called over my shoulder as I hustled Morgan, Sophie, and Ella out of the yard. We dashed around the corner, not pausing until we reached a church which was about a block away. We collapsed on a stone ledge that ran along the side of the building.

"Is everyone all right?" I asked when we had caught our breath. Nods all around, although Sophie and Ella did not look like they could have run much farther.

"What now?" Morgan asked.

"We get these girls back to their families. But…"

"But?"

"We can't just walk into the station with them. I'm supposed to be locked up, and Ward suspects you're involved, too. We have to think this through. But the first thing we need to do is get off the street."

I patted down the pockets of my vest. Miraculously, I still had my phone, and it had a charge. I now had to hope for one more miracle. I held my breath while I dialed the phone.

"Trav, what the hell?" Sam asked a moment later. "They let you keep your cell phone?"

I started breathing again. "Thank God. I was afraid Ward had locked you up."

"He tried. Right now, he has about twenty forensics guys trying to bust into my laptop."

"Can they?"

Sam made a farting sound. "Don't be ridiculous. They'll be collecting their pensions before they break my encryption. But where are you calling me from?"

"I'm... uh, not where they put me. Long story. I'll fill you in later. Can you get to your car?"

"Oh, yeah. I'm not at the station anymore."

"Ward let you go?"

"He didn't have any choice. I got a message to Clark, who sent an attorney over to make sure they didn't try to hold me. But what about you? When Ward realizes you slipped the leash, there's gonna be hell to pay."

"One crisis at a time. Right now, some ladies and I could use a ride."

"You found them?" he crowed. "Awesome! Where are you?"

"By that church near the Physics building. You know the one?"

"Yes! I'm out the door. Be there in a flash."

"Make one stop before you pick us up." I explained to him what I needed.

The street in front of the church was a busy one, but where we were crouched was pretty well hidden from traffic. We rested, trying to look inconspicuous, until Sam pulled up in his Prius. It was a tight fit, but Morgan and the girls were able to squeeze into the back. I slid into the passenger seat.

"Where to?" Sam asked.

"City Park."

He swung into traffic, the Prius' hybrid engine humming softly.

"Did you get it?" I asked.

He nodded. "On the floor in front of you."

I felt around until I located the small plastic sack. It contained a prepaid phone, and a three-pack of men's t-shirts. I tore open the blister pack for the phone and powered it up.

"That what you need?" Sam asked.

"Yeah."

"Want to tell me what you have in mind?"

"When we get there."

He pulled into the park, and putted up a hill until we came to a small playground. The weather was warm, but it was supper time, as I had hoped, we were alone.

I hopped out as soon as Sam stopped the car, and helped Morgan get the girls out. I told Sam what I needed the t-shirts for and he went to work. Morgan and I sat the girls between us on a park bench.

Morgan caught Ella looking at the swings. "Do you want to go play, honey?" she asked.

Ella heaved the kind of world-weary sigh only a eight year old can achieve. But the effect was spoiled by the huge yawn that followed. "Maybe later," she mumbled, and put her head in Morgan's lap. Morgan stroked her hair and fifteen seconds later she was sound asleep.

Sophie was looking at Sam thoughtfully.

"He was the one with the knife, who grabbed me," she said. "But he was older."

I nodded.

"And I saw eight different men who looked exactly like you. I counted."

"You're very observant."

"I'm a genius."

"Really."

"Oh, yes," she said matter-of-factly. "Mom and Dad had me tested."

"I knew you were smart."

"Really?" Curiosity lit her face. "How did you know?"

"By the way you took care of Ella. And you never panicked. Even though things were very weird."

"You can say that again."

We sat in silence for a moment.

"Ella thinks you're all brothers."

"Uh huh."

"But you're not, are you?"

"Not exactly."

"Can you tell me what you are?"

"It's a very long story, and the police are going to be here soon. I need to be gone before they get here."

"Will you get in trouble for helping us?"

I shook my head. "I think I can keep that from happening. But if I'm here, it will lead to a lot of questions that will be hard to answer."

She nodded but looked at me with a frown. "If I tell the police the kidnappers looked just like you and your friend, they'll think you did it, won't they?"

"Probably."

"I won't tell them. I promise." She made a cross over her heart. "And I'll make sure Ella doesn't either."

I smiled, my throat suddenly tight. "Sophie, I'll tell you a secret. When Ella wakes up, she will probably remember very little of what happened. And it will take a little longer, but it will get really foggy for you, too."

"I find that very difficult to believe," she pronounced, so grown up it made me want to laugh and cry at the same time.

She screwed up her face in deep thought again. A sly smile lit her face, and she looked up at me.

"This is like that one *Stargate* isn't it? The one where the SG-1s from all the parallel universes started showing up and it got so crowded?"

I stared at her. My mouth opened and closed a couple of times. I didn't dare look at Morgan, but out of the corner of my eye, I could see her shoulders shaking as she tried to stifle a fit of giggles.

"*Stargate*, huh?" I finally said.

She nodded. "It's my dad's favorite show."

I ruffled her hair. "You tell your dad he's raising you right. Any more questions?"

She shook her head.

"I have to go. Morgan will stay with you, okay?"

She nodded, but before I could stand, she threw her arms around me and crushed me to her with all the strength her small frame possessed.

"Thanks, Mr. Becker," she whispered.

"My pleasure, Sophie. Take care."

"Will I see you again?"

"Anything's possible." I gave her a final squeeze and disengaged her arms. Morgan lifted Ella's head from her own lap and moved her to lean against Sophie.

"Can you watch her a minute?"

Sophie nodded.

Morgan rose. She came over and stood very close to me.

"Got your story down?" I asked.

"I was taken right after I left you" she recited. "I never saw the kidnappers' faces. They held us in a dark room. I never saw anything to identify its location. A little while ago, they blindfolded us, brought us here, told us to count to one hundred before taking the blindfolds off, and that someone would come."

"Sounds good. Sam?"

He had finished cutting up the t-shirts into strips that would pass for blindfolds. He tossed them to me, and I handed them to Morgan. She tossed them to the ground, and rubbed them into the dirt with the heel of her shoe, to dirty them up a little.

"Will they believe me?" she asked.

"They'll be confused. But even though Ward is a suspicious son of a bitch, there really isn't anything to tie you to the kidnapping. Mainly they'll just be glad to close the case."

"If you say so," she said doubtfully. "But what about you?"

"Me? They'll find me safely in my cell, where I couldn't possibly have had anything to do with any of this. Ward won't be real happy, but he'll go for the simple explanation."

"One that involves organized crime, not parallel realities."

"The FBI doesn't believe in parallel realities."

"And you're sure the girls will forget?"

We looked over at them. Sophie had her arm around Ella, whose head rested on the older girl's shoulder in angelic slumber. Sophie was looking pretty drowsy, too.

"Sophie won't want to forget you," Morgan murmured.

"What do you mean?"

"Oh for God's sake," she said, rolling her eyes. "You are completely clueless. You rescued her. You're her hero."

"I look exactly like her kidnappers."

"She knows the difference." Morgan looked in the direction of the girls, but this time didn't seem to see them. "Or will for a little while, before she forgets."

Her voice dropped to a whisper, so faint I wasn't sure I made out her next words.

"Will I forget, too?"

I shrugged. "You're asking the wrong guy. Dick and Gear seemed to think they could turn memories off. But Sam remembers what happened to us last year. My guess is, you will, too."

"Shit."

"What?"

"Nothing. I mean, it's just that, now we pretend none of this ever happened, don't we? I mean, that's what you did last time, right?"

I nodded.

"Okay, then," she said firmly, echoing my nod with a jerk of her chin.

"What's the matter?" I asked.

"Nothing," she sniffed. "It's just that…"

She gave a watery giggle, reached up and touched my cheek.

"I've grown accustomed to your face."

"Oww," I groaned. "How long have you been saving that for?"

"A long time." She smiled sadly. "But it's like you said, on this stream we hardly know each other. I know I have to go back to that, but…"

I opened my mouth to speak, but she held up a hand.

"You don't have to say anything. If you were the kind of guy to go looking around when he was already in a happy relationship, I wouldn't want anything to do with you in the first place. Go back to her. Be happy. Don't think of me as the path not taken.

"In fact," she sniffed, "You should know, I would never date you. You are so not my type."

She tried to glare at me, but it only lasted about ten seconds before we both broke into quiet laughter.

Our chuckles faded after a minute, and we looked at each other for either ten seconds or ten years.

I finally broke the silence. "Morgan, I…"

"Shut up," she whispered hoarsely. She stood on her tiptoes, slid a hand around the back of my neck, and pulled me into a kiss.

Which also lasted either ten seconds or ten years.

"Goodbye, Trav Becker," she whispered, releasing me. She walked quickly back over to the park bench and bent over Sophie and Ella.

The place on my cheek where her hand had lain felt very cold.

I turned and walked to the car. Sam leaned against the fender, watching me.

"Everything okay?"

"Yeah. Hand me the phone." I covered the mouthpiece with a piece of one of the t-shirts, and dialed 911.

When the dispatcher answered, I pitched my voice into a low growl. "You'll find the girls and the psychic at the north end of City Park. Don't come looking for us. We got what we wanted, and we'll be long gone by the time you get here."

I hung up, powered the phone off, and removed the battery.

"Let's go," I said. "They won't waste any time."

We hopped back in the car and retraced our route back out of the park. We had just reached the river when a parade of black and whites, along with two Feebmobiles, screamed past us. Like the good citizens we were, we pulled over to the side of the road to let them pass. While we were stopped, I took the opportunity to toss the burn phone over the bridge railing.

A few minutes later, we pulled up to the station.

"How are you going to get back in?" Sam asked.

"Jails are designed to keep people from getting *out*. Getting *in* won't be a problem."

"Are you sure?"

"Well, I will probably use my extra talents to help."

"Of course."

"That reminds me. Remember what you told me about your quantum algorithms, how you were worried they might be affecting the streams?"

He nodded.

"Well, I'll go into the whole thing when we have some time, but long story short, you may be right."

"That can't be good. But what can we do about it at this point?"

"Those algorithms can't go live, Sam."

He looked stricken. "Clark is not going to want to hear that."

"I don't think we have a choice."

"Well, crap." He slumped into his seat. "Do you suppose he'll take back all that money he gave the university?"

"Sorry, man."

"No," he waved a hand. "I thought my file storage was secure, but Sanjana was still able to get in. It's on me. I'm just lucky all hell didn't break loose." He stopped, and looked at me in a sudden panic.

"Did all hell actually break loose? On some other stream?"

I shook my head. "Not because of your algorithms, at least. I'll tell you about it later."

"I can hardly wait. Okay, you better get in there. They'll be looking for you pretty soon."

"I hope so."

We bumped fists and, after looking around carefully to make sure no one I knew was nearby, got out of the car and made my way over to the building.

You know, it *is* a lot easier to break into jail than out. Especially, if you can re-arrange probability just enough to make sure people are in the rest room, or watching YouTube videos when you need to slip past them.

But at the same time, I was cognizant of what Boss Sam had said. That the fact that it got easier shifting streams was not due to my increased skill, but to the weakening of the barriers between realities. I wondered if one Trav's resolve to not contribute further to that weakening would make much difference.

I was certainly willing to try.

I thought about the other things the Boss had told me. That somehow on this stream, Sam and I had created a third way, a new line of probability that avoided so much conflict and pain.

On the one hand, it seemed the height of hubris to say I knew better than the Boss, than Buck, and all the Travs and Sams who had sacrificed up to now. On the other hand, there was no way I could join either one of their sides. I had left all of this behind a year ago. I could do it again. Their war would just have to go on without me. It seemed to me preserving this third way needed to be my priority.

These thoughts kept me company as I waited in my cell. As I had hoped, the difference in the rate of time in the Treehouse and Arkham had worked in my favor. On this stream only a couple of hours had passed, and apparently no one had checked on me. Of course, I had shoes on, not to mention I was no longer wearing the hospital scrubs. I just had to hope no one would notice.

It was nearly two hours before I heard rustling outside my door. A moment later, it swung open to reveal Adam Yount.

"Hey," I said.

"Hey yourself. Let's go."

"Go?" I tried to look confused. "Adam. Tell me you did not pay my bail."

"Bail?" he said with a chortle. "You don't need bail. They found the girls!"

I stood up. "Found them? Where?"

"The kidnappers dropped them at City Park and split. We got a call a little while ago."

"Are they all right?"

He nodded. "And get this. That psychic, Morgan Foster, was with them."

"Really?"

"Yeah. And she backed up your story completely. Said she was taken after you and she went your separate ways."

"I bet Ward was happy to hear that."

He laughed. "Sure he was. Now, are you ready, or have you taken a liking to this place?"

I followed him out, but not before flipping him off.

He had expedited the process of my release, so it was just a matter of picking up my personal items. A few minutes later I was in the bullpen, facing Leon and Ward. The latter glared at me. Leon's face was carefully neutral.

Ward leaned in very close and said softly, "I know you were involved in this, Becker. I don't know how you got to the psychic and the girls, but you are dirty, and I will prove it. That's a promise."

"Knock yourself out," I whispered back.

He glared at me for a moment more. "I'll be downstairs," he muttered.

"You made a friend for life," Leon observed.

I shrugged. "He saw what he wanted to see."

"Regardless," my boss said, "there are some pretty big holes in your story. Internal Affairs will have some questions for you before you return to duty."

"Fair enough," I replied.

Leon was no dummy, and I had hurt him earlier with my stonewalling. I wasn't in the clear yet.

But for now, his relief at finding the girls safe was contagious.

"There's a media conference in a couple of minutes," he said. "The families are downstairs. They want to see you."

"Great," I said, although what I really wanted was a shower and about a week's worth of sleep. He nodded, and I started to think maybe everything was going to be okay between us.

"Any word on the kidnappers?" Adam asked.

Leon shook his head. "The call came from a burner. Turned off right after. We're watching the bus station and the airport, but the Feebs think they were independent contractors, brought in just to make the snatch. Probably hired by some of the less savory backers of El Juego's competitors to throw a monkey wrench into the launch. Important thing is the girls are safe."

"Amen."

We reached the first floor, and could hear the muted hubbub of the media gathering for the news conference. But instead of heading out to the reception area, Leon steered us to a conference room crowded with happy people.

Michele Day sat in the corner, Ella perched on her lap, cheek rested against the top of her daughter's head. Her eyes were closed as she rocked back and forth. Ella looked at us curiously as we entered, but didn't spend any more time looking at me than she did Adam or Leon.

Sophie and her parents stood nearby. She was in the middle, wrapped in her mom and dad's arms in a tearful, grinning tangle.

Sophie also looked up as we entered. She frowned when she saw me, staring just a little too long. But then her dad said something, and she turned back to him.

Morgan sat by herself in a corner of the room. A blanket lay around her shoulders, and her hands were wrapped around a steaming mug of the department's atrocious coffee. She looked tired and small.

I started toward her, but turned around when I heard my name.

"Trav!"

Mary leapt into my arms.

She kissed me long and hard. When we finally came up for air, she rested her forehead against mine.

"Are you okay?" she asked.

"People keep asking me that. I'm fine."

"I was going crazy," she said. "No one would tell me anything. I finally said to Leon, 'I am waiting here until you either let Trav go or tell me what is going on.' Just about that time, all hell broke loose, and everybody left in a huge hurry. I came in here and sat down. I must have dozed off, because the next thing I knew, Adam was shaking me, and said you were coming down soon."

"You were waiting here all this time? Why didn't you go home?"

"You promised me a date night. You think I'd let a little thing like a murder charge stand in the way?"

"You're a nut," I said. Any other time, I would have kissed her. But I settled for putting an arm around her waist. I told myself it had nothing to do with the fact that Morgan sat nearby, deliberately not looking in our direction.

Ward asked for everyone's attention.

"I know you all want to go home," he said. "So we'll keep the news conference short. Maybe if we feed the media beast now, they'll give you some peace. Any questions before we go out?"

Morgan raised her hand.

"Yes, Ms. Foster?"

"The media doesn't have my name, correct?"

"That's right," Ward replied. "You weren't missing long enough for it to come up."

"Then I can go?"

He frowned. "You don't want to attend the news conference?"

She shook her head.

"I'm sure your station would like the publicity for your program."

"It's not up to them."

Ward concealed his bewilderment, finally saying, "We will have some more questions for you."

"I understand. But we can do that tomorrow?"

Ward nodded.

"Can someone give me a ride home?"

Before I could even think about whether I should volunteer or not, Larry Kudej beat me to it. "I'll do it."

Leon nodded. "Thanks, Kooj."

"This way, Miss," he said.

She brushed past me on her way out of the room.

"Detective," she murmured.

I tried to catch her eye, but she swept out of the room without saying anything more.

Mary watched her leave. She turned back to me, and opened her mouth to say something. Then she closed it again.

"What?" I asked.

She shook her head. "Nothing. What about you? Do you have to be at the news conference?"

"No. With everything that's happened in the last twenty-four hours, it's probably better for everyone if I make myself scarce."

"Good idea. Want to be scarce at my place?"

"Yes, please."

I told Leon I was taking off. He nodded absently, already composing himself for the press.

"I gotta run upstairs and collect my stuff," I said to Mary. "Then we can go."

"Can I trust you out of my sight? Or do you need an escort to make sure you find your way back to me?"

I couldn't think of a retort, so I just gave her another kiss and ran up the stairs, two at a time. It seemed like I had spent the last month at Central Station, and I couldn't have been more anxious to split.

I got to the top of the stairs and entered the bullpen. Something was off. For a second, I couldn't figure out what. Then I realized pretty much everyone in the building was downstairs. But this room was practically full. Where had all the people come from?

With a chill, I realized why.

Because the room was full of Trav Beckers.

Somehow, I was back in the Treehouse.

23

AS I LOOKED around the room, I realized Trav Becker's was not the only face I could see. There were a few Sams.

And two Morgans.

Fay stood next to Buck. Next to them, Parker held Morgan's arms, preventing her from running to me.

The unconscious body of Larry Kudej lay in the corner.

"Big," Buck said.

"This is a pretty neat trick," I said, waving a hand to encompass the room as well as the people. "Care to tell me how you did it?"

"You wouldn't understand," Gear said.

"We were worried when you didn't return," Buck said, "especially after Igraine failed to return with Fay and me. I'm glad to see you're both all right."

I nodded. "But I'm not thinking you invited us to this party just to make sure we were okay."

"Well, I have to admit I wish you would have reported in. Then we wouldn't have had to come looking for you."

"I've been a little busy, creating a chain of events that did not involve me telling Leon I had to rescue two kidnapped girls and my friend the psychic from a parallel universe."

"Good point," he replied. "So, now that you got everything straightened out, you were on your way back to us?"

"I told you I would work with you until we found the girls. But that's it. I'm out."

He nodded. "I see. Tell me about meeting the Boss."

"Before Morgan shot him, you mean? Nutty as a fruitcake, just like most of the others I've met."

"Hey!" three Sams cried in unison.

Buck silenced them with a raised palm. "Then what is your plan?"

"My *plan* is to go back to a normal life, and try to keep your private little war from doing any more damage to my stream."

Buck nodded again. "But Sam made a hard pitch for you to join his team, didn't he?"

I shrugged.

"Is there anything I can do to convince you to help us instead?"

"Look, Buck. I know that you believe you're doing what needs to be done. But so does Sam. And meanwhile, there is more and more damage to the streams."

"Then you think Sam is right."

"I don't know. Even if he is, he seems fine with the trail of bodies he leaves behind him. No way am I okay with that."

"And what are you going to do about it?"

"He was bleeding pretty good when we split. I think it will be a while before he's any trouble for you."

"But you know he'll be back."

"It's not my problem. I told you. I'm out."

He actually looked surprised. I wondered if any version of us had ever turned him down before.

"All right," he said slowly. "Fair enough. I'm not going to force you to join us. But Sam won't quit so easily. And he's not above getting nasty to achieve what he wants."

"I can handle Sam."

"I wish I could believe that. Parker, take his bracelet."

"Gladly." Parker signaled two of the Sams to take his place near Morgan.

"Wait. What?" I said.

"I told you, I'm not going to force you. If you don't believe in our cause, that's your right. But I can't trust Sam to give you a pass, too. He might blackmail you, or do something else to convince you to take his side. I can't have you someplace where he can find you."

Morgan got it before I did.

"NO!"

She threw herself toward me, but the Sams grabbed her arms.

"Hush, child," Fay said. "This is what has to be done."

Gomez and Emdall had taken up station on either side of me. Parker took my arm, and removed the bracelet.

Buck looked over at Gear, who was staring at his tablet. With a chill, I realized he was preparing to scramble, or maybe it was unscramble, the nano machines that allowed me to retain my memories of Traveling.

After a moment, the little man nodded.

"It's working. Just a minute while I reset the causality parameters."

"What are you doing?" I demanded.

"I'm giving you your wish," Buck said. "You want out. You'll be out. It will just be on a stream where you can't do any harm, and where Sam won't be able to find you."

Morgan turned to Fay. "You can't let them do this!"

The older woman shook her head. "It's you who doesn't understand," she said sadly. "We've been fighting this war for years. What gives you the right to wade in here and tell us everything we're working for is wrong?"

"He won't be hurt," Buck said to her. "But I can't risk him undoing everything we've worked for."

He turned to me.

"Last chance."

I shook my head.

He sighed, his shoulders sagging a little. He waved a hand at Gear.

"Let's get this over with so we can go back to work."

"What about Morgan?" I asked.

He frowned. "What about her? She goes back where she came from. Without her bracelet, that's where she'll stay."

"What about her memory?"

"Hmm." He looked thoughtful. "I hadn't thought of that. Gear?"

Gear didn't look up from his tablet. "One head at a time, please."

"Travis William Becker," Fay said sharply. "I forbid it. You just said there will be nothing she can do. Besides, the accommodation will cause her memories to fade."

"It would be kinder to just make them go away all at once," Buck said to his wife.

"She has been through enough. I will not have you scrambling her brain, too."

"The absence of Trav will greatly accelerate the adaptation," Gear said. "With him gone, I'll be surprised if she remembers much of anything."

Buck nodded. He suddenly looked every one of the years he had on the rest of us.

"I have your word she'll be okay?" I asked.

"As okay as any of us will be," Buck said. He turned to Gear again. "We're running out of time."

"This would go a lot quicker if you would shut up and let me work."

"Fine. Just hurry up."

"*Please*." Morgan pleaded. "Don't do this. Listen to him!"

"It'll be all right," I told her.

And I stomped down as hard as I could on Emdall's instep.

He let go of my arm, howling. I snapped my hand around and grabbed the back of his head. Before Gomez, on my other side, could react, I banged their noggins together. Their lookalike faces slammed into one another with a dull crack, and they both went down.

Gear looked up at the commotion and saw me coming for him.

"Eep!" He frantically pushed and swiped at his tablet.

Stepping over the two unconscious bodies, I leapt at the little man. He was even lighter than I expected, and made his own satisfying thud as I slammed his body into the wall. He stared at me for a minute, then his eyes lost focus, and he slid slowly to the ground.

I looked at the other two. They were down for the count as well.

"Very efficient," said a voice from behind me.

I turned around and looked into the smiling face of Anton Kaaro. He put an arm around my shoulders.

"You are not a large man, Travis," he mused, "but you never seem to have any difficulty putting down our troublemakers."

I shrugged. "That's what you pay me for."

"Always a man of few words."

"Shall I throw them out?"

He shook his head. "Bill will take care of it. You were just about done for the day, yes?"

I nodded.

"Let me buy you a drink."

I let him lead me over to the bar. The Kremlin had been quiet until that trio of young men had shown up, waving obnoxious wads of cash around, accosting the women, who they assumed were prostitutes.

Which they were, but Kaaro liked people to do business with a little more discretion.

The crowd had gone silent as I put the idiots down, but like the Mos Eisley Cantina, the noise level ratcheted back up after the show was over.

I rubbed my left wrist. I apparently had walked out of the house without my watch, and it felt naked.

"I will need you to come in early tomorrow," Kaaro said as we picked our way across the dimly-lit room.

"I think I'm working the door tomorrow," I said.

He gave a dismissive wave. "We will find someone else to check IDs at the door. I have a special task, and it requires a senior employee."

"Whatever you need," I replied.

Amy was bartending. When we reached the bar, she was ready with two highball glasses filled with four fingers of Stolichnaya over ice.

"You promised I could have him tonight, Anton," she admonished our boss with a pout. "He's worked late every night this week."

"So I did. Well, find Robert and have him take over. You two can leave anytime."

She bustled off, but not before giving me a smoldering look that indicated if I was anticipating sleep, I should adjust my expectations.

I watched her hips sway as she threaded her way to the back of the bar. Kaaro raised his glass. *"Budem zdorvy."*

Absently, I clinked glasses with him. I had been thinking about something when those three had started making their commotion. But for the life of me, I couldn't remember what it had been.

With a mental shrug, I tilted the glass to my lips. If it was important, it would come back to me.

The icy liquid turned to fire as it slid down my gullet. I gave a pleasant sigh as the vodka erased the cares of another day.

The Traveler Chronicles Conclude In

TRAITOR

THIS STREAM'S version of the cell did not feature a Slavic crime boss, but instead was occupied by a small man with red hair, cropped close to disguise the fact he was starting to go bald. He lay in the bottom bunk, head and shoulders propped against a pillow, reading.

He closed the book, keeping his page with one finger, and calmly looked me up and down, as if people appeared out of thin air in front of him every day.

"Aren't you supposed to be dead?" he asked.

"Not for lack of trying on your part."

Sam shrugged. "I think the way you arranged things to stick me in here balances the scales."

"You got what you deserve."

"I can yell for the guard," he mused. "And you'll get to explain how the man I allegedly murdered is not only still alive, but managed to get into my jail cell without showing up on a dozen security cameras."

"Do that and I'll disappear long before anyone can get here."

"Then why are you here, Trav? It can't be to gloat. That's not like you."

Sam was playing it cool, but his eyes burned with curiosity. He stared at me for what seemed like a long time. Then he smiled. But it wasn't the goofy grin I knew. This smile was hard, even predatory. I reminded myself that this Sam not only had succeeded in killing multiple Trav Beckers, but had spent the last year in prison. He was not the Sam I knew and trusted. Or even the one trying to remake the universe in his own image.

Of course, the last few months had changed me as well.

"You need my help," he said. "That's why you're here." A triumphant glint came into his eyes. "What's the matter? Did you finally realize I was right all along?"

"Let's just say I realized that the best way to hunt Sam Markus was with the help of Sam Markus."

"Interesting." He jumped up. "Well, what are we waiting for?"

He had no sooner stood than I was across the room. I slammed him into the wall, using his throat as a handle. The bravado faded from his face as I squeezed. His face began to turn the same shade of scarlet as his hair. His mouth worked, but all that came out was a low gurgle.

I leaned in very close. "Yes," I said softly, "I need your help. But make no mistake. Step out of line, or hesitate one fucking second when I tell you to do something, and I will *end* you. Understood?"

He nodded.

I released him. He straightened his collar.

"Anything you want to take with you?" I asked.

"You're kidding, right?"

"Then let's get moving."

He gave me an appraising look, rubbing his throat. "So who else is in on this gig?"

I told him.

"Awesome!" he crowed. "We're putting the band back together!"

TRAITOR

Coming soon from Dennis W. Green

AUTHOR'S NOTE

A couple years years prior to the publication of *Traveler*, I began meeting regularly with two friends, Rob Cline and Lennox Randon, in a writers group to complete novels we all had on the shelf.

Randon (he goes by his last name) was at the time in remission from stomach cancer, and publishing a book was on a bucket list he was no longer putting off. He recruited Rob first, who then got me involved.

When the guy with cancer says he is going to make writing a priority, it's hard to make excuses for not also doing the work.

This association has resulted in all three of us publishing books, a better average than most writing groups, I think.

At the time of this writing, Randon's cancer has returned. But he has completed his second book, a little weaker perhaps, but staying positive and being an inspiration to Rob, me, and everyone who meets him.

There would be no *Traveler* without Lennox Randon.

If you enjoyed *Traveler*, please check out Randon's new book, a time-travel thriller called *Memoirs of a Dead White Chick,* or his first effort, *Friends Dogs Bullets Lovers*. Rob Cline's hilarious pizza murder mystery is called *Murder by the Slice*. Both are available in the usual formats online at Amazon and Barnes & Noble.

Feedback and reviews are always welcome, on book review sites as well as my own web page, *www.denniswgreen.com*.

The character of "Kooj," is named for my friend and fellow Rotarian Larry Kudej, who won the honor at a silent auction in support of KCCK, the non-profit jazz radio station where I work. Ever since, he's been asking me how "our" book is coming. I hope you like it, Larry!

I continue to be grateful to my publisher and friend Karen Matibe, who believed in Traveler before anyone outside my family had even seen it, along with an awesome community of book bloggers, led by Terri LeBlanc and Candace Robinson.

I have also fallen in with a delightful bunch of authors who have become my friends and collaborators. Each has given valuable feedback which has made both both Traveler and Prisoner better books. If you like good stories in a variety of genres, you will immediately start Googling A.R. Miller, Michael Koogler, Jed Quinn, Rachel Aukes, Aaron Bunce, Adam Whitlach, Christian Schoon, David Suski, Rachel Eliason, and Tamara Jones. Then buy all of their books. You won't be disappointed.

THE MUSIC OF TRAVELER

Music is important to Trav Becker, and to me. Each of us has a personal soundtrack of songs that conjure up a certain feeling, or time in our lives. Part of the fun of writing these books was thinking about songs that have been important to me, and weaving them into Trav's story.

Here is the music mentioned in the Traveler books:

• "Miami 2017 (Seen The Light Go Down on Broadway)" from *Turnstiles* - Billy Joel

• "Take Five" from *Time Out* - Dave Brubeck Quartet

• "Freddie the Freeloader," from *Kind of Blue* - Miles Davis

• "I Shot The Sheriff," from 461 Ocean Boulevard - Eric Clapton

• "Too Many Nights Too Long" from *Rose of Cimarron* - Poco

• "Buffalo River Home," from *Perfectly Good Guitar* - John Hiatt.

• "Birdland," from *Heavy Weather* - Weather Report

• "In The Court of the Crimson King," from *In The Court of the Crimson King* - King Crimson

• "Thunder Road," from *Born To Run* - Bruce Springsteen

If you purchase any of the songs or albums from the above links, a few shekels will go to KCCK-FM, the public radio station where I work. It's a little payback for the time I spent thinking about the book when I should have been working. Oh, and if you like jazz and blues, check it out. It probably doesn't surprise you that I think there is no Pandora channel or iTunes playlist that compares to music programmed by a real person.

I've posted a playlist of these and some of Trav's other favorite songs at http://denniswgreen.com/the-music-of-traveler/

ABOUT THE AUTHOR

Dennis Green's first novel, the sci-fi detective thriller, *Traveler,* ranked in the Top Ten in the 2014 Ben Franklin Independent Publishing awards, and has a 4.9 review average on Amazon. Trav Becker's saga concludes in the final volume of the trilogy, *Protector.*

A popular radio personality in his native Iowa, Dennis's adventures as a DJ were covered by newspapers from Anchorage to Los Angeles. He has also worked on the stage, TV, and independent film.

Dennis's writing has appeared in the anthology *Sadistic Shorts,* magazines including *Grift,* and *Romance and Beyond,* as well as his own blog at denniswgreen.com.

By day, he is the general manager of Iowa's only jazz radio station, KCCK-FM. And if it's 5:30 am, you can probably find him in the pool, working out with the Milky Way Masters swim club.